"I'm sorry, Nick, this isn't going to work out."

Erin took a deep breath and started to walk away, heart pounding.

"Wait!" He strode after her and put a hand on her arm. "I don't understand. What happened between Saturday evening and this morning to change your mind?"

Lifting her eyes to his, she answered, "I—I've had time to think. You know how people in small towns talk."

"You're not going to tell me you're worried about the town gossips. What could anyone say that could possibly harm either of us?"

She conjured up a vivid image of herself hugely pregnant, and Nick cast unfairly as the father. She couldn't put him in such an untenable position.

Nor could she bear to sit and wait for him to reject her.

She shrugged, forcing herself to appear nonchalant. "I'm sorry. I just don't want to get involved. Please accept my decision."

Shutting her heart to the hurt and anger in his eyes, she put her chin in the air, straightened her shoulders and walked out of his life....

Dear Reader,

Kids—you gotta love 'em. They say that mothers always know who their children are, but a father can never be certain. Until the advent of DNA testing, that is. The idea for *Child of His Heart* came by playing around with the writer's favorite creative tool—what if? What if suddenly you discover that the child you always thought was yours might not be?

Nick Kincaid's wife confessed on her deathbed to having an affair around the time their daughter was conceived. The galling knowledge doesn't diminish Nick's love for his daughter, Miranda, but he does think twice about getting romantically involved with Erin Hanson, who is pregnant by her ex-fiancé. The last thing he wants is to raise another child that isn't his. Or does he?

Child of His Heart explores what it means to be a parent. Is fatherhood purely genetic? Or is a commitment to a child's welfare on a daily basis just as important, perhaps more so? I think any parent, biological or adoptive, knows the answer to that.

Erin figures out pretty quickly that Nick would make a better father to her child than the biological father, despite Nick's protestations. Nick gets there in the end, with Erin's help, but not before he risks losing those he holds dearest. It's a happy man who knows that, child of his loins or not, the child he loves and cares for is a child of his heart.

I hope you enjoy this story as much as I did writing it. I love to hear from my readers. You can contact me c/o Harlequin Enterprises, 225 Duncan Mill Road, Don Mills, Ontario, Canada, M3B 3K9; or e-mail me at www.superauthors.com.

Joan Kilby

Child of His Heart
Joan Kilby

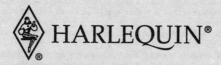

HARLEQUIN®

TORONTO • NEW YORK • LONDON
AMSTERDAM • PARIS • SYDNEY • HAMBURG
STOCKHOLM • ATHENS • TOKYO • MILAN • MADRID
PRAGUE • WARSAW • BUDAPEST • AUCKLAND

ISBN 0-373-71030-5

CHILD OF HIS HEART

For the children of my heart—Ryan, Gillian and Matthew

CHAPTER ONE

THE PHONE WAS RINGING when Erin entered her Seattle apartment late one Sunday night in early August. She longed for a hot shower and a quiet finish to the weekend with her fiancé, John.

Correction—her *ex*-fiancé.

"Hold on," she muttered at the phone. "I'm coming."

Slipping off her Prada slingbacks, she tossed her overnight bag onto the living room sofa and moved through the dark to the granite-and-oak kitchen. Three of her seven clocks chimed the quarter hour and she automatically looked at her watch—11:45.

The phone clicked onto voice mail. "Hi, Erin. It's Kelly. Call me—"

At the sound of her sister's voice, Erin snatched up the phone. "Kel? I'm here. I just got in."

"Erin, thank God. I've been calling since yesterday morning."

"I was away for the weekend with John. What's up?" Stifling a yawn, she flicked on the lights and wriggled onto a bar stool, pushing back the spiraling blond strands that fell around her shoulders.

"It's Gran," Kelly said. "She's fine now—"

"What do you mean *now?* What happened?" Erin hugged the cordless phone to her ear, one arm wrapped around her waist. *Please, God, not Gran.*

"She had a slight heart attack," Kelly explained.

"Oh, my God." Erin slid off the stool, her free hand pressed against her forehead. "Where is she? Is she okay?"

"She's back home. She's fine, honestly," Kelly reassured her. "The doctors did all kinds of tests and they say there's no serious damage to her heart. But I'm worried, Erin. When it happened, I was at work. She felt pain in her chest, and instead of going to the doctor she went around the house and penciled a name on the back of all her needlepoint pictures so we wouldn't fight over them in case she died."

"As if we would." But Erin could just see Gran doing that.

"Well, Geena might," Kelly said. "You know she's always coveted the one of the lighthouse."

Erin chuckled, and Kelly joined in. Laughing was okay because they both knew that like them, Geena wished Gran could live forever. No amount of needlepoint pictures would make up for her loss.

"I asked her to come and live with us," Kelly continued. "She refused."

"I'm not surprised—that house is her home." Erin opened the fridge door and reached for the carton of orange juice. "She and Granddad built it over sixty years ago. I can't imagine her living anywhere else. And we grew up there. I'd hate to see it go out of the family."

"What should we do?" Kelly asked.

"I agree she shouldn't be alone." Erin pictured Gran suffering another heart attack, reaching for the phone and collapsing before she could dial 911. "Maybe we could get her a live-in housekeeper."

"I suggested that, too. She doesn't want a stranger in her house. I got her a Medic Alert tag, but she won't wear it. I don't know if she's in denial or just forgetful."

Erin drank some juice while she considered their options; there weren't many. "I could come home," she said slowly.

"But how?" Kelly objected. "What about your job? And John?"

Erin's shoulders drooped. "John and I broke up."

She barely finished speaking before clocks began to sound the hour from their various locations around the apartment. As she waited for the chimes to cease, her mind flitted back over the weekend at John's cabin. *She'd* gone with the expectation that they'd plan the wedding; *he'd* come to tell her he wanted to postpone it—*again.* After two days of arguments, lovemaking and tears she was drained, emotionally and physically.

"Oh, Erin. I'm sorry." Hesitantly, Kelly added, "To tell you the truth, I'm glad. He wasn't right for you. But are you okay?"

"Yeah." Erin put down her glass and moved into the darkened living room to stand before the picture window. From her twelfth-story apartment the lights of Seattle twinkled around the dark fingers of Puget

Sound. "I'm running on empty, but I'll survive. John's not a bad guy—"

"He's manipulative. I don't know why you can't see it. What did he do—put off the wedding again?"

"This is a bad time for him, workwise. As prosecuting attorney he has responsibilities, and now he's thinking of running for Congress. Maybe I'm being too pigheaded. Gran isn't the only stubborn one in the family."

Kelly snorted impatiently. "All you wanted was a June wedding. After being engaged for over two years you'd think he could fit that on his agenda. You shouldn't have to do things *his* way all the time. Love is about mutual respect and compromise—"

"I know. I know," Erin cut in. She was grateful for Kelly's support, but her sister had a blind spot about John. "It might do us good to have a break from each other for a while."

"I thought you just said you'd split for good!"

"This could blow over given a little time." Gut instinct told her John was never going to change, but she'd invested so much time and emotional energy in the relationship that letting go was hard.

"Oh, Erin." Kelly gave an exasperated sigh and switched topics.

Leaving her new position as manager of the Loans Department would be a sacrifice, Erin had to admit. She'd worked hard for three years and had finally been rewarded with the promotion. Job opportunities appropriate to her qualifications weren't exactly thick on the ground in Hainesville. Not only that, she loved the vibrancy, the variety a larger city like Seattle offered. She enjoyed the anonymity and the freedom to do what she wanted, to be who she was, without fear of censure or gossip.

Yet sometimes, like now, when her mind was weary and her heart sore, she longed for the cozy comfort of the small town she'd grown up in. A place without traffic jams and road rage, where the air smelled of blossoms and freshly cut grass, not diesel fumes; where people who'd known her as a child stopped on the street to chat. A place with memories and continuity, where life proceeded at a user-friendly pace.

"A job is just a job," she told Kelly. "Family is everything."

"YOU'VE RUINED MY LIFE. You know that, don't you?" Miranda complained from the passenger seat of her father's Suburban. She tugged irritably at a purple-streaked strand of curly auburn hair. "I'm not even thirteen and my life is over."

Nick Dalton ignored his daughter's histrionics and kept his eyes straight ahead on the northbound lane of the interstate freeway. Puberty. Would it never end?

Usually he laughed off her over-the-top statements because they were underscored with humor and affection. But she was more furious than he'd ever seen her, and he was *tired*. Instead of finishing his last week as battalion chief for Orange County with paperwork, he'd had to contend with a major blaze that had broken out at a chemical plant and had been on duty around the clock, coordinating three battalions of firefighters. Now he and Miranda had been on the road for three long days and she'd been at him every waking minute. According to her, he'd "ruined" her life so many times it was a wonder she'd survived preschool.

"So sue me," he teased, trying to pull her out of the despair she apparently loved to wallow in. "Taking you out of a smoggy, overcrowded, crime-ridden city and into fresh air and open spaces ought to be good for at least a million dollars." When she didn't even crack a smile, he added, "Don't be so negative. I grew up in a small town."

"Exactly," she said, as if his origins accounted for his every deficiency. Miranda slumped in her seat, arms crossed over her recently blossomed breasts. "Hicksville isn't small—it's microscopic."

"Hainesville," he corrected her wearily. He rubbed his jaw, his fingers rasping over the stubble of his heavy beard. "People are friendly in small towns. And I hear the fishing in the area is fantastic."

She rolled her eyes. "Is there a mall? Or a movie theater?"

"Maybe you can get a horse. Join a sports team."

"I still don't see why we had to leave L.A. I only got a navel ring. You can't punish me as though I were a little girl. You didn't freak out like this over the nose ring or the eyebrow ring."

True, he had controlled his anger over the first two rings, telling himself that what was done was done and sooner or later she'd grow out of this ridiculous phase. But the navel ring had been the last straw. Curving provocatively from her bare midriff, it drove him crazy with paternal anxiety. Even now, he couldn't keep his voice from rising when he spoke of it. "What the *hell* is a young girl doing with a ring in her navel? Huh?"

"You're afraid I'll look sexy," she taunted. "You're afraid I'll start *having* sex."

The smirk in her voice sent his blood pressure soaring. She'd pushed his hottest button. Nick gripped the wheel with both hands and forced himself to breathe deeply. You weren't allowed to strangle your daughter. Nor could you lock her up until she was over thirty.

He'd taken the job at the Hainesville Fire Department partly to get Miranda away from the gang of older kids she'd started hanging with. Sex, drugs— who knew what those lowlifes got up to. Grounding Miranda hadn't tamed her; more than once she'd snuck out of the house after he was asleep. Even the housekeeper he'd hired hadn't been able to control her. The only solution, in his mind, was to distance her from bad influences.

Twelve-going-on-twenty, Miranda was trouble with a capital *T*. The older she got the more she looked like her mother, all lush curves and pouty lips. And if she *looked* like Janine, he couldn't help think she would end up *acting* like Janine. His late wife

had always been flirtatious, but until she lay dying in
the hospital from injuries sustained in a hit-and-run
accident, he'd never seriously thought she had de-
ceived him. Before she'd passed away she'd confessed to having an affair around the time of Miranda's conception. The memory was a slap in the face
every time he looked at his daughter—if she really
was his daughter.

"This move isn't only about you," he reminded
her. "I got a promotion, don't forget. You should be
proud of your old man. At thirty-six I'm probably the
youngest fire chief in Washington State."

"Only because no one else wanted to come here!"

"Miranda, that's *enough*." The warning edge to his
voice still had the power to subdue her—just. This
move may have been sparked by concern for Miranda, but the change would be good for him, too. In the
two years since Janine's death he'd turned into a her-
mit. He needed balance in his life just as much as
Miranda did.

A meeker voice said, "You look tired, Dad. Want
some coffee?"

Nick glanced over to see Miranda, contrite after her
outburst, screwing the lid off the thermal jug.
"Thanks, honey. Any of those doughnuts left?"

She handed him a travel mug, then picked up the
paper bag at her feet and offered it to him. "Don't
eat the blueberry one."

Grinning, he tickled her behind her ear. "Who's
going to stop me?"

Reluctantly, she giggled. "Da-a-ad."

ERIN TURNED INTO Linden Street and parked in front of Gran's house. The two-story Victorian home, set on a wide, deep corner lot, was painted white with blue trim. Lilac bushes flanked the steps, and colorful petunias lined the footpath. In the center of the front yard grew a tall maple, in whose sturdy limbs she'd spent half her childhood.

Erin entered quietly in case Gran was sleeping, and was assailed by the deliciously spicy aroma of home-made gingersnaps. She stooped to set her suitcases on the runner protecting the polished hardwood floor just as the antique grandfather clock in the foyer began to strike noon. Reverently she stroked the polished mahogany and listened to the booming brass chimes. If she coveted anything in Gran's house, it was this clock, brought west from Chicago by her great-grandfather, Henrik Hanson, more than a hundred years earlier.

The last vibrating note died away. She walked down the hall and into the kitchen. "Gran! I'm here."

Sunlight streamed through the window overlooking the backyard, bringing a rich glow to the warm yellow walls. Ruth Hanson was pulling a freshly baked pan of Erin's favorite cookies from the oven, her glasses fogged with heat. In her tracksuit she looked smaller and frailer than Erin remembered, her gray wig almost too large for her angular features. Her skin was stretched tightly over the bones of her face, but her smile was warm and welcoming. "Erin, honey!"

"What are you doing baking cookies?" Erin scolded. "You should be resting." She grabbed an oven mitt from the table, took the hot tray and set it on a cork mat so she could hug her grandmother.

"I've been doing nothing *but* resting since I got out of the hospital. Oh, it's so good to see you." Gran's hazel eyes became watery and she dug into her pocket for a tissue. "But you shouldn't have quit your job to look after me. You've got your own life to live."

"It hasn't been much of a life lately, to tell you the truth. I'm glad to be here." She hugged her again. "Really glad."

Gran held her at arm's length. "I like your dress. That smoky blue matches your eyes. You look good."

Erin grinned. "Who wouldn't in one of Geena's designer outfits?"

"You're lovely enough to have been a model, too, except that would have been a criminal waste of brain power." Gran picked up a spatula and scooped the hot cookies off the pan and onto a rack. "Before I forget, as soon as you've settled in, go down to the bank and see Jonah Haines. I wouldn't have suggested you do that on your first day home, but Jonah's a hard man to pin down. He's always in some important meeting."

"Sure. Do you have some banking that needs to be taken care of?"

"No, he's looking for an assistant manager. Edna Thompson mentioned it when she brought around a casserole after my little spell."

Assistant manager. It would beat flipping burgers at the Burger Shack. Erin dug a finger into the bowl of cookie dough. "Thanks for putting in a good word for me."

Gran batted her hand away from the bowl with an oven mitt and smiled indulgently. "Erin, there aren't enough good words in the Bible to describe you. But you never did learn to keep your hands out of the cookie dough."

Something brushed Erin's ankles. She glanced down to see a fluffy gray kitten with enormous blue eyes staring up at her from the black-and-white linoleum floor.

"Well, hello there. Who are you?" Erin crooned. She picked up the kitten and rubbed its soft fur against her cheek. The kitten meowed and climbed onto Erin's shoulder, digging her sharp little claws into Erin's skin through the thin fabric of her cotton-knit dress.

"That's Chloe," Gran said, rolling lumps of dough into balls and placing them on the cookie sheet. "Kelly brought her over to give me company."

The front door opened and a woman called, "Gran? Erin?"

"Speak of the devil," Erin said with a grin, then yelled, "we're in the kitchen."

Small feet raced down the hallway. "Auntie Erin. Auntie Erin." Kelly's youngest children, twins Tammy and Tina, charged into the room and flung themselves at Erin's knees.

"Hi, kids," Erin said, crouching to hug her blond, brown-eyed nieces. Tina's features were a little finer, Tammy's hair a fraction darker; otherwise the girls looked alike. The kitten scampered off Erin's shoulder and into Tina's arms, getting tangled in the little girl's long hair and making her giggle. "How are you guys? Where are Robyn and Beth? And your mom?"

"I'm bringing up the rear, as usual." Kelly, her shiny chestnut-brown hair swinging around the shoulders of her navy-blue suit, bustled into the room. "Robyn and Beth are playing at friends' houses for the afternoon. I'm dropping these two off at day care on my way to work, but I had to stop in and say hi." She threw her arms around Erin. "It is *so good* to have you back."

Erin, half a head taller, embraced her sister. Even though they saw each other every few months, the time apart always seemed too long. "Do you have to go to work today?"

Kelly tilted her head in a gesture of apology. "I'm trying to close on a riverfront property. If I can nail this deal it'll be my third sale this month."

"Fantastic," Erin said, then noted with surprise her grandmother's pursed lips. "Isn't it, Gran?"

"Kelly knows my thoughts on the subject. I've said all I'm going to say." Gran slid the tray of cookies into the oven, then went to the fridge for a jug of lemonade. She set it on the table along with a couple of cookies each for the children, admonishing them kindly, "Sit up at the table so you don't spill crumbs on my clean floor."

"Gran thinks I spend too much time working and not enough with my kids," Kelly explained, then added with a shrug, "I stayed home for fifteen years. It feels great to be out there, earning some money."

"I can understand that." Kelly's two older girls, Robyn and Beth, were in grade four and grade two, respectively. Kelly had started back to work six months ago, when the twins turned three, but Erin hadn't heard about this small friction between her sister and Gran. "How does Max feel about you working long hours?"

"He'll get used to it. He'll have to." Kelly bit into a fresh cookie. "These are delicious, Gran, but you're supposed to take it easy. Erin, you're going to have to keep an eye on her. See that she doesn't do too much."

"That's why I'm here."

"You girls! I'm not an invalid."

"Hello? Who's just spent time in the hospital? You need to take care." Kelly wrapped one arm around Gran's waist and carried on speaking to Erin. "I had to give up coaching the junior girls' basketball team at the YWCA. If you're interested, the position's still open."

"I haven't played in years."

"That won't matter for an ace player like you." Kelly glanced at her watch. "Come on, kids. We've got to go."

Amid clamors of protest from Tammy and Tina, Erin walked her sister to the door. "When can we get together? I have an appointment at the bank, but that won't take all afternoon."

"Drop by the office. I'll be in from two o'clock

on.'' Her smile turned sly. ''The new fire chief is coming by to pick up the keys for his rental houseboat.''

''New fire chief?'' Erin said, disentangling the kitten's claws from Tammy's sweater. ''What happened to Chief Roland?''

''He retired in July,'' Gran explained as she slipped each of the children another cookie. ''Steve Randall's been acting chief since then. He applied for the position but didn't have enough experience.''

''So who's the new guy?'' Erin asked.

''A total babe,'' Kelly said, rolling her eyes dreamily. ''If I weren't married... I met him last winter when he came to interview for the job and look at rental houses. He's a widower from Los Angeles with a young daughter. You'll have to check him out.''

Erin shook her head. ''I'm not interested in meeting anyone.''

''You'll be interested in this guy,'' Kelly predicted. ''See you later.''

Erin and Gran waved them off from the porch.

''Why don't you go on upstairs and put your things away,'' Gran said as she closed the door. ''I'll clean up the kitchen.''

''You've exerted yourself enough for one day,'' Erin said firmly, taking Gran's arm and leading her to her first-floor bedroom. ''I'll clean up after my appointment at the bank. *And* I'll make dinner tonight. No, don't say a word.'' She smiled gently. ''I'm here, Gran. Everything's going to be okay.''

Erin carried her suitcases upstairs to her old room.

It looked the same as it had in high school—high ceiling, pale cream wallpaper sprigged with rosebuds, white-painted iron double bed covered with a patchwork quilt. Her heels tapping on polished floorboards, she crossed to the wide bay window, where as a girl she'd curled up on the window seat and read, or stared out at the full moon to dream. Many was the time she used to push up the sash and crawl onto the huge old maple, or nimbly descend its broad limbs rather than mundanely take the stairs.

Nostalgia flooded through her, warring with a niggling sense that she was going backward in life. When she'd left Hainesville for college she never thought she'd return here to live. Had she done the right thing in coming home? She'd been happy in the small town as a child and a teenager, but she was an adult now, and used to a wider world. What kind of future could she have in Hainesville?

The move was only temporary, she reminded herself. She would stay as long as Gran needed her, and long enough to rejuvenate her spirits.

She began to unpack. One suitcase was devoted to her shoe collection—*part* of her shoe collection, that is. Jimmy Choo, Dolce and Gabana, Manolo Blahnik, Prada—she adored them all. She lined up the shoes in neat rows in the closet and hung her clothes above. On top of the old maple dresser she placed her favorite clock, a brass turn-of-the-century German mantel clock decorated with cherubs. Beside her bed she set an Aynsley china arch clock, white with pink roses. The rest of her clocks and shoes she'd packed for shipping; they would arrive tomorrow.

When she'd finished unpacking, she went down the hall to shower, then changed into a skirt and fitted jacket in gray linen. After some consideration she chose a pair of black crocodile skin pumps with kitten heels. She brushed her long hair, letting it fall in loose waves over her shoulders. Then, checking that her briefcase held a copy of her résumé, she slipped quietly downstairs.

Outside, her gaze went to the basketball hoop above the garage door. She hadn't played since college, basketball being one of those things she never found time for in Seattle. Coaching might be fun.

She walked toward the center of town beneath the cool dappled green of overarching shade trees. Past the Contafios' next door, with their orchard and horses; past the monkey puzzle tree on the corner. Children's laughter, a distant lawn mower and the tinkling bell of the ice cream truck accompanied her. The fragrance of roses, warm grass and ripe apples drifted on the soft breeze. All at once she didn't miss Seattle one bit. A spring came into her step and she smiled, thinking of her earlier doubts. Truly, life seemed to be taking a positive turn.

On the outskirts of the town center, Erin went by the fire hall and waved to Steve, who was out in the yard, washing down one of the trucks. There was no sign of his new boss. She continued on, past Knit 'n Kneedles, where Gran got her yarn and patterns, past the health food store and the bakery, then crossed the street at the single set of traffic lights.

Between Blackwell's Drugstore and Orville's Barbershop stood the imposing stone building bearing the name Hainesville First National Bank on a brass plaque. Hainesville's *only* bank, national or otherwise. With luck this would be her new place of employment.

CHAPTER TWO

EDNA THOMPSON, Gran's oldest friend and Erin's erstwhile piano teacher, was just leaving the bank. Erin held the heavy glass door open while Edna hobbled out, leaning heavily on her cane.

"Erin, how nice to see you." She clasped Erin's hand and beamed. "I was hoping I might run into you. Ruth has been looking forward to having you home to stay."

"Thank you. It's nice to see you, too," Erin replied. She wasn't surprised that news of her arrival had already spread through town. She would probably make the front page of the *Hainesville Herald* this week. "How have you been?"

"Well..." Mrs. Thompson paused only long enough to take a breath before launching into a recitation of her ailments. "My arthritis pains me something fierce. I have to go in for a cataract operation next week, and yesterday I had another gallbladder attack. This morning I woke up with a pain here." She pointed to a spot on her right side, below her ribs. "But, I can't complain," she said with a cheerful smile. "No, I never complain. Goodbye for now, my dear."

Erin smiled to herself and started through the open door. The bank was empty but for the tellers, who eyed her with obvious curiosity. A beautiful black woman she didn't recognize stood at one window, while at the other lounged a pimply faced young man she was afraid she did. Could that possibly be Bobby Murchison, a boy she used to baby-sit?

"Bobby?" she said, moving across the carpeted lobby to the counter.

"Oh, hi, Erin." He straightened anxiously, as though Erin might even now punish him for putting that garter snake in her tennis shoe so many years ago.

"I've come to see Mr. Haines. He's expecting me."

"I'll tell him you're here." Bobby wove past a cluttered desk, a photocopier and a check-printing machine to knock on a corner office.

Erin smiled at the other woman. "Hi, I'm Erin."

"Tracy." She regarded Erin frankly. "So you're the paragon I've been hearing about all week. Straight-A student, star athlete, girl most likely to succeed." She grinned. "I don't even know you and already I hate you."

Erin grimaced. "People exaggerate."

Tracy leaned over the counter, winked and in a low voice confided, "Don't get me wrong, I'm looking forward to having another female around the place." Then she spotted Erin's crocodile-skin high heels. "Man, I love those shoes! Where'd you get those, girlfriend?"

Erin recognized a fellow devotee when she met one. "There's this fabulous little shoe boutique in Seattle—"

Jonah Haines's door opened, causing her to break off. He looked exactly as Erin remembered, like a big absentminded teddy bear. He wore a moss-green cardigan over a navy blue shirt with a clashing mustard yellow tie, and his brown suit pants were baggy and creased. Gray hair puffed above his ears on either side of his balding dome.

"Erin, my dear, wonderful to see you." He peered at her over half glasses perched midway down his nose. "Come in."

Erin followed him into his office and took the seat he indicated with a vague motion of his hand. Oil paintings of river scenes with herons and fishing boats decorated the walls. On his desk, hooks, fishing line and wisps of colored feathers were laid out on tattered blue felt.

He sat down heavily in his creaking leather swivel chair, picked up an unfinished fly and resumed tying a bright red feather to the hook. "I still remember the day you opened your first bank account. You were only five, and already so grown-up and responsible."

Erin well remembered coming into the bank clutching her savings—$6.50. Her mother and father had died in a car crash a month earlier, and to take Erin's mind off her loss, Gran and Granddad had given her chores to do around the house. They'd paid her for her efforts and encouraged her to deposit her pocket money.

"I was so proud of that little blue passbook," she

said, adding with a chuckle, "although later I regretted not keeping out a nickel for an ice cream. I certainly never thought that twenty-five years later I'd be in here applying for a job."

"You were at City Bank in Seattle until recently, I understand. I always knew you'd amount to something."

"I managed the Loans Department." Erin opened her briefcase and handed him a copy of her résumé. "Before that I worked with a financial consulting firm in New York. Please feel free to contact any of my supervisors for a reference."

Still holding the fishing fly in one hand, Mr. Haines glanced at her résumé. "You did a double major in business administration and economics. Impressive." He regarded her over his glasses. "Hainesville will seem a bit of a backwater."

"I'm sure you're aware I came home to take care of my grandmother while she recuperates from her heart attack." She paused. "I'll be honest with you, Mr. Haines. My stay is unlikely to be permanent."

Jonah Haines concentrated on winding the feather onto the hook with a length of fishing line. He tied a complicated knot, snipped off the loose end with a pair of scissors and set the hook aside. "To tell you the truth, I haven't had a lot of applicants with your qualifications. Can you manage people? It's important you be able to handle the bank in my…uh, absence."

"That wouldn't be a problem, sir. I supervised staff in my previous position."

He picked up another fishing hook and a new bit

of feather. "I can't give you the kind of salary you were probably getting in Seattle."

"I understand. What are you offering?" He named a figure not quite as low as she'd expected. "That'll be fine."

"Good. When can you start?"

"Tomorrow?"

"Excellent." He shook her hand across the desk. Then he rose, clapped a fishing hat bristling with flies onto his head, grabbed the rod propped in a corner and walked her to the door. "I don't want to rush you but I've an important meeting with the mayor."

"Certainly." Erin managed to keep a straight face. "Thank you very much."

"Tracy, Bobby," Mr. Haines said to the tellers. "This is Erin. She'll be assistant manager, starting tomorrow. You'll report to her in my absence."

Tracy's eyebrows lifted as she gave Erin a thumbs-up. Bobby gazed at her, his mouth parted in awe.

"Oh, Mr. Haines," Tracy called as he made his way to the exit. "The roof sprang a leak in the back room when we had that big rainfall last week. When I turned on the computer this morning, there was a *pffft* sound and a puff of black smoke."

Mr. Haines turned to Erin. "Sounds like the outlet blew. Can you take care of this?"

Her first executive decision, and a no-brainer. "No problem. Bobby, look up roofers in the phone book and make me a list of names and numbers. I know a good electrician in town. I'll call Mike Gordon and ask him to get over here first thing in the morning."

"Excellent." Mr. Haines beamed at her as though she'd just solved the national debt. Then he glanced at his watch and hurried toward the door. "See you all tomorrow. Tracy, I know I can count on you to lock up."

When he'd left, Tracy turned to Erin. "With the salmon derby coming up in a couple of weeks we hardly see the boss anymore. Thank goodness we're going to have someone responsible around here." She glanced at Erin's shoes again and rubbed her hands together with glee. "Someone with style!"

Erin laughed. Becoming assistant manager of the Hainesville bank might not be one of her more challenging career moves, but she had a feeling she would enjoy working here. She leaned toward Tracy. "My sister Geena sent me the most beautiful Pashmina shawl...."

ABOUT AN HOUR NORTH of Seattle, Nick exited the highway and headed west toward Hainesville. The area looked a lot more inviting than the soggy gray landscape he'd seen during his visit last January. Now, in mid-August, the sky was a deep dreamy blue, and thistledown floated on a sultry breeze. He wound down the window and put his face into the wind, breathing deeply of the warm, humid air and the earthy scents of summer.

To his left was a small dairy farm with a barn and a silo and creamy Jersey cows dotting the green fields. To his right, thick stands of alder and birch hid the river from view. Closer to town, where the river broadened on its way to meet the ocean, assorted light marine industry lined the banks and fishing boats mingled with houseboats. One of those houseboats would be their home, and he was as excited as a kid at the prospect of living on the water.

Pretty soon the town itself came into view.

"Look, Miranda," he said. "We're here."

She sat up and gazed out the window. "What a dump."

Nick couldn't have disagreed more. The streets were wide and lined with shade trees. The houses they'd passed were neat and well-cared-for, their lawns trimmed and the gardens bursting with color. Farming and fishing had clearly made for stable growth since the town's inception a hundred years earlier. Nick felt as though his cares were dropping away as he cruised down Main Street, with its central grassy boulevard and diagonal parking on both sides. He admired the old stone buildings and turn-of-the-century wooden structures identifiable as the courthouse, library and museum. Benches set into the broad sidewalk every twenty paces or so seemed a deliberate invitation for citizens to slow down.

"They built to last in the old days, didn't they?" Nick commented, stopping at a set of traffic lights. The *only* set of traffic lights, he realized, glancing ahead down the street.

Miranda glanced around. "I see a video store, but where's the McDonald's? Is this place for real?"

"Forget chain restaurants. I'll bet there's a coffee shop or a drive-in somewhere in town that serves the best burgers you've ever tasted.'' The light changed and Nick continued slowly, watching for the realty office.

A woman coming out of the bank caught his eye. Elegantly slender, with shiny blond hair and a stylish suit, she walked with a grace that made her stand out among the moms in tracksuits, teenagers on skateboards and elderly men leaning on canes. Nick couldn't help but turn his head as he passed, his elbow resting on the open window as though he were a teenager out cruising on a Saturday night. The woman must have felt his stare, for she slanted him a look. He smiled at her. Coolly, she nodded back. Once past, he checked her out in the rearview mirror. She was noticing his California plates.

''Da-a-ad. *Hello*. Isn't that the realty office?''

''Huh? Oh, right.'' Nick pulled into the curb and parked opposite the town clock in the middle of the boulevard. ''Wait here,'' he said to Miranda. ''I should only be a minute.''

When he got out of the car, the blond woman paused to peer into a store window, her black briefcase held in both hands behind her back. Her gaze slid in his direction, but she saw him watching and focused on the window again.

The bell over the door of the realty office tinkled as he entered. A young woman with dark brown hair was standing behind a desk, talking on the phone. She saw him and held up a finger to indicate she'd only be a minute. ''Yep. You got it, Mrs. Fontana. I'll be out tomorrow with the contract. Thank you *very* much.''

She set down the phone and came out from behind her desk. "Hi, I'm Kelly Walker. You must be—"

"Nick Dalton. Nice to meet you." He shook her hand. "Nice town you've got here."

Her wide smile expressed delight. "Population 3,376—give or take a few—and I'm sure every one of us is looking forward to meeting you and your daughter. I know we're grateful to have someone of your experience as our new fire chief. Can I offer you a cup of coffee?''

"Thanks, but I'll have to take a rain check. My daughter's waiting in the car," he explained. In spite of what he'd told Miranda, he was surprised to encounter such immediate friendliness and warmth. But he liked it very much. "We've had a long drive and the moving van's not far behind," he went on.

"Of course." Kelly plucked a set of keys from a pegboard on the wall behind her desk and handed them over, along with a sheet of paper. "Your keys and a map of Hainesville. Hard to get lost around here, mind you. I've marked your houseboat," she said, pointing to a spot on the map. "You're going to love living on the river. It's a really nice little community and there's a launching place for your boat. Didn't you say you had a boat?''

"Just a small runabout. I like to fish."

"Well, you've come to the right place. If there's anything more I can do, just holler." She walked him to the door and right out onto the sidewalk. "Oh, there's my sister."

Kelly waved to the elegant blonde who'd caught his eye. The woman hesitated before slowly proceeding toward them. Nick scrubbed a hand through his short hair, wishing he'd had a shower and clean clothes and maybe a few hours' sleep to erase the dark circles below his eyes.

Inside the Suburban, Miranda beeped the horn.

"I'll let you go," he said reluctantly to Kelly, and moved toward the vehicle. He didn't want Miranda creating a scene on their very first day in town. "Thanks for everything."

"What took you so long?" Miranda demanded when he'd got back inside and started the engine.

"Courtesy," he replied shortly. "Something *you* could use a little of." He sketched a wave to the two women standing on the sidewalk and drove off with the distinct impression they were talking about him.

Two blocks down he saw the concrete tower of the Hainesville Fire Department. A bright red-and-white fire engine was parked outside, wet and gleaming from a recent washing. Nick pulled in at the curb, ignoring Miranda's groan at yet another stop. A young blond fireman wandered out from behind the engine, saw Nick and came over to the vehicle with a friendly smile. "Hi, there. Can I help you folks?"

Nick put a hand through the open window. "Nick Dalton, your new chief. Steve Randall, right?"

Steve wiped a damp hand on his regulation navy

pants and shook. "Welcome to Hainesville, Chief. Sorry I didn't recognize you at first."

"That's okay. We only met once. My daughter and I just arrived." He glanced around at the silent street. "Slow day?"

Steve grinned. "No other kind around here."

Miranda made a small noise of disgust.

"This is Miranda," Nick said. "She's looking forward to the peace and quiet of a small town."

"Da-a-ad."

Nick eased the truck into gear. "Guess I'd better be moving. The furniture van is right behind us."

"I'll stop by after work and give you a hand unloading," Steve said.

"I wouldn't want to put you out."

"Oh, it's no problem," Steven informed him cheerfully. "I'll bring over the casserole my mom made for you. She figured that on your first night here you wouldn't be set up for cooking."

"That's really nice of her," Nick said, taken aback at the kindness of a complete stranger. "I'll see you later."

He found River Road again and drove out the other side of town toward the marina where his houseboat was moored, his thoughts echoing Miranda's earlier comment—was this place for real?

God, he hoped so.

BY THE END OF THE FOLLOWING week, Erin had familiarized herself with the bank's corporate accounts and met many of the individuals who entrusted their money to the institution. She'd set herself up in the office next to Jonah Haines, put fresh flowers on her desk and hung one of her two Regulator clocks on the wall.

At 11:55 a.m. she closed the file on an application for a home loan and leaned back in her chair to stretch. Through her partly open door she could hear the quiet hum of voices as Tracy served a customer. Then the front door opened and closed as the person left. Silence. She glanced at the clock. Minutes seemed to tick by more slowly here in Hainesville.

Tracy's voice, good-natured and strident, roused her. "Hey, Erin," she called. "Sally Larkin over at the drugstore reckons our new fire chief wears boxer shorts. I say briefs. What do y'all think?"

Half scandalized, half amused, Erin rose to stand in the doorway. "Are you gawking at that poor man again?"

"Every chance I get," Tracy said, blatantly unrepentant as she peered through the slats in the venetian blind at the front of the bank. "If I weren't already engaged to the sweetest man west of the Rockies I'd be knocking on the front door of the luscious Mistah Dalton. I can't believe he's been here over a week and you haven't met him yet."

The truth was, Erin had deliberately *avoided* several opportunities to meet him. Although she was intrigued, he made her nervous. He was pure male energy, his sexuality restrained but undiminished by old-fashioned good manners. Her heart was already in traction; God knows what further damage a man like Nick Dalton could inflict.

"I've been busy catching up with Gran and Kelly. Not to mention the fact that I've just started a new job," Erin protested. "If I meet him, I meet him. I'm not going to go out of my way to do so. Frankly, I'm a little sick of him already. Nick this, Nick that. He's just a man."

"Well, you're the only one who thinks so."

Tracy was telling the truth. Nick Dalton had every woman in town talking. Already it was common knowledge that the chief ordered pastrami on whole wheat for lunch at Rosa's deli, took Mrs. Thompson's arm to help her across the road and had left Los Angeles to get his twelve-year-old daughter away from bad company. Most important, as a widower in a small town with a limited number of attractive bachelors, he was single. And to the women of Hainesville, that meant *available*.

Which of course was irrelevant to Erin. Only a few weeks had passed since her breakup with John. The memory of their emotional last weekend together was still fresh in her mind. He hadn't called her yet, but he would, if she just gave him some space. She owed it to herself to give him a chance to make things right.

"He's heading this way," Tracy announced. "Bet he's goin' on down to Rosa's. Come quick, or you'll miss him."

Erin tucked a long strand of blond hair behind her ear and crossed her arms over her chest. "Ogling a man is demeaning," she said severely. "You're viewing him purely as a sex object."

"Hoo boy, you got that right." Tracy wiggled her behind in appreciation. "Hurry up, girl. Goin', goin'…"

Erin glanced around. Bobby was chewing gum and checking out a new pimple in the reflection of the glass above his teller cage. Jonah Haines was in another "meeting" with Mayor Bob Gribble out on the river. The bank would be empty of customers for at least five minutes until the lunch rush. She shouldn't be tempted to take a gander, but with all the hype, who could blame her?

To heck with it. There was no harm in a peek.

She lifted the hinged counter separating the tellers from the customers and joined Tracy at the window. Through the venetian blinds half closed against the sun she saw Nick Dalton strolling past in front of the bank.

With easy muscular grace, he threw an orange into the air and caught it in one hand, then repeated the motion. Beneath his crisp white short-sleeved shirt his biceps flexed, and when he tilted his head back, his near-black hair glinted auburn in the sun. Erin had glimpsed him working out on a set of weights in the recesses of the fire station. As she remembered his sweat-sheened muscles, her mouth lost some of its moisture.

Tracy nudged her in the ribs. "Isn't he gorgeous?"

Just then, Nick turned his head toward the bank and caught Erin peering through the blinds. He grinned and tipped two fingers to his temple in a lively salute. Erin's cheeks flamed. She slapped the slats shut and stepped away from the window, mortified.

"He's probably got an ego the size of Texas," she snapped.

"And you, girlfriend, are in denial if you think you're not attracted." Tracy's grin spread wide. "What are you so worried about?"

Erin ignored her and strode back through the opening in the counter. "Did those roofers say when they'd be over?" she demanded of Bobby. "Mike fixed that outlet, but if those wires get wet again, they could short out and we could have a fire in here."

Bobby straightened away from his reflection. "They said they'd try to get here this afternoon but couldn't promise anything."

"Call them again. If they're busy, call someone else."

Erin went into her office and shut the door. Damn Nick Dalton, grinning at her like that.

She slumped against the door and forced herself to acknowledge the truth. Since the day he'd breezed into town like a hot Santa Ana wind, his dark eyes and white grin had sparked feelings she wasn't able to control while apart from John. As handsome and suave as John was, he'd never, even in the early days of their romance, made her feel so...so restless.

Erin paced the small room. What was wrong with her? She wasn't one to avoid difficult situations, yet she was being held hostage, as it were, in her own town. *She* used to buy her lunch at Rosa's until she'd found she was in danger of running into *him* there. Now when she saw him coming she crossed the street, entered a store, ducked into her car, *anything* to escape.

This couldn't go on. She simply had to face the man, speak to him, reduce him to human proportions.

She grabbed her purse from her desk drawer and marched through the bank. "I'm going to lunch," she announced to Tracy and Bobby.

"She's going to Rosa's to meet him," Tracy crowed with delight.

"Looks to me like she's getting ready for a show-down," Bobby said.

Erin lifted her chin, refusing to dignify their remarks with a reply. "I'll be back at one o'clock."

CHAPTER THREE

SHE MARCHED DOWN the block, head high, the stacked heels of her Versace loafers clicking briskly on the sidewalk. But as she drew nearer to Rosa's, her palms began to feel damp. This, she reminded herself, pressing her hands to her narrow skirt, was *her* town.

Entering Rosa's deli was like dropping into a corner of Italy. Erin breathed in the mouth-watering aromas of prosciutto and sun-dried tomatoes, pungent cheeses and fresh and dried herbs. Strings of garlic and red chili peppers hung from the ceiling alongside whole salamis and cured hams. Behind the counter, Rosa, plump and smiling, and her statuesque daughter, Nina, filled orders for the hungry regulars.

Mrs. Thompson was pointing out to Nina exactly which three slices of Black Forest ham she wanted. Toby Conner, from the gas station, known to Erin's graduating class as "Tubby" Conner, handed over money for an extra-large container of potato salad. Greta Vogler, fifty-six and never married, asked Rosa for a tuna sandwich, then flirted over her shoulder with Nick Dalton. Perfectly polite, he smiled fixedly, not quite looking Greta in the eye.

Conversation paused as Erin entered. The towns-people she'd known for years greeted her with friendly waves and hellos. Nick Dalton registered Erin's presence with a slow blink, a subtle double take. His smile widened and became genuine.

"Hi," she said in a general greeting. She let her gaze rest momentarily on Nick, including him but not singling him out. Very good, she commended herself, friendly without being gushy.

Now for the next step.

"I don't believe we've met," she said, extending her hand to Nick, cool and collected. At least she hoped she appeared that way. Her heart was beating like a mad thing. "Erin Hanson. I work at the bank."

His hand, large and warm and strong, wrapped around hers, inspiring a feeling of confidence and se-curity. If she were trapped in a burning building she'd like those hands to be pulling her free.

"Nick Dalton. Nice to meet you—at last." Amuse-ment colored his low voice, as though he was teasing her with an inside joke.

So he'd noticed her avoidance tactics—how em-barrassing. Then she became aware of Toby staring openly at the two of them, and Greta's sharpened fea-tures. "You've met my sister Kelly, I believe."

"She was very helpful with the rental houseboat. In fact, the whole town's been welcoming. I'll prob-ably be calling on you soon—"

Erin's thoughts took flight. How to say no to a date. Dare she say yes?

"—about a home loan."

"Oh! A home loan. Of course. Anytime." She laughed.

Mrs. Thompson tucked her package of ham into her string shopping bag, smiled at Erin and left. Toby took his potato salad and roast beef sandwich to one of the stools at the counter along the window. Greta laid a hand on Erin's forearm and said in a funereal tone, "I was so sorry to hear, my dear."

"I beg your pardon? Hear what?"

"You know." Greta's gaze flicked to Nick and back. "Your breakup. Why you had to leave Seattle. Don't worry, we're on your side."

Erin did a slow burn. Greta Vogler had been teaching English at the high school since the dawn of time and was the nosiest woman in Hainesville. Erin couldn't begin to imagine what atom of information Greta had gotten hold of, or what monumental work of fiction she'd blown it into. As pleasantly as possible, she replied through gritted teeth, "I came back to take care of Gran."

"Of course you did," Greta said, oozing understanding. She picked up her sandwich and swept out of the store in a rustle of shopping bags. "Marriage is highly overrated, or so I've been told. We spinsters live longer."

Rosa scowled after her, then turned to Erin. "For two cents I'd spit in her tuna fish. You want me to put the evil eye on her?"

Erin shook her head. "Somehow she would turn it back on you."

"Who's next?" Rosa said, looking from Nick to Erin.

Nick gestured to Erin.

"Oh, no. You were here first."

"Please. I insist." He touched her elbow, gently pushing her forward.

"Thank you." Flustered by the warmth of his fingers on her bare skin, she stepped to the counter. With Nick Dalton blotting coherent thought from her brain, she shouldn't have been surprised that she blurted out the first thing that came to her—his favorite sandwich. "Pastrami on whole wheat, please."

Rosa's eyes opened wide. "That's amazing! Nick here, he orders pastrami on whole wheat every day."

Erin felt sick when she realized what she'd done but was too embarrassed to take it back. "Is that right?" she said weakly.

"It's a fact," Rosa said with an emphatic shake of her head. "Most people ask for pastrami on rye, roast beef on whole wheat," she elaborated effusively. "Hardly ever pastrami on whole wheat. First him, now you. Amazing."

"Astonishing." Nick had a twinkle in his eye.

"Usually, Erin orders turkey or egg salad. Never pastrami," Rosa continued, this time to Nick. "Hey, maybe this means you two are meant for each other."

"Let's not get carried away," Erin objected. "I…I felt like a change. It's just a sandwich."

"Ah, but what a sandwich," Nick put in. He kissed his fingertips in the deli owner's direction. "Rosa makes the best pastrami on whole wheat I've ever tasted. No wonder Erin wants one, too.''

''You better watch out. He's a charmer,'' Rosa told Erin with a sly smile. ''Hot mustard or seeded?''

''I'll bet she likes it hot,'' Nick said with a wink at Rosa.

''Seeded, please,'' Erin replied coolly. This wasn't turning out at all the way she'd planned. She handed over the money in exchange for the wrapped sandwich. ''Thank you.'' As quickly as she could without appearing to rush, she headed for the exit.

Before she reached it, Nick was there, holding open the door and handing her a paper cup. ''Don't forget your dill pickle.''

Now was the time to snub him, but he spoke with such insouciant goodwill that she couldn't think of a single dampening comment. With his glittering dark eyes and curving smile, he looked like a cross between a handsome devil and a guardian angel. She'd been mistaken about one thing—there wasn't a trace of egotism in that sinfully attractive face.

Something inside her melted and she laughed. ''Thanks.'' She took the pickle and backed out the door. ''Nice meeting you. See you…sometime.''

Nick watched her move away down the street. Then he turned to Rosa. ''How fast can you make a turkey sandwich?''

''Faster than she can walk back to the bank.'' Rosa smiled at him and slapped sliced meat onto bread and piled it with lettuce and tomato. ''Erin is a very nice girl. Very pretty.''

"Very." He grabbed the wrapped sandwich and threw down some money. "Thanks, Rosa. Oh, and two coffees, to go."

"Sure thing. Erin likes caffe latte."

Nick grinned. "Make it two."

By the time he reached the sidewalk Erin had disappeared from sight. He walked in the direction of the bank, glancing into side streets. And then he saw her, strolling down a lane toward the park by the river. He caught up with her just as she was settling onto a wooden bench.

"Well, what do you know? This is my favorite bench, too," he said, sitting down beside her.

"Are you following me?" she demanded, but a hint of a smile warmed her voice.

"Just another amazing coincidence." He handed her a foam cup with a wisp of steam curling from the hole in the plastic lid. "Caffe latte?"

"Thank you. Or should I thank Rosa?" She slanted him a sideways glance from under lowered lids, reminding him of the first day he'd seen her.

"You and I are on the same wavelength, can't you tell?" Nick hoped she wouldn't think him rude for staring. Her long, gently waving blond hair, parted in the middle, contrasted sexily with her business outfit, but seemed to suit those ultra-long legs, which ended in multicolored suede high heels. He glanced at the still unwrapped sandwich in her lap. "Aren't you going to eat?"

She smiled ruefully. "This is embarrassing to admit, but I hate pastrami."

He held out his sandwich. "Trade?"

"Pastrami for pastrami? What's the point?"

"I've got turkey."

"Why?" she asked, suspicious but obviously tempted.

Smiling, he held her gaze. "Sometimes words just pop out of my mouth. You got me so flustered that before I knew what I was saying, I asked Rosa for turkey on sour dough with lettuce, hold the mayo."

Laughing, she traded sandwiches with him. "You're a case."

"I'm sure you mean that in the nicest possible way," he said as he unwrapped his sandwich. "You don't seem like the kind of lady who would insult a virtual stranger."

Erin took a bite, then pulled off a corner of her crust and threw it onto the grass for the ducks. A mallard family waddled over, quacking hungrily. "The whole town's talking about you. You're hardly a stranger anymore."

"How boring. You already know everything about me." He peered around her at the paper cup sitting on the bench. "Planning on eating that pickle?"

She handed it to him with a glance hinting of mischief. "Not everything."

"Oh?" The dill crunched beneath his teeth. "Is there something you'd like to know but don't?"

Pink suffused her cheeks, bringing out the blue in her eyes, and she laughed silently. "I could win a bet...."

"Just ask. I'll tell you anything."

Sobering, she sipped her coffee. "Don't say that. The local grapevine can be intrusive. People here are genuinely caring, but you have to guard your privacy."

"I guess you're right," he said, remembering the pinched-faced woman in the deli and her snide remarks to Erin.

They ate in silence for a few minutes. Across the river, Nick spotted a familiar figure clothed in tight black flares, a midriff-baring white top and clunky red platform sandals ambling toward the footbridge. "Miranda!" he called, and waved.

"Is that your daughter?" Erin asked, starting on the second half of her sandwich.

"Yes. Frankly, I'm surprised to see her outside. All week she's been slouched in front of the TV."

Miranda saw him and lifted her hand in a half-hearted wave.

"She's tall for a twelve-year-old," Erin remarked.

"She's a child in a woman's body." Familiar worries gnawed his insides. "All she thinks about are boys, clothes and makeup. Although you'd never know about the last two by the awful way she dresses."

"She'll grow out of it. I made some unbelievable fashion mistakes when I was a teenager."

Nick glanced at her suit. He didn't know much about women's clothes, but he could tell quality when he saw it. "That seems hard to believe."

She smiled. "My little sister Geena is a model. Whenever she visits, she goes through my closet and throws things out, then takes me shopping. Sometimes she passes on designer outfits she's worn once or twice. Our feet are exactly the same size so I really score on shoes.''

To Nick, Erin looked beautiful enough to be a model herself. Her face was long and oval, with wide blue eyes and a slight bump in the middle of her nose. Her full mouth showed a lot of perfect white teeth when she smiled. "You don't mind her taking over like that?"

"Are you kidding? I love it! I like to wear nice clothes, but I don't usually have a lot of time to shop. Besides, she's my sister,'' she added, as though that explained everything.

Miranda reached their side of the footbridge and hesitated, as though unable to decide whether to grace them with her presence. Nick waved her over again. To his embarrassment, she simply lifted a hand before taking the path to town. For an instant he saw his daughter through a stranger's eyes—sullen and unlovely. The thought no sooner crossed his mind than it was replaced by a wave of protective love.

"She's a good kid," he said to Erin. "Smart as they come, especially at math. But sometimes she can be a little rude.''

"You don't have to apologize. Twelve is a tough age.''

"Tell me something I don't know.'' He took the last bite of his sandwich and chewed in silence.

"I hear you like fishing,'' Erin said. He glanced at her, eyebrows raised, and she added with an apologetic smile, "Walt, who owns the sporting goods store, mentioned to Kelly's husband, Max, that you'd been in to buy some fishing lures."

Nick crushed his empty foam cup. "I wish Walt were as free with information on fishing spots. He acted awfully cagey when I asked him to recommend some good places."

"The locals are very protective of their fishing holes." Her smile turned dreamy. "My sisters and I used to fish with my grandfather. He had a secret spot on the river not even Jonah Haines or the mayor knows about. I caught my first fish there. Granddad used to bring in the biggest steelhead of anyone in these parts."

"I don't suppose you'd join me fishing tomorrow morning and show me where it is?" Nick said hopefully. He'd like to find that fishing hole, but more than that, he'd like to get to know Erin better.

Erin was quiet as she tucked her empty sandwich wrapper inside her cup. Finally she said, "I'm pretty busy helping my grandmother."

She brushed a few crumbs off her skirt, pushed back her hair. Another second, Nick realized, and she'd be getting up to leave. "Would you have dinner with me sometime?"

He felt her retreat even before she got to her feet and tossed her cup into a nearby trash bin. "Thanks, but I don't think that's a good idea."

Nick rose, too, shaking out the creases in his pants. Damn. They'd gotten along fine until he'd asked to see her again. Maybe she was still hung up on that guy in Seattle, whoever he was. Well, he could be patient. In a town this small it was inevitable they would run into each other again.

When they reached the main street, Erin paused. "I'm going the other way. I want to stop in at Kelly's office."

"No explanation necessary," he said, holding up his hands. "Thanks for your company. I hope now that you've gotten to know me a little you won't be afraid of me."

Her creamy cheeks turned rosy. "I was never afraid of you."

Of yourself, then, he thought suddenly. He didn't say it aloud in case she became more embarrassed or even indignant. But if true, it would confirm what he hoped—that she was attracted to him, too. "See you later, then."

He'd started walking toward the fire station when she called, "Nick?"

He turned on his heel. "Yes?"

"If you've got a minute, come with me to my sister's office. I'll show you on a map where Granddad's fishing hole is."

He grinned. "Great."

"On one condition," she warned. "Don't tell anyone else."

"Don't worry," he said. "Your secret's safe with me."

"YOU AND YOUR CLOCKS," Gran said, settling into her armless chair by the window in the living room.

She dug through her needlework bag while Erin went around the room carefully winding her most prized possessions.

"You don't mind them, do you, Gran? I'll turn the chimes off at night if they keep you awake." She had three mantel clocks and four wall clocks—minus the one she'd taken to the bank and not counting her bedside clock. The grandfather in the hallway made seven at home. Seven sets of chimes ringing through the big house every hour on the hour.

"The chimes don't bother me, and I find the ticking soothing," Gran said, pulling out a large square of tapestry with an intricate pattern depicting a stag in a forest. "The two you left behind when you went to New York years ago kept me company and reminded me of you."

Erin started to sit in one of the overstuffed wing chairs opposite the fireplace. "Did you take your blood pressure medicine after dinner?"

"I don't need that stuff—"

"Yes, you do." Erin went to the kitchen, poured a glass of water from the jug in the fridge and grabbed the bottle containing Gran's medicine from the counter. Back in the living room she handed it to her grandmother and stood over her while she took it. "I came back to take care of you and that's what I'm going to do."

"Bully," Gran said mildly, but she swallowed the tablets.

"It's for your own good." Erin smiled fondly at

her. "How many times did you say that to me when I was growing up?"

"You never liked taking medicine, either. Not even those flavored children's pain relievers Kelly popped into her mouth like candy." Gran smiled as she threaded green yarn through a large needle.

"She used to sneak them when you were in the garden."

"Did she think I didn't know that? You girls were a handful. There was fourteen months between each of you, but you behaved more like triplets."

"True," Erin said. "Whatever one of us did, the others followed. Piano lessons, Girl Scouts, basketball..."

The chiming clocks drowned out her words. It was seven o'clock on a Friday night. If she were in Seattle she'd be getting dressed to go out to dinner with John or to a club with friends. Erin pulled back the lace curtain to gaze out the window at Linden Street. It was one of those golden late-summer evenings when the light fades slowly and children play outside till long past their normal bedtime.

"Why don't you call up one of your old friends?" Gran said. "Laura Emerson still lives over on Vermont Street."

Erin heard a tiny meow at her feet and bent to pick up Chloe, rubbing the kitten's soft fur against her cheek. "Not tonight. I've still got the laundry to do. And I'm a little tired."

She was very tired, in fact. Unusually so. The week had seemed long what with adjusting to her new job and settling in. She wondered what Nick was doing right now. Sitting on his deck on the water enjoying the fine evening? Out on a date? The thought rankled unexpectedly.

"Is Granddad's fishing gear still in the garage, Gran?"

"I expect it is." Gran glanced at her with mild curiosity. "Planning on going fishing?"

"Sometime. Maybe." Part of Erin wished she were going with Nick tomorrow. He made her laugh, and she'd had far too few laughs in recent months. But getting to know him would complicate her relationship with John and distract her from caring for Gran.

"I hear our new fire chief is a keen fisherman." Gran's fingers dexterously pushed the needle in and out of the tapestry. "What did Kelly say his name was again?"

"Nick Dalton. I ran into him at Rosa's the other day. I told him where he could find Granddad's fishing hole."

"I see." The older woman's mouth curled into a knowing smile.

"It's not like that, Gran. I was just being neighborly to a newcomer."

Gran tied off the green and reached for a ball of yellow yarn. "Whatever you say, dear."

"RISE AND SHINE." Nick rapped on Miranda's shut door. "It's six o'clock."

A loud groan issued from the bedroom. "I can't believe you're making me go fishing."

"Oh, come on. You love it, you just can't admit it." He leaned on the doorjamb and inspected his nails while he waited for the biting reply.

"Yeah, right."

Nick set his head on one side judiciously. "The contemptuous tone is outstanding, but the verbal display fails to dazzle," he said, mimicking the patter of a sports commentator. A second later her slipper hit the door. Nick chuckled. It was either laugh or yell, and he disliked yelling, even though sometimes she goaded him into it. The only way to deal with Miranda and emerge sane was to tease her into doing what she was supposed to do. A mention of forthcoming treats never hurt, either. "Fish with me today, and next week we'll go into Seattle and get you some school clothes."

"I don't want to go to school." Her token grumble sounded muffled beneath her pillow.

"You're a little old for that line. If you want breakfast before we go you'd better get up now." Then he walked off before she could make another smart remark. These "discussions" could go on endlessly, and although a little was amusing, too much was not.

"Why are you in such a good mood?" she demanded ten minutes later over the scrambled eggs he'd set before her.

"Must be your charming company—which I miss, by the way." Nick took his own plate to the sink. Outside the window, beyond the river, the sun had risen above the distant mountains. Water lapped at the edge of the deck from the wake of a passing gillnetter, gulls screeching noisily. "You've been on your own all week and this is a chance for us to do something together."

She scooped some egg onto her fork. "Fishing is boring."

"You didn't think so the time you caught a salmon up in British Columbia." He filled a thermos with freshly brewed coffee and tipped the remainder into his cup.

"I didn't know any better," she said. "I was only ten."

"A mere child," he agreed. In so many ways she still was. But once again he acknowledged how her heart-shaped face and green eyes were rapidly maturing and her developing bust and hips made her look less like a child every day. Certainly less like *his* child and more like her mother's. And once again his stomach constricted as the memory of Janine's deathbed confession came to mind like a recurring nightmare. Had she told the truth when she'd said their daughter might not be his—or had she only wanted to hurt him?

"What day are we going shopping?" Miranda asked.

"Next Saturday." He sipped his coffee. "Maybe Erin can suggest some good stores."

"Who's Erin? That woman you were with in the park?"

"Yes, and you will be nice to her if and when you happen to meet her." So far Miranda hadn't been kind to the few women in his life since Janine had passed away. "Erin works in the bank." Craftily, he added, "One of her sisters is a fashion model."

Miranda lifted her head. "A supermodel?"

"Probably." If Erin was anything to go by.

Thinking of Erin made him lean against the counter with his coffee and zone out. If her grandfather's fishing hole was all it was cracked up to be, he would be on her doorstep before the day was through, luring her to dinner with the prospect of fresh fish. He had a bottle of white Zinfandel in the fridge. Would candles be too much? Maybe one, in the center of the table.

"Earth to Dad. Come in, Dad."

He blinked and saw Miranda waving a hand in front of his face, her empty plate in her hand. "A few minutes ago you were dragging me out of bed. Are we going, or what?" she demanded.

"Sorry, I must have been daydreaming."

"You've been acting very weird the last couple of days, you know that?"

CHAPTER FOUR

ERIN DIDN'T WAKE UP until ten on Saturday morning. Although she'd gone to bed early and slept soundly, she still felt tired. As she swung her legs over the side of the bed, her stomach lurched queasily. With an involuntary moan, she clutched her midsection. She hoped she wasn't coming down with the flu.

Later that afternoon, Erin was in the backyard, digging well-composted horse manure into the flower bed. Her stomach had settled down after breakfast. She'd weeded and mulched the mixed beds of perennials and colorful annuals, keeping a watchful eye out that Gran, given the job of trimming dead heads, didn't overtax herself.

After lunch Gran had gone in for a nap and Erin carried on. She ought to wash the floors when she was finished gardening. Then there was the vacuuming, the bathroom to clean and the laundry. She'd suggested hiring a cleaning lady, but again Gran had been so upset at the thought of a stranger in her house that Erin had given up the idea. Weekdays she got up early and did at least one chore before breakfast so Gran wouldn't have anything to do. Keeping her grandmother resting was a job in itself.

At the front of the house, the doorbell rang.

"Coming," she called, scrambling to her feet. She hurried around the side of the house, hoping the ringing hadn't wakened Gran.

Her heart gave a little leap. Nick Dalton stood on the porch in hip waders and a fishing vest, holding a string of steelhead trout. His wide white grin contrasted sharply with the five o'clock shadow on his strong jaw. "Look what I pulled out of your grandfather's fishing hole."

Erin climbed the stairs, pushing at straggly wisps of hair that had broken free of her ponytail, and self-consciously brushing bits of compost off her baggy-kneed, shiny-bottomed track pants. Pants she'd hidden in the back of the linen closet so Geena couldn't get her ruthless hands on them.

"Three steelhead," she exclaimed. "Congratulations."

"I've got more. These are for you and your grandmother."

"Why, thank you." She started to reach for them, then withdrew her hand when her stomach roiled at the faint but distinctive fishy odor. Her "bug" was back. "You caught them, keep them for yourself."

He thrust the fish toward her. "If it wasn't for you I might not have caught any."

"Really, I insist." She backed away from the fish and into the front door just as it opened from behind. "Wha— Oh, Gran!"

"Well, what do we have here?" Bright-eyed and

sprightly after her rest, she glanced from the string of fish to Nick.

"Nick Dalton, ma'am." He shook her hand, then presented her with the trout. "My respects to your late husband. I brought you ladies an offering from his fishing hole."

"Why, thank you. Call me Ruth. I'm pleased to meet you." Gran gave him a friendly smile. "Erin, why don't you ask this nice young man in for coffee."

"Well, he probably has to get back." She glanced at the dark green Suburban parked at the curb. "Is that your daughter waiting in the car?"

Gran waved a hand. "She can come in, too."

Nick gazed at his vehicle and thoughtfully stroked his jaw. "Miranda's wet and muddy. She wouldn't want to go into anyone's house."

"Another time," Erin said.

"Go home and change first," Gran suggested hospitably.

"Actually, I was wondering if Erin would like to join us for dinner," Nick said, speaking to Gran but looking at Erin.

Erin crossed her arms over her rebellious stomach. If Gran wasn't standing there she was sure she could think of a little white lie. "Uh…"

Before she could speak, Gran reminded her, "Kelly will be here tonight."

Saved. "That's right." She turned to Nick. "Thanks, but I can't."

Then Gran's eyes lit behind her outsize glasses.

"Nick and his daughter can come over here and we'll have ourselves a big old fish fry."

Erin stared at her grandmother. "I'm sure Nick has other things to do today. Shopping, for example. It's Saturday." She'd heard from Kathy down at the grocery store that Nick bought his weekly supplies on Saturday afternoons.

"I went last night, just to keep people on their toes," he told her with a wink. "But I don't want to intrude on your family dinner."

She wasn't feeling well; she could beg off. But as he backed away, all at once she found herself saying, "No. Please join us."

Then she glanced at the trout and covered her mouth. She wasn't up to dealing with fish. "Are they cleaned?"

"They are. But I'll take them home and wrap them and the others in foil. Ma'am," he said, retrieving the fish from Gran. "Thanks for the invitation. We'll see you shortly."

As he walked back to his car, Gran nudged Erin in the ribs. "I think he likes you."

ERIN RUMMAGED THROUGH boxes and assorted junk in the garage for the barbecue starter fluid. From the backyard she could hear the tumbling clatter of the briquettes Nick was pouring into the barbecue. Despite telling herself she wasn't trying to attract or encourage the man, she'd showered, washed her hair and changed into a flowing summer dress that brought out the blue in her eyes. The floors and the laundry could wait.

"Here's the starter fluid," Erin said when she rejoined him a moment later, and watched as he poured a liberal dose over the briquettes with a satisfied grin. "You're enjoying this."

A playful light in his eyes, he capped the tin of starter fluid. "I'm a fireman."

Miranda, who sat cross-legged on the grass teasing Chloe into leaping at a dandelion, glanced up. "He's a firebug. He loves fire."

These were the first words the girl had uttered besides hello. Erin eyed Nick curiously. "Is that true?"

"I don't light them, but yeah, I get a buzz out of fighting fires. Most firefighters do."

"Water—now, that's a different story," Miranda said sagely.

"*Miranda.*"

The ring through Miranda's nose quivered as she gleefully ignored the warning. "He's from California and he can't even swim. He loves boats, but hates being in water."

Nick laughed it off. "She keeps me humble."

Erin could have cheerfully smacked the girl. "I can't ski, even though Mount Baker is barely an hour's drive away," she confessed. "I'm terrified I'll break a leg."

"Have you two got that barbecue going yet?" Gran called from the back porch. "Kelly and Max and their brood will be here soon."

Nick held a lit match above the briquettes. "Stand back."

Whoosh! Orange flames leaped into the air and a burst of intense heat drove Erin back a pace. Through the flames she could see Nick's face lit by the fire, his hair lifting with the breeze from the backdraft, and his grin of delight. She had to laugh. As annoyed as she'd been with Gran for orchestrating this event, she had to admit she was enjoying his company.

Nick moved around the barbecue and stood beside her. His gaze on the flames, he leaned sideways, his bare arm brushing hers, and the faint scent of his woodsy after-shave came to her over the pungent smells of charcoal and starter fluid. "I appreciate you having us over. It's nice to be made welcome in a new town."

She smoothed a hand over her skin where her arm had touched his, wondering if she should move away. Staying put ensured more contact, which seemed to be what he wanted, but was she ready for it? "You'll soon get to know everyone. And once Miranda starts school she'll make friends."

"I hope you're right. Miranda can be pretty disdainful about small towns." He shoved his hands in his pockets, effectively increasing the distance between them.

Erin glanced at the girl. She'd put on headphones, and the tinny beat of techno music mingled with the determined chirping of a robin sitting on a branch of the cherry tree above her head. "Raising a daughter on your own must be difficult."

"Teenagers are like another species altogether. We used to be close, but now it's hard to find activities we can do together and both enjoy."

"She went fishing with you."

"And whined the whole time."

"Does she like sports?"

"Sure. Let's see, there's Internet *surfing,* telephone *marathons*…oh, yeah, and she loves *racket* sports— MTV at top volume."

Erin chuckled. "I'm coaching the junior girls' basketball team this year at the YWCA. If Miranda's interested, I'd love to have her on the team. Our first practice will be a few weeks after school starts."

"Did you hear that, Miranda?" Nick called.

"What?" she answered lazily.

"Do you want to join Erin's basketball team?"

"Basketball's boring."

Nick picked up the poker lying on the grass and pushed the briquettes around. "According to her, everything's boring these days except video hits and clothes and—" he paused to shudder "—makeup." He shook his head and smiled wryly. "I'd give her a few tips but we have completely different coloring."

Erin glanced at Miranda's inexpertly applied eyeshadow and dark purple lipstick. Underneath the paint was a pretty, if insecure, young woman. "True, she doesn't look anything like you," she said, and added jokingly, "are you sure she's not the milkman's child?"

Nick's smile faded abruptly and he lapsed into

stony silence. He gave the briquettes a jab with the poker, raising a shower of sparks.

"I'm sorry. I didn't mean—" Erin broke off; she was making her blunder worse by apologizing.

When Nick glanced up, he was smiling again, his face blandly cheerful. "You wouldn't happen to have a beer, would you? It's a little hot here at the coal face."

She smiled tentatively. "Sure. I'll get you one and be right back. Miranda," she called to the girl, "would you like a soda?"

"Yes, please."

Erin ran up the back steps and into the kitchen, where Gran was mixing a batch of coleslaw in a big stainless steel bowl. Half a dozen foil-wrapped fish lined the counter. "Gran, what are you doing! I said I'd make the salad. Why don't you take a cool drink outside and find a seat in the shade."

Ruth gave the mix a final stir and dropped the spoon into the sink. "How's Nick going to ask you out if you're in here and he's out there?"

"Gran, you're being silly. No, Gran, look at me. Don't start matchmaking. It's embarrassing. Anyone would think I'm the old maid the family is trying to marry off."

"Aren't you?" her sister teased from the doorway. Kelly came in carrying a plastic-wrapped bowl in one hand and a cake tin in the other. Tammy and Tina milled around her skirt, while her older two, Robyn and Beth, followed carrying extra lawn chairs.

"Here, let me help you." Erin unloaded the bowl

and gave Kelly a hug. "Hi, girls. Robyn, Beth, are you looking forward to going back to school?"

Her question elicited loud groans from nine-year-old Robyn and a shy nod from seven-year-old Beth. Both girls had inherited their mother's dark hair and brown eyes, though they'd likely be tall like their father.

"Where's Chloe?" the smaller children demanded.

"Outside," Ruth said, taking off her apron. "Shall we go find her? Come on, everyone." She and the children went out the back door.

"I'm glad we could get together today," Erin said to Kelly. "I've hardly seen you since I've been back." She went to the fridge for the cold drinks. "Where's Max?"

Kelly's mouth dropped at the corners, the way it did when she was trying not to cry. "He's not coming. We had a fight. He's ticked off with me because I worked again last night. But he sends you his love."

"Oh, Kel." Erin put the drink cans on the counter. She closed her arms around Kelly again. "It'll be okay. Say hi to Max for me."

"I will." Kelly's voice quavered; she was definitely not her usual happy-go-lucky self. "Sorry. I didn't mean to fall apart."

"Shh," Erin whispered. "What's a sister for? Today's not a good time for a heart-to-heart, but let's make a time to talk, just us, really soon."

"I'd like that." Kelly reached for a tissue from the box on the counter and blotted her eyes. "I've got a pretty busy schedule this week. I might be able to squeeze in an hour for lunch on Thursday.''

''You know, you're ruining my image of the slow-paced small town,'' Erin teased as she brushed the hair out of her little sister's eyes and straightened the collar of her blouse. ''If there's anything I can do to help, such as baby-sitting, call me. You and Max could go out for a wild night on the town.''

Kelly's smile returned, full of mischief. ''I'd have thought you'd be more interested in your own wild night out—with our gorgeous new fire chief. I saw the way he looked at you the other day.''

Erin rolled her eyes. ''Don't *you* start. And keep your voice down. He's in the backyard.''

''You're kidding!'' Kelly went to the window and peered out. ''Gosh, Erin, how can you not be interested?''

''He *is* nice.'' She put the cans and some tall glasses on a tray. ''Grab that bag of chips, would you?''

''Nice?'' Kelly repeated. ''That's all you can say? Nice?''

''Okay, *really* nice. But John isn't totally out of the picture. Come on. Let's take this stuff out. I promised the man a beer.''

THEY ATE AT A CLOTH-COVERED table in the shade of the big old cherry tree that spread its thick limbs across half the backyard. The mellow afternoon was warm and golden, rich with the aroma of barbecued fish and the honeyed scents of late-summer flowers.

The queasiness that had dogged Erin on and off all day had abated. Replete and content, she placed her knife and fork atop her empty plate and sat back.

"That trout was the best I've ever tasted," she pronounced with a smile for Nick. "My compliments to the chef."

He raised his glass, holding her gaze across the table. "Thank you."

Erin didn't miss Kelly's and Gran's quick exchange of glances, but she hoped Nick had. Her sister and grandmother had thus far resisted embarrassing her, but she had a horrible feeling that was about to end.

"I hear there's a new movie on at the theater," Kelly said with a casual innocence Erin recognized as one-hundred-percent calculated. "A romantic comedy."

"Sounds like just your sort of film, Erin," Gran said, picking up her cue like a pro.

Erin silently began stacking empty plates together.

"What type of movies do *you* like, Nick?" Kelly continued in the same innocent tone.

Erin leaned over to take her sister's dish and whispered in her ear, "Cut it out."

Before Nick could say anything, Miranda spoke up. "Dad likes action movies. Car chases and explosions. Guy stuff."

"Thank you, Miranda," he said good-humoredly. "I have been known to branch out on occasion."

"Perhaps dining out is more your style," Gran suggested. "Nearby Simcoe has several fine restaurants and Seattle is only an hour away."

"Erin lived there for years. She's familiar with all the best spots," Kelly chimed in.

Erin sighed. There was no stopping them.

"Dad hates to eat out," Miranda countered quickly. "Plain home cooking—that's what he likes."

"Erin's a wonderful cook," Gran and Kelly said together.

Miranda's beringed nostrils flared as she clearly tried desperately to think of a comeback.

Erin glanced sideways at Nick and burst out laughing, relieved to see the humorous twinkle in his eye. "Isn't family wonderful?" she asked him, rising from the table.

"Gotta love 'em," Nick agreed. He rose, too. "I'll help you clear up the dishes."

"I'm sorry about that," Erin apologized when they'd reached the kitchen. "Gran and Kelly have no idea when to quit."

"They mean well, which is more than I can say for Miranda."

"She doesn't need to feel threatened."

Nick set his stack of bowls in the sink. "I know, although try to convince her of that."

Erin heard the click from the New Haven shelf clock that signaled the hour. If Nick heard it, he didn't realize the significance, because a second later he jumped as the house resonated with the melodious combination of bells and bongs.

"What the hell?" He turned in a slow circle, trying to locate the source of the echoing chimes. He stopped in front of the shelf clock, with its wooden front carved in the shape of a church. "This isn't making all that noise."

"It's only one of seven. I collect clocks," Erin said, pitching her voice above the chimes. "MTV has nothing on me as far as racket goes."

"That's an unusual hobby. I bet you never miss an appointment. You'll have to show them all to me someday, but speaking of time..." Nick eyed his watch. "Miranda and I had better get going."

Erin went with him to the back door. "If she changes her mind about playing basketball, let me know."

"I'll do that." He paused, head lowered in thought. Then he glanced up, his mouth serious. "Erin?"

Erin found herself looking for the twinkle that lurked in his eyes. "Yes?"

"Would you like to trade sandwiches again on Monday?"

Decision time. Part of her had been hoping he would ask to see her again, but now that the moment was here, she let a beat go by, then another. Hands loosely linked in front of him, he waited, confident but not arrogant. Exuding masculinity. Regarding her curiously, patiently.

"My fiancé in Seattle...*ex*-fiancé," she amended painfully. "It's only fair to warn you, we may get back together."

Nick spread his hands. "This isn't a marriage proposal. Just an invitation to lunch."

Only lunch. Yet deep down, she knew there was more to it than they were pretending; otherwise why would accepting seem so significant?

In spite of her reservations, she found herself saying, "In that case, I'd like that very much."

THE NEXT DAY, SUNDAY, Erin felt queasy most of the day. It couldn't be Kelly's potato salad, she reasoned, because Gran had eaten some and she felt fine. And it couldn't be the flu because she had no other symptoms.

A sudden thought made her palms dampen.

That last weekend with John... No. No way! They'd used protection every single time. She was too cautious not to, and John was too averse to children. She must have a stomach bug. Erin ignored the mild nausea as best she could and went on with her day.

Monday morning, she threw up in the toilet.

Her bare toes curling against the tile floor, she shivered inside her flannel bathrobe. But not because she was sick with food poisoning or gastroenteritis.

Inside she knew with cold certainty exactly what her condition was. She couldn't bring herself to voice her suspicion. Not yet. Not until the evidence was before her.

She dressed quickly and slipped out of the house before breakfast to drive thirty miles down the highway to Simcoe to buy a pregnancy testing kit. Once home again, she ran up the stairs to the bathroom before Gran could ask her where she'd been. With trembling fingers she administered the test and sat on the closed toilet seat to wait for the results.

The procedure was a mere formality. Erin knew even before the indicator strip turned color that she was pregnant. Now that she thought about it, her period was over a week late—she, who'd always been as regular as a Swiss timepiece. Yet she stared at the stick of damp paper with numb disbelief.

She was going to have a baby. A tiny thread of delight curled inside her heart. And then disappeared as she contemplated the reality of her situation.

She and John were anything but a couple. Raising a child by herself? She adored her sister's kids, but the thought of being responsible for children of her own was daunting. Babies, especially, terrified her. They weren't like numbers, predictable and compliant, staying put in neat columns and always adding up the same. Erin tried to recapture the shred of delight, but it was gone, overwhelmed by a host of fears for the uncertain future.

She forced herself to adhere to her morning routine—shower, dress, makeup and hair. Everything went wrong. She applied conditioner first instead of shampoo and wondered why it didn't lather. Then she ripped three pairs of stockings before she thought to file down a ragged nail. Her hand shook and pins rained onto the tile floor as she fumbled to roll her hair flat against the back of her head. By the time she hurried out the door, her clocks were chiming nine, the hour at which she should have been at the bank.

All her life she'd put one foot in front of the other, always knowing where she was headed. This morning when she stepped onto the sidewalk to go to work she felt as though the universe had shifted. Nothing looked familiar. Not the cream picket fence that bordered Gran's house or the broad-leafed maples that lined the street. Next door, Mrs. Contafio waved to her from her front step, where she was retrieving her milk and newspaper. Erin walked past, aware only of the knot in her stomach.

She was going to be a mother. And she was scared spitless.

Despite being late for work, her footsteps slowed as she approached the fire station. What guy would be interested in a woman who was pregnant by another man? The answer came to her with the swiftness of instinct—*not Nick.* Her mind flashed back to her joke about Miranda and the milkman and how Nick had reacted. She didn't know what that was all about, but she'd obviously touched a sore spot.

She walked softly, not wanting to attract attention, but he must have been watching for her. Even before she was abreast of the station, he strolled out of the truck bay. He glanced at his watch, then thrust his hands in his pockets as casually as if he were merely taking a breath of air. On the sidewalk, he awaited her approach.

His dark hair and freshly shaven jaw gleamed in the morning sunlight. "Good morning. Beautiful day."

She felt his gaze absorbing her hair, her face, her

legs. *Beautiful woman,* his eyes added silently. He couldn't see the nervous flutter in her stomach. Or the baby in her womb.

"It's lovely," she agreed.

"Perfect for lunch in the park."

Be firm but nice, she told herself. He would know the reason for her backing off soon enough. For now he would just have to think of her as fickle. "I was going to call you. I..." Despite her resolve to be brave, her voice wobbled. Hoping he hadn't noticed, she cleared her throat and said more firmly, "I won't be able to make it."

There was a moment's pause, and then he said easily, "No problem. We'll do it tomorrow."

"Tomorrow's no good, either." Her hands wanted to twist themselves around the strap of her leather handbag. She forced them to be still, and radiated calm and certainty. Aloofness.

A tiny frown line appeared between his eyebrows, but his voice was even. "What day would be good?"

Erin took a deep breath. "I'm sorry, Nick. This isn't going to work out. I...I've got to go. I'm late."

She started to walk away, heart pounding.

"Wait!" He strode after her and put a hand on her arm. "I don't understand. What happened between Saturday evening and this morning to change your mind?"

She couldn't stand it; her gaze dropped. For some inexplicable reason, the sight of her Jimmy Choos with the kitten heels toe to toe with his polished black leather brogues filled her with loss. Lifting her eyes to his, she answered, "I...I've had time to think. You know how people in small towns talk."

"You are not going to tell me you're worried about the town gossips," he said, hands on his hips, blatant disbelief in his voice. "What could anyone say that could possibly harm either of us?"

She conjured up a vivid image of herself hugely pregnant, and Nick cast unfairly and unwillingly as the father. She couldn't put him in such an untenable position.

Nor could she bear to sit by and wait for him to reject her.

She shrugged, forcing herself to appear nonchalant. "I'm sorry. I just don't want to get involved. Please accept my decision."

Shutting her heart to the hurt and anger in his eyes, she put her chin in the air, straightened her shoulders and walked out of his life.

CHAPTER FIVE

NICK STARED AFTER ERIN. She'd broken their date! With no explanation, barely an apology. He watched her graceful sway, her trim, muscular calves flexing above tapered ankles, her feet striding firmly despite her high heels.

He hadn't misread the signals on Saturday; he was positive. *He'd* asked and *she'd* said yes. What could be clearer?

"Nick." Steve was calling him.

"Yeah?" he said distractedly, still gazing after her receding figure. All those clocks to remind her of the time, yet she was late. That tough cookie act didn't fool him; something had happened to upset her. He had half a mind to go after her...

"Dave's here. All the volunteers are ready."

For a second, Nick wondered what Steve was talking about. Then he caught sight of a burly guy in his early fifties, silver-blond hair in wispy tangles around his collar. Oh, *that* Dave. One of the volunteers, an aging hippie and ex-lawyer from Mendocino who was sure he and Nick had something in common because they were both from California.

"I'll be right there." He'd met all the volunteers

the previous week, but this was the first of their monthly training sessions he was to participate in. He sent one more glance down the street. Erin was crossing at the traffic lights, walking into the bank....

He turned abruptly, glancing at the sky. It was going to rain.

He went through the truck bay to the empty lot behind the station where the volunteers had assembled. Besides Dave, there were Rick and Rob, car salesman brothers in their forties; Frank, a retired Navy Seal, who held his grizzled head with military bearing; and last but not least, Angela, a thirty-something manager of the local pizza parlor, who clearly did weight training.

Nick surveyed his ragtag band. "Are those all the volunteers?" he asked Steve in a low voice.

Steve nodded. "We used to have about twenty, but the old chief was such a pain in the butt he drove most of them away over the years."

"Okay, let's see how they do on some routine ladder work."

Nick donned a raincoat and watched while Steve put the group through their paces. The weather wasn't the only cause for gloom. The volunteers were awful. They didn't work as a team, they barely knew which end of the ladder was up and if fire did break out, heaven help the victims because the Hainesville volunteers sure wouldn't be much use.

By the end of the session the rain was coming down steadily. Nick waited while Rick and Rob worked the controls to retract the extension ladder.

When the group had shuffled into a semblance of order, he stood before them, legs splayed, hands behind his back.

"We've got some work to do before we're working efficiently as a team. This fire department relies upon volunteers. If the school is burning and children are trapped inside, their anxious parents are depending on *you* to save little Timmy or little Alice. So from now on, we'll have weekly training sessions. In the meantime, if you know anyone who's interested in becoming a volunteer, tell him or her to come and talk to me. That's all for now unless there are any questions. No? Then you're dismissed."

Frank snapped a salute and turned smartly on his heel as if he were on the parade ground. The others drifted away through the rain.

Back inside the station, Nick and Steve hung their wet jackets on hooks inside the truck bay and went to the day room for a coffee. On one side was a small kitchen with a table and chairs; on the other side was a battered couch, a coffee table piled with magazines and dog-eared paperbacks, and an ancient TV.

Steve made coffee and they carried their steaming mugs to the table. "They're not usually quite that bad," Steve said, pouring sugar from a container into his cup and stirring. "They were nervous because you were watching."

"A few more sessions and I'll have them working like pros," Nick said as he sipped his coffee. "But we need to recruit more volunteers. Another paid firefighter wouldn't go amiss, either."

Steve tipped back on his chair. "Good luck. Hainesville isn't exactly rolling in dough and council members are notoriously tightfisted. Watch out for Greta Vogler. She's not only on the council, she's got her finger in every pie around town. Nothing gets passed without her approval."

"Greta Vogler," Nick mused. "Is she that prune-faced biddy with the tight curls and her blouse buttoned up to her eyebrows?"

Steve nodded, chuckling. "She teaches English over at the high school. Lived here all her life. My granny says she had a tragic love affair when she was young that turned her sour."

"Hard to imagine someone like her being young and in love," Nick said. "You got a girlfriend, Steve?"

"Sort of. Angela."

"What do you mean, sort of?"

Steve pushed his cup away and began to draw circles in the condensation left by the hot mug on the Formica tabletop. "We went out once or twice. I thought things were going great. I thought she *liked* me. Then one day about a month ago she broke our date with no explanation."

"That would put a crimp in a relationship," Nick commented dryly, thinking of his exchange with Erin that morning. "Did she say why?"

"Nah, just some bull about not being ready to get serious. Heck, all I did was invite her bowling." He dragged his cup back and took a sip, adding gloomily, "I think she's seeing someone over in Simcoe."

The boyfriend in Seattle. Maybe Erin had heard from him over the weekend. Well, hell, she could have told Nick. He wouldn't have liked it but he'd have understood. And at least he'd know what he was up against.

"So what should I do?" Steve asked.

"I'm not exactly the best person to ask," Nick replied. "Not having much luck myself."

"But you must have some ideas," Steve persisted. "I'm desperate."

"Isn't Angela a little older than you?"

Steve shrugged. "Five or six years. Doesn't bother me."

Try seven or eight, maybe even eight or nine. "Might bother *her.*"

Nick chewed on the end of the wooden coffee stirrer. What if it wasn't the boyfriend? What if Erin was bothered by something about Nick? Such as his rebellious preteen daughter. What woman in her right mind would want to jump feet first into his problems? If so, that was too bad, because he and Miranda were a package deal. Not that he was serious yet; he just wanted to get to know Erin, have some fun and enjoy her company.

All at once he couldn't wait a minute longer to find out why she'd blown him off.

Nick rose and headed for the door. "I'm going for lunch. I'll be back in about an hour."

Now, where would Erin go to eat her sandwich on a wet day?

IN A WINDOW BOOTH at the Bluebird Café, Erin was listening to Kelly's domestic problems and feeling terrible, partly for Kelly and partly because she'd had no idea things had gotten so bad between her sister and brother-in-law.

"We're fighting all the time now," Kelly said, sniffing. "I walk in the door and he thrusts Tina at me and says something horrible like 'Your daughter's crying for you.' I mean, just because I've got a job, why does he have to lay this big guilt trip on me? He makes me feel like I'm a bad mother."

Panic trickled like icewater down Erin's spine. If *Kelly,* who doted on her children, was a bad mother, then what would she, Erin, be?

The waitress arrived and Erin ordered soup and salad for both of them, since Kelly was much too upset to talk.

"We should have gone somewhere else, Kel," Erin said, handing her sister a wad of paper napkins from the dispenser.

"I only have half an hour," Kelly said, dabbing at her eyes, trying not to smudge her makeup. Not that her efforts made much difference thanks to the dark circles already beneath her eyes.

"Gran's right. You're working too hard. You're wearing yourself out. You'll have a nervous breakdown or something."

Kelly glared at her. "Why don't you all join forces against me—you, Gran and Max."

"We're just worried about you. You shouldn't neglect your family, Kel," Erin said gently. "Or yourself.'' She put a hand on her empty stomach as if that would quell the now familiar feeling of nausea. ''Oh, miss,'' she called to a passing waitress. ''Could I have some crackers, please?''

''Sure thing, honey.''

The waitress dropped off little packages of Saltines the next time she went past and Erin ripped open the cellophane as though she hadn't eaten in a week. She just hoped she wasn't too late to prevent herself from throwing up in the café washroom.

''Have you sat down and tried to talk things through with Max?'' she asked between mouthfuls. Erin wanted desperately to tell Kelly about the baby and try to figure out what on earth she was going to do, but how could she spill out her problems when Kelly's were so much more immediate?

''You must really be hungry,'' Kelly said, distracted by the crackers. ''I've never seen you eat so fast.''

''I, uh, missed breakfast. So, what about Max? Have you two talked?''

Kelly shook her head, her mouth twisting disconsolately. ''He never listens. He's angry because suddenly I'm not there every minute of the day to take care of the kids so he can work whenever *he* wants. It's not fair. Why should his job be more important than mine?''

Erin knew Max had worked long hours for many years to build up his home-based architect business. ''Because he's the primary breadwinner?''

''If I had half a chance, *I* could make a significant

contribution to the family finances. Does he consider that? No."

"Maybe he feels threatened by your success." Erin looked up gratefully as the waitress deposited their salads on the table. But when she picked up her fork, she found she had no appetite for the greenery she normally thrived on. Her knotted stomach seemed to *know* cellulose was impossible for humans to digest.

"If he's threatened, he'd never admit it," Kelly said, stabbing into a pile of baby spinach leaves. "Listen to that rain come down. You'd never believe it was August."

Erin glanced at the streaming windows. And saw Nick walk past, his shoulders hunched into his jacket, rain coming off his hood in sheets. Quickly she turned back, praying that Kelly wouldn't notice and invite him to join them. But Kelly was too involved in talking about Max.

"He's always saying these are the best years, rah, rah, and we should spend the time with the kids while we can, but does he practice what he preaches?"

"Kelly, don't you like being a mother?"

"'Course I do," Kelly replied. "I just want to be *me,* as well. Can't anybody understand that? Getting ahead in my profession requires putting in the hours. What's my boss going to think if I'm always running home to care for my children? He wouldn't take me seriously. He'd give the big commissions to other agents."

"I guess you're right." Erin picked at the bacon bits on top of her salad, items she usually discarded as having too many calories. Would she be able to hang on to *her* job once she had the baby? Who would take care of it during the day? She couldn't ask Gran. She hadn't even told Gran. "What's the day care center like?"

"Good. Tricia Morrisy runs it. Remember her? She was in Geena's class in high school. Tina and Tammy love her."

"Great." But did she want her baby loving a surrogate mother? What did spending eight or nine hours every day in day care do to a child's emotional development? Erin sighed. Mother's guilt obviously began with conception.

"So I said to Max—" Kelly broke off. "Erin? Are you with me? What's wrong? I don't think you've heard a word I've said in the past five minutes."

"Sorry, Kel. I've…got something on my mind."

Kelly's pretty mouth turned up. "Could that something be a certain fire chief?"

Erin pushed away her uneaten salad. "I just found out I'm pregnant."

Kelly blinked. "That was fast. You almost had me convinced you weren't even interested in Nick. Now you're having his baby."

"Don't be ridiculous," Erin hissed. "The baby is John's. And keep your voice down. Greta Vogler just sat down at the counter."

She was sure now that she'd done the right thing in breaking her lunch date with Nick. If Kelly, who ought to know better, could jump to the conclusion that he had fathered Erin's baby, so might the whole town. She felt bad about letting him down, but he would find someone else to exchange sandwiches with. Angrily she ground the heel of her hand into her moist eyes. Stupid hormones. She hated being pregnant.

"You're pregnant!" Kelly said in a thrilled whisper as though she'd only just taken it in. "That's so exciting."

Erin gazed miserably at her. "Yeah, right."

"Well, it would be better if you were committed to someone long term, but still... A baby. Wait till I tell the kids they're going to have a new little cousin."

"Kelly! Don't you dare!"

"Why not?" Kelly stared at her. "Are you thinking of terminating?"

"No, I just don't know how I'm going to manage."

"You will, somehow. I'll help."

"Oh, Kelly." Erin gazed at her sister with affectionate exasperation. "You don't have enough time for your own family."

"Have you told Gran?"

"No," Erin said slowly. "And I'm not going to just yet. She pretends she's back to normal but she's still fragile. I don't want to trigger another heart attack."

"She's not *that* fragile." Kelly chased the last spinach leaf around the plate and finally speared it. "Have you seen a doctor? How far along are you?"

"I'm going to see my doctor in Seattle this Saturday. As far as I can figure, I'm only a few weeks along." She paused. "I'm also going to see John and tell him."

"Promise me you won't do anything stupid like marrying him for the sake of the baby." When Erin didn't answer right away, Kelly became alarmed. "Erin? Tell me you won't."

"Would it really be so bad to give my baby a mother *and* a father?"

"*Yes,* if the father is John. It would be totally stupid. Has he even called you since you moved back here?"

"He's really busy, Kel. Give him a chance."

Kelly snorted in disgust. "A chance to hurt you."

"Kelly, I'm scared stiff of being a single mom. Not of having to do without. That doesn't bother me because we never had much when we were growing up. But what do I know about raising children? And Gran will be so disappointed when she finds out, maybe even ashamed. She had such high hopes for me."

Kelly leaned over and squeezed her hand. "Don't worry, Erin. And don't underestimate Gran. Everything will turn out okay. At least you're healthy and have a good job to fall back on. And you have family."

Erin smiled shakily. "I know. I'm sorry. I should quit whining and count my blessings."

Kelly glanced at her watch and dropped her crumpled napkin beside her half-eaten bowl of soup. "Yikes, I've got to run."

"But your lunch," Erin protested.

"Have it. You're eating for two."

Erin forced herself to finish her soup even though she had little appetite. She left a tip and went to the cash register to pay, giving Greta a cool smile as she passed, hoping the older woman wouldn't pump her for information.

"How's your grandmother?" Greta inquired while Erin waited for her change.

"She's well. Thank you for asking." Erin said politely.

"And how's Kelly? She works *so* hard, poor girl. I don't know how her husband manages those poor tykes on his own."

"Kelly's *fine*," Erin replied emphatically. "Really good. And Max *adores* his kids."

"And Geena? Have you heard from her lately?"

Erin stifled a sigh of impatience. The truth was no one in the family had heard from Geena for months and they were all a little worried. But Erin wasn't about to tell Greta that. "Geena's fine, too. Oh, dear, look at the time. I must get back to the bank. Nice talking to you, Greta."

She turned quickly. And ran smack into Nick Dalton. His raincoat dripped onto the tile floor of the café and his dark hair was plastered to his head.

"Erin, I've been looking all over town for you. Can we talk?" He gestured to an empty booth.

Erin cursed silently. If she refused to talk to Nick, Greta would be very interested to know why not. If she *did* talk to him, Greta would hang on every word. "Outside," she muttered.

"What?" Nick looked back at the steady downpour in dismay.

"Outside." Erin slipped into her jacket and hustled him back through the door. She held her umbrella to shelter both of them and caught the scent of rainwater on warm male skin. "What did you want to talk about?"

Brooding eyes gazed at her from under black lashes spiky with water. "I would like to know why you broke our date."

Beneath the dome of the umbrella the air was humid and the steady drumming of raindrops on taut nylon nearly drowned out the swish of car tires on wet pavement. His mouth was within kissing distance, his eyes the warmest she'd ever seen. There were so many things she could say. But her vocal cords couldn't seem to make the sounds that meant *I'm pregnant.*

"It's a very long story." She glanced at the café and saw Greta watching them. She had to wrap this up quickly.

"I have time to hear it this weekend," Nick said. "Saturday I'm taking Miranda shopping in Seattle for school clothes, but Saturday night, or Sunday, I could be all yours."

"My life is pretty complicated right now...." She trailed off. Nick's intense focus made it hard for her to concentrate on saying no. Her doctor's appointment was at three, and she wouldn't catch John until late afternoon since he usually worked Saturday.

"I'm going to Seattle this weekend, too," she

found herself telling Nick. ''I could spend a few hours with you and Miranda in the morning, show you some good places to shop.''

His flashing smile sizzled through her; evaporating, she felt sure, the raindrops as they hit her overheated body,

''Fantastic.'' He wrapped his hand around hers on the curved wooden handle, lowered the umbrella around them and, before she knew what was happening, kissed her quick and hard on the mouth.

She was still catching her breath when he growled softly, ''See you Saturday,'' and ducked out from under her umbrella to stride off through the rain, whistling.

Erin touched her fingers to her still-tingling lips. What on earth had she done?

''I'm taking my own car!'' she called after him.

He spun on his heel and walked backward a pace or two, giving her a nod and another brilliant smile.

This was a big mistake, she thought, twirling the umbrella between her fingers, trying to suppress an answering grin.

But a thrillingly delicious one.

NICK SHIFTED IMPATIENTLY between two racks of skirts in the Juniors section of a major department store. At least, he assumed they were skirts. They were cut shorter than the rag he used to wash the Suburban.

Miranda came out of the fitting room wearing a scrap of fluorescent pink that barely covered her rear end, and thrust a hip at the mirror. "Cool. I've never had a skirt like this."

"Turn around, Miranda," Erin instructed, and the girl obediently twirled on her toes.

Was Erin *serious?* As if he would *ever* allow Miranda to buy that outfit. "I can see her underwear, for God's sake."

"Da-a-ad. Keep your voice down." Miranda's gaze darted in search of witnesses to her humiliation, but none of the other shoppers was paying them any attention.

Erin threw him a quelling glance, then turned to Miranda. "Sit down on that chair."

Miranda complied. As meek as a lamb, Nick noticed grumpily. Why wasn't she like that with him?

"Comfortable?" Erin asked Miranda. "Can you cross your legs?"

"Sure." Miranda stretched one leg over the other, revealing acres of skin, or so it seemed to Nick. She tugged at the skirt hem. "It's fine, see?"

Nick clapped a hand to his face, shutting out the sight of his daughter's bare limbs. Although still coltish, she had her mother's legs—shapely and attractive.

"You are *not* buying that skirt," he snarled, not caring who heard.

Erin cut him off with a sharp clearing of her throat and turned back to Miranda. "Stand up again. Let me see... Lovely color, nice fabric." Then Erin joined her at the mirror. "Turn around...look at the back."

Miranda twisted to peer over her shoulder at her image. "Okay, now bend over."

Nick spun away so fast he almost toppled a revolving rack of belts. Then he heard Miranda say "Ohmigod," and he glanced across to see her streaked hair flopping upside down with her backside facing the mirror.

Red-faced, she straightened, tugged down the skirt and looked ruefully at Erin. "Maybe not. I wouldn't even be able to pick up a pencil if I dropped it."

Erin gave a theatrical sigh. "I guess you're right." She pointed Miranda toward the fitting room. "While you're changing, I'll find you something else to try, shall I?"

"Okay," Miranda said happily, and off she went.

Nick extricated himself from the belt display and followed Erin to a clothes rack holding longer skirts. "You had me worried for a minute. You know how she hangs on your every word—"

"I understand why you want Miranda to have clothes that are reasonably modest," Erin said, slipping a hanger off the rack and adding it to the ones in her hand. "But she's got to like them, too, or she won't wear them, and you'll have wasted your money. We can get her into nice outfits, but it's got to seem like *her* idea." She gave him a stern glance. "So, please, no more outbursts."

Put in his place, he could only say, "Yes, ma'am."

"That's more like it," she said, still brusque. Then her lips curved in a teasing smile that set his adrenaline pumping as fast as the water lines at a three-alarm fire.

After that Nick prudently kept his mouth shut. Given the job of holding the "keepers," he soon had a double armful of skirts, pants and blouses. One or two midriff-baring tops crept into the bundle, but Nick decided he could live with them, considering that the rest were respectable.

"Thank goodness that's over," he said as they went through the checkout, only wincing a little when he saw the total.

"Oh, we're not done yet," Erin informed him. "She'll need shoes to go with those new clothes."

"Ooh, yeah," Miranda chimed in enthusiastically.

Nick groaned. "All right. Anything to get her off those stilts."

"I *love* these shoes," Miranda declared, glancing down at her worn red platforms. "I want another pair just like them."

"Let's see what they've got," Erin said, who was every bit as eager as Miranda. She led them through the crowded store, Miranda hurrying after her and Nick trailing behind carrying the shopping bags.

As they passed the cosmetics department, Miranda slowed at a counter displaying rows of lipsticks. *Oh, no,* Nick groaned to himself, almost choking as another customer spritzed copious perfume onto her wrists, *not more makeup.*

"You know, Miranda," Erin said, pausing beside her. "If you're going to wear makeup, you might as well learn how to apply it properly, find out what shades go with your coloring.''

"Cool. What do you suggest?''

"Just a moment.'' Erin turned to Nick. "Why don't you get a coffee and meet us in half an hour in the shoe department.''

No way did he want to stick around for a makeover session, but *more makeup?* "Erin...'' he began.

She tilted her head and gave him that look. "Trust me.''

Well, she'd done fine with the clothes. "Okay. I'll take these bags to the car and see you shortly.''

As he walked away he heard Erin say to Miranda, "A good rule of thumb when it comes to makeup is, less is more,'' and knew his daughter was in safe hands.

So he was a little surprised when he returned from the carpark to find them in the shoe department trying on a pair of red platform shoes nearly identical to the scuffed ones Miranda already owned. High heels were fine on a grown woman—on Erin they looked sensational—but he'd been hoping for a nice flat loafer or saddle shoes for Miranda.

"Shouldn't you wear something more sensible for school?''

Two pairs of eyes turned on him, Miranda's horrified, Erin's mildly appalled.

"Da-a-ad.'' Miranda's cakey mascara was gone and her lipstick was barely more than a sheer gloss, but her attitude to shoes clearly hadn't altered.

"Sensible?" Erin looked scandalized. "We're talking *shoes.* You don't want sensible. You want *style.*"

"Okay." Nick held up his hands in surrender. He was definitely not going to win this one. "I'll be over in Sporting Goods. Come find me when you're done." He glowered at Miranda, needing to assert some authority. "Nothing over two inches, young lady. And stick to the budget we agreed on." He turned to Erin. "I insist on at least one pair of flat shoes."

Erin and Miranda exchanged inscrutable female glances. They seemed to come to some silent conclusion, because they turned to him with compliant nods.

"Okay, then." He left them to it, only partially reassured.

When they showed him Miranda's purchases at lunch he knew why his intuition had raised alarm bells. The flat shoes were as soft as bedroom slippers and as frivolous as the sparkly plastic high-heels Miranda had worn as a fairy princess at the age of five.

"They were on sale," Erin said, digging into her shrimp salad with an apparently clear conscience. Seeing his face, she added, "Miranda still has her running shoes for casual wear."

"Why is it that the more impractical the shoe, the better women like them?" he asked, without expecting an answer. He could hardly criticize Erin when the sight of her slender ankle in a fashionable shoe was enough to turn his head. But his daughter was another matter.

"If she ends up with orthotic inserts I'll hold you

personally responsible.'' Then he softened. ''But thanks. You've been an enormous help. I couldn't have done what you did today.'' He reached across the table and laid his hand over hers.

Erin smiled, her cheeks turning pink. ''I had fun.''

Miranda glanced up from her clam chowder and noted their linked hands. ''Are you guys, like, going together?''

Erin withdrew her hand. ''We're just friends.''

Just friends. Nick stabbed at a piece of fried halibut. She still hadn't told him why she was putting him off. He'd hoped they would have a chance to talk, but that wouldn't be possible with Miranda around.

''We're going to the aquarium this afternoon,'' he said to Erin. ''Can you join us?'' Maybe with Miranda's nose pressed against the glass of the beluga exhibit he and Erin would have a chance for a few quiet words.

''I'm sorry. I have an appointment.''

''Afterward?''

Her face clouded as she picked through her salad for the shrimp. ''I...I'm going to see a...friend.''

She was meeting her ex-fiancé; Nick would bet his life on it. ''I see. Are you and this friend...renewing old ties?''

''What are you talking about?'' Miranda interrupted, her radar picking up on the change of tone.

''Nothing that concerns you, sweetheart. Finish your soup.'' His gaze locked with Erin's, challenging and penetrating. *Please tell me you're not.*

''Maybe.'' She pulled her gaze away from his.

With hands that trembled slightly, she buttered a slice of sourdough bread.

Hell. Nick threw down his fork. So far, nothing he said or did had the power to change her mind. He caught Erin's regretful glance laced with—could it be *longing?* She felt something for him, he was certain, but wouldn't, or couldn't, act on it. Frustration might be eating him up, but she was obviously going through an emotional crisis. He felt bad for grilling her, especially in front of Miranda.

Fine. He would bide his time. Again.

CHAPTER SIX

ERIN WAITED ON THE EDGE of the cream love seat for John to finish making coffee. The sudden hiss of the espresso machine through the open kitchen door made her shift nervously on the cold leather. She went over again in her mind the words, the tone, in which she would relay what ought to be the happiest news of a couple's life together. But they weren't a couple, and John, at least, wouldn't be happy to learn he was going to be a father.

Bearing a lacquered tray holding two frothy, steaming cups, John entered the room. Erin waited until he'd set the tray on the coffee table; then, casting aside all her emotion-loaded phrases, she said matter-of-factly, "John, I'm pregnant. The baby is yours."

John jerked upright, his hand catching the edge of the tray and setting the cups rattling in their saucers. He backed into the matching sofa opposite. "Are you sure?"

He didn't sound quite as horrified as she'd feared, but neither did he look as though he wanted to hand out cigars to his buddies down at the courthouse. "My gynecologist confirmed it this afternoon." She sipped her cappuccino. "Is this decaf? Caffeine isn't good for the baby."

"What? Oh, yeah. The regular stuff upsets my stomach these days." Ignoring his coffee, John moved to the sideboard, where he poured Jack Daniel's neat into a crystal tumbler. He swallowed a big gulp, grimacing.

Erin was glad she'd decided to play it cool. John wasn't fond of emotional scenes and she didn't want to prejudice him against the baby because she was a hormonal mess. But the fact that he needed a stiff drink didn't bode well for her or the baby.

John sat across from her and leaned forward, elbows on his knees. He had himself under control now, and his voice was gentle, even caring. "How've you been, Erin?"

"Fine. I—" She'd started to say "I've missed you," then stopped, wondering how true that was. With all the changes in her life lately—Gran's care, her new job, Nick—she hadn't had time to miss him. She waited. The ball was still in his court.

John loosened his silk tie, ran his long fingers through his well-cut dark blond hair, careful not to muss it. He was elegant and cultured, appreciated fine art and good food; she missed that. In the mirrored lobbies of restaurants he used to watch the pair of them go by and admire how well they looked together. She'd chided him for his vanity and secretly agreed.

"Are you sure it's mine?" he said.

That hurt. "We were engaged for over two years. I haven't been with anyone else in all that time. The baby can't belong to anyone but you." Tears were perilously close to the surface. Hormones again. She pushed herself to her feet. "I'll go. I just thought you had a right to know that you were going to be a father."

"Erin, wait." He put his drink down and reached for her as she attempted to brush past him on her way to the door. "I'm sorry," he said, folding his arms around her.

She couldn't bring herself to pull away. The longing to believe he cared about her and the baby was too strong. "I didn't plan this, John."

"It's just such a shock. Do *you* want the baby?"

"What do you mean?"

"You may still have a choice," John said carefully. "How far along are you?"

"You mean, I should have an abortion? Never."

He chuckled. "Ms. Pro Choice refusing to have an abortion?"

Her opinion on the subject had swung one hundred and eighty degrees practically overnight. "I still believe in choice, but I could never abort my own baby. *You* don't want the baby, is that it?"

"I didn't say that. The thing is, I'm going to announce I'm running for Congress soon. If the media get hold of an illegitimate pregnancy in my background I can kiss my election chances goodbye."

It obviously didn't occur to him that he could fix this by making her pregnancy legitimate. "I'm talking about a life created by the two of us. We have a responsibility to our baby."

"I have a responsibility to the people of Washington,'' he remonstrated gently. ''I can do so much good for the state, but not if my personal situation is put under the spotlight. You can see that, can't you?''

''In a way, but—''

''I'm going to ask you a big favor. Don't mention my name as the father.'' Her shock must have shown in her face. ''Just temporarily,'' he said, planting soft, tender kisses that brought tears back to the surface. ''Please, babe, just for a while. You know I care about you. And the baby.''

''If we were married, no one would question your morality.''

She felt him stiffen. His hands moved from her back to her arms, stroking them. ''Now isn't a good time to discuss marriage. Or anything, for that matter.'' He glanced at his watch. ''I was getting ready to go out when you showed up.''

''Are...are you seeing someone else?''

''No, it's just a campaign fund-raiser. Boring old business thing.''

''Okay.'' She blotted her eyes from a well-worn tissue. ''We'll talk another time.''

''That's the spirit. Everything's going to be fine. You'll see.''

The doorbell rang. John left her to answer it. Erin reached for her coat on the back of the sofa.

''Hello, John,'' a female voice purred from the doorway.

''Right on time,'' he replied briskly, ushering in a tall brunette in a black evening gown. ''Erin, you remember Andrea, from my office.''

"Hello, Andrea." Erin forced a smile for the aggressive young lawyer, who throughout Erin's relationship with John had flirted blatantly and relentlessly with him. Had Andrea finally won? Or was this truly just a business dinner?

John put his arm around Erin's waist, reassuring her, and led her to the door. "I'll call you. I promise."

Erin kissed him on the cheek.

Whether they ended up together or not, she and John were bound forever by this baby. He was the father. That had to mean something.

ON THE FIRST DAY OF SCHOOL, Nick dropped Miranda a block away from Hainesville Secondary. This concession was in exchange for her *not* wearing a midriff-baring T-shirt.

"Don't pick me up," she warned before climbing down from the Suburban. "I'll walk to the fire station to meet you."

Nick watched her stride away, kicking through the first yellow leaves of autumn that had fallen from tall oak trees bordering the football field. Her footsteps slowed as she caught up to the drifts of students gradually moving toward the entrance. He could tell she was nervous, even though she would have died rather than admit it. Would she loosen up and make friends? Or would she put everyone off with that falsely superior attitude?

She passed a group of kids about her own age and he saw her toss her magenta-streaked locks and lift her nose in the air. The kids paused in the conversation and laughed unkindly. Nick winced for her sake. With a sigh, he put the truck into gear and drove off. Hard as it was to quell his fatherly angst, some battles she had to fight on her own.

AT LUNCHTIME ERIN PASSED clusters of high school students heading for the Burger Shack and wondered how Miranda's first day was going. Not that she was likely to find out; she was back to avoiding Nick. Instead of getting a sandwich at Rosa's, she'd started going home for lunch. It meant she had a little less time for her break, but at least she could make sure Gran was taking her medication and eating properly. Shortly after arriving home, she had lunch prepared.

"Let's sit in the dining room," she suggested, carrying their plates of reheated quiche to the polished mahogany table; there they could enjoy the view of the front yard through the big bay window.

Gran sat and went to work cutting her lunch into bite-size pieces. "You never did say much about your trip to Seattle on the weekend. Did Miranda get some clothes that won't keep her father awake at night?"

"Let's just say we found outfits they could both live with." She smiled a little sadly, remembering a day that likely wouldn't be repeated. "I had fun."

"I'm sure you did. They're nice people." Gran paused. "How did things go with John?"

Erin poured water from a jug into two glasses, avoiding Gran's sharp gaze. She hadn't told her the real purpose of her trip to Seattle. "Fine," she fibbed.

"He's running for Congress, so we didn't get to spend much time together."

"He's welcome to visit you here."

"Thanks." Erin flashed her a grateful smile that just as quickly faded. "But we didn't make any plans to see each other again."

Gran put a hand on her arm. "I'm sorry to hear that. I prefer Nick myself, and I know Kelly doesn't like John, but if *you* care for John that's enough for me." Then, ever practical, she added, "He's got a good job and could provide for you."

"I've got a good job and can provide for myself," Erin pointed out.

"True, but someday you'll settle down and start a family. When that happens you'll be out of the workforce, at least for a while."

Out of the workforce. Would she still be at the bank when the baby was due? Erin took a bite of quiche. She dreaded having to tell Mr. Haines she was pregnant. She dreaded telling *anyone*. Damn it, she didn't want to be pregnant.

Gran took a bite of quiche and chewed daintily. "I heard from Dorothy Atkinson, who heard from Mary Gribble, that Jonah Haines thinks the sun shines out of your you-know-what."

"Gran!" Erin scolded with a giggle. "He did not say that."

Her grandmother's eyes sparkled behind her glasses. "I may have interpreted Mary's words a little loosely, but that's the general idea. Apparently you've got things running as smooth as a top over at the bank and he's grateful.''

"Tracy is smart and fun to work with, and Bobby falls all over himself to do things for me. They make my job easy.'' She passed a plate of sliced tomatoes and carrot sticks. "Eat your vegetables.''

Gran made a face and took some. "Well, I guess you have plenty of time before you need to start worrying about having babies. I wouldn't be surprised if Jonah passed over the reins to you in a year or so when he retires.''

"I'm not sure I'd want that,'' Erin said. "Once you're completely better I might go back to Seattle to live and just come out on weekends.''

"Oh.'' Gran tempered the disappointment in her voice with an understanding smile. "It's a pity we can't find something or someone to tempt you into staying if things don't work out with John. Nick, for instance, is a fine man.''

"Don't get your hopes up where Nick is concerned, Gran. As I said, I won't be seeing him again.''

Gran, about to bite into a carrot stick, lowered her hand. "Why not?''

"Well…'' Erin was saved from having to explain by the sight of a speck of gray fluff scrambling up the trunk of the maple tree. "Chloe!'' she exclaimed, leaping to her feet. "She's climbing the maple.''

Gran pushed back her chair and joined Erin at the window. "How on earth did she get out? That kitten doesn't have a lick of sense. She'll get stuck up there.''

"Don't worry, Gran. I'll get her."

Erin went to the door, slipped her stocking feet into a pair of tennis shoes and ran down the front steps, across the grass to the tree. Chloe was already beyond reach, her tiny limbs splayed against the trunk as she dug in with her claws. Erin hesitated only a moment, then grasped one of the massive lower limbs and lifted a foot, finding purchase against the rough bark with the toe of her tennies. Luckily her skirt was cotton-knit and stretched with her.

Holding tightly to the handrail, Gran descended the steps as fast as she could. "Don't you go doing anything foolish like climbing that tree. You'll give me another heart attack."

Erin paused, crouching on the first limb. "Don't worry, Gran. I've climbed this tree a million times. I'll have Chloe down in a jiffy."

"Oh, Erin, I don't think you should be doing this." Gran stood at the bottom, looking up and wringing her hands.

"Piece of cake." Erin stretched for the next limb. "Chloe, come here, sweetheart." The kitten meowed piteously and moved higher.

Erin climbed easily until she reached the branch level with her bedroom window. As a child and a teenager, she'd gone right to the top of the tree. So far this was no big deal.

Or was it? Fifteen feet below, the ground seemed to shimmer in the heat, and she was beginning to feel a little light-headed. Between the branch she was standing on and the next one up there was a big gap.

As she recalled, bridging the two meant shinnying up the trunk.

"Chloe. Here, girl," she crooned, trying to entice the kitten to reverse direction. The cat's fluffy gray-blue fur stuck straight out and her ears were flattened to her skull. She looked at Erin, meowed and went higher.

"Erin, come down," Gran called. "We'll call the fire department to get the cat."

"Don't do that!" The last thing she wanted was Nick over here.

Erin took a deep breath. Stretching her arm high, she curled her fingers around the next branch. She hugged the trunk with her other arm, placed one foot high against the trunk and heaved herself up. Once on the next limb, she clung to the trunk, blood pounding in her ears while she caught her breath and waited for her courage to return.

"Erin!" Gran's thin wail seemed to come from far away. Susan Trembley from across the street came out of her house and joined Gran below the tree.

"I'm fine, Gran," Erin called back, but her words were a hoarse whisper that Gran couldn't possibly have heard. Why was this so hard? True, she hadn't climbed this high in five or so years—okay, maybe ten—but surely it was like riding a bicycle, something you never forgot. Above her, Chloe's continuous, staccato meows betrayed her fear.

"I'm coming, Chloe." Erin renewed her grip on the branch above and put all her effort into lifting herself. Her bare legs scraped painfully on the bark, a fingernail broke, and she heard a rip along the side seam of her skirt. But she made it, gasping for breath, onto the limb. With her last ounce of strength, she reached up, grabbed Chloe by the scruff and dragged her off her branch, stiff-legged and mewling.

"I got her," she called to Gran, and snuggled the trembling kitten to her breast. Now that she had Chloe safely in her grasp, the danger of her situation became apparent. She was perched precariously on a narrow branch twenty-five feet above the ground, light-headed through a combination of exertion and fear, without the least idea of how she was going to get down.

What had she been thinking? What if she'd fallen and injured the baby? In her effort to reach the kitten she hadn't given a thought to her own safety, much less the safety of her unborn child. She could *still* fall. She hadn't wanted this baby, but now some primal instinct made her fiercely protective of it. Dizzy at the thought of miscarrying, she hugged the trunk and Chloe and squeezed her eyes shut.

Faintly, she could hear Susan talking to Gran, no doubt discussing her predicament and how to get her down. Soon the whole street would be here, maybe even a reporter from the *Hainesville Herald*.

"Don't worry, Erin," Gran called up to her. "Susan saw you and Chloe in the tree and phoned the fire station. Hang on, honey. Nick will be along any minute."

The words were barely out of Gran's mouth when Erin heard the siren's wail. She could have sunk through the earth with humiliation—if the earth hadn't been so far below her feet. With a last effort at saving herself, she loosened her death grip on the trunk and stuck out a foot to begin her descent. Her foot dangled in thin air, and when she glanced down the tree seemed to sway. *Oh, dear.* Beads of sweat popped out on Erin's brow and her stomach did a somersault. Renewing her hold on the tree, she decided she wasn't going anywhere.

The siren's wail became louder, deafeningly so, and then abruptly ceased as the big red ladder truck pulled up at the curb. Nick hopped down from the driver's seat. He wore his usual white shirt and black pants—plus a big grin.

There was nothing Erin could do but wait with as much dignity as she could muster while Nick worked the automated controls that sent the extension ladder shooting up. He swiveled the base around until the top rested next to her against the tree trunk, and then he was nimbly running up the rungs. Seconds later, his shoulders and head appeared against a backdrop of leafy green.

"Fancy meeting you here." His deep voice was rich with unspilled laughter as he plucked a twig from her hair. "Are you okay?"

"Fine." Suddenly she was aware, not just of the debris in her hair but of the rip in her skirt and the scratches on her legs. Dignity was a state of mind, she told herself. "I want you to know I've climbed up and down this tree a million times."

"I believe you. Probably not always with a kitten

in your arms, though. May I?'' He pried Chloe from Erin's knit top and tucked the animal inside his shirt, wincing as her claws dug into his skin.

''Since you're an old hand at tree climbing, I guess you don't need help getting down,'' he added, his dancing eyes at odds with his bland expression.

''Ordinarily, I wouldn't...'' Erin began.

Nick saluted her and started down the ladder.

Panic squeezed the air from her lungs. She looked at the ground. An elderly man had joined Gran and Susan, and a little way off stood a woman with a baby buggy and an excited four-year-old. Every face was upturned; every eye waited and watched.

''Damn it, Nick! You can't leave me up here.'' She glared at him, silently demanding him to stop teasing.

His probing gaze turned grave; his smile became gentle. ''On the other hand, it's not often I get a chance to rescue a damsel in distress. How about letting me play hero, seeing as how I'm new in town and need all the PR I can get.''

Erin relaxed a little, enough to release her hold on the tree and accept his outstretched hand. ''Since you put it that way...''

Instantly Nick became a trained professional, calmly coaxing her into completely letting go of the trunk. ''Put your arm around my neck. That's right. Now step away from the branch. I'm right here. I've got you.''

Going from branch to ladder involved a leap of faith, but with Nick's steady gaze and strong arms closing around her, she felt as secure as if they'd been standing on the sidewalk below.

At the top of the ladder she clung to him, not caring what he, or anyone, thought. Her long hair spilled over his shoulder and her cheek scraped across the faint stubble of his jaw. She breathed in a whisper of some masculine-scented soap, starched cotton and clean sweat.

He held her long enough for her to catch her breath. "Are you ready to climb down the ladder?"

His voice was a warm murmur against the buzzing of blood in her ears. Then he moved his head and she was gazing into intense dark eyes. She looked at his mouth, with its crooked upper lip and full lower one, and nodded, ready to do anything he asked.

His hands, firm and impersonal, slid to her waist, maneuvered her so she faced the ladder. He descended two steps and gripped the sides of the ladder so that he was behind and below her, protecting her and controlling her descent. She could feel Nick's body heat from her calves to her shoulders and every tingling inch in between.

The rest was over in a blur, and before she knew it, Nick was lifting her off the truck and setting her on the ground. Gran rushed over and felt her forehead with the back of her hand as though she were five years old instead of thirty. Susan clucked away in the background, and the elderly gentleman continued to gaze up into the tree as if hopeful someone or something else might emerge from its branches. The four-year-old tugged on Nick's pant leg wanting to know if he could ride on the fire engine.

Erin wobbled a little, then sank to her knees beneath the tree. When she felt the cool grass and the solid earth, she gave thanks that despite her foolishness her baby was going to be okay.

Nick pulled Chloe out of his shirt and handed her to Ruth. Then he bent so that he was eye to eye with the little boy. "Get your mom to bring you to the fire station sometime and I'll show you *all* the trucks, okay? Right now I have to make sure the lady is all right."

The boy nodded vigorously and tugged on his mother's hand. They moved off down the street, followed by the shuffling old man. Gran supported herself on Susan Trembley's arm. "If you'll help me back inside, Susan, I guess Nick can take care of Erin."

Erin wanted to groan with embarrassment. If only Gran knew how useless throwing her at Nick was now. She struggled to stand, but Nick crouched on the grass in front of her, pushing aside locks of hair to cup her cheek in the warmth of his palm. "You're white!"

With his other hand, he picked up her wrist and pressed his fingertips to her pulse. "Lots of people react badly to heights," he said. "I'll buy you a hot fudge sundae after work. Deal?"

"I can't," she whispered, moving her head away from his hand.

"A movie to take your mind off your ordeal? I'd

even sit through a romantic comedy if you were beside me.''

"Please don't keep asking. I hate turning you down. You're too nice.''

"*Nice*—that's the kiss of death if I'm not mistaken. Look, I don't want to be a pest, but I thought we connected, right from the start. If you're getting back with your boyfriend, just tell me.''

"I'm not.''

"Then what is it?'' He must have seen something in her face, for he added, more urgently, ''What's wrong, Erin? You're upset, and not just about getting stuck up the tree. Am I right?''

Mutely, she nodded. Suddenly it wasn't fair *not* to tell him. Though their acquaintance was short, already he felt like a friend. Maybe she was overreacting. Maybe her pregnancy wouldn't matter. At any rate, she couldn't hide the truth from him forever. Better he learn about the baby from her rather than someone like Greta Vogler. For some reason, telling him seemed easier than telling people she'd known all her life.

"I'm pregnant.''

He recoiled as if she'd slapped him in the face. One second he was crouched before her, his fingers loosely linked with hers. The next instant, he was on his feet, striding over to the ladder truck. His back and shoulders rigid, he stabbed at the controls and cursed when the ladder jammed and didn't retract right away.

Erin stared at him, trying very hard not to dissolve into tears. She hadn't expected him to be overjoyed at her news, but she hadn't expected this angry withdrawal, either. She felt more hurt than she would have imagined possible, considering she'd known him such a short time. Slowly she got to her feet, brushing at her clothes, pushing the hair out of her face. Stiff and polite, she said, "Thank you for getting me out of the tree."

Jaw tight, eyes cold, he walked back to her. "I take it the baby is your ex-fiancé's. So this past weekend didn't result in reconciliation?"

"No." The trace of bitterness in her voice came as a surprise.

Nick glanced away, the throbbing vein in his temple the only sign he was struggling to control his feelings—whatever those feelings were. She didn't think he'd be confiding in her any time soon.

"I know this is a shock," she said. "I only found out the day we were supposed to have lunch."

He stared at the ground, hands on his hips. "I've got a very impressionable twelve-year-old daughter who thinks you're pretty cool."

All of a sudden she was angry that he could make her feel humiliated, even ashamed. And here she'd thought they were friends. "Don't blame *me* because you can't control your daughter. I'm *glad* I'm having this baby."

And to her surprise, it was true. The moment of danger had shown her how important the life growing inside was to her. Thank God for her safe escape, for the chance to nurture her baby and to feel her own joy at becoming a mother.

His gaze swung back to her, dark and explosive. "I like you, Erin—a lot. And I'm very attracted to you. But we've only known each other a few weeks. Suddenly we're talking diapers and midnight feedings for a child who isn't mine."

"*Who's* talking diapers and midnight feedings?" she demanded, outraged. "I didn't ask you to be my baby's father."

"Good, because I've done my time. I don't want any more children."

"Didn't you hear me? I don't expect anything from you. I don't *want* anything from you." Burning with a perverse desire to drive him away for good, she pushed at his chest, backing him off her lawn and onto the sidewalk. "*Goodbye,* Mr. Dalton. And *good riddance.*"

NICK POPPED THE TAB on a can of beer and climbed the gangway to the upper deck of the houseboat. The stunning view of the sun setting over the broad reaches of the river delta was lost on him. Instead of relaxing he paced the deck, taking long slugs of his drink as the sky and water turned from silver-blue to purple in the twilight.

Erin was pregnant. *Pregnant.*

He pulled one arm across his chest and stretched out his triceps. After Erin's revelation, he'd gone back to the fire hall and spent the rest of the afternoon working out. He was tired and sore, but all the exercise in the world couldn't work off the shock and betrayal, or the sense of having taken a blow to his male ego, inappropriate as that might be.

His mind kept flashing back to Janine drifting in and out of consciousness, and in one lucid moment blurting out the devastating news that Miranda might not be his real daughter. The baby he'd cradled in his arms, the toddler he'd swung upon his shoulder, the young girl who placed her hand so trustingly in his— the child whom he loved more than his own life— might have been fathered by someone else. In one second his world had turned upside down and had never been quite right since. The most basic element in his life, the thing that had seemed rock solid and immutable, suddenly was as insubstantial as a mirage.

Nick propped his elbows on the railing, his gaze following a heron as it lifted off from a mud flat exposed by low tide and flapped lazily across the river to the salt marsh. As shaken by Janine's revelation as he was, he'd never sought a paternity test or searched out his wife's lover. He was damned if he'd hand Miranda over to a stranger, even if that man was her biological father.

CHAPTER SEVEN

ERIN HELD THE FIRST practice session for the junior girls' basketball team the third week in September. Two weeks had passed since she'd gotten stuck up the maple tree, and now its leaves were changing to orange and brown. Miranda didn't show up for basketball practice, but Erin hadn't expected her to.

Nor had Erin talked to Nick during those two weeks, or seen him except at a distance. Now he was avoiding her, too. Part of her was angry that he'd turned his back on her so completely; part of her thought she understood—a relationship needed time to grow. How could they discover if what they had was special and lasting when the responsibilities of parenthood loomed?

Responsibilities Nick had no personal stake in.

She still felt nervous about becoming a single mother, but the fierce, protective love for her unborn baby sparked by the tree incident was growing steadily. She'd gotten into the habit of talking to the baby at night in bed, one hand resting gently on her still-flat stomach. And when she turned on the radio she tuned into classical music, instinctively certain her baby would find Debussy more soothing than Eminem.

One day after work, Erin dropped by Kelly's house to pick up some books on pregnancy and childbirth. The cedar-and-slate home that Max had designed had a Japanese-influenced elegance and simplicity that couldn't disguise the fact that four active young children lived there. As Erin walked up the footpath she righted a shiny red tricycle and stepped over roller skates discarded outside the front door.

"Hi, Max," Erin said when her brother-in-law answered her ring. The pencil stuck above his ear was lost in disheveled wheat blond hair and his blue corduroy shirt was rolled up to the elbows. "Are you working?"

"Yeah. Come on in, stranger. Kelly's in the sunroom." He gave her a hug before retreating to his studio. "See you later."

Erin walked through the house, poking her head into the family room to say hello to the girls before making her way to the glass-enclosed, plant-filled room that doubled as Kelly's home office. Her sister was seated at a small secretary desk, going through her listings.

"Hi, Kel."

"Erin." Kelly removed her reading glasses and swiveled her chair around. "Sit down. The books are on the side table. Do you want coffee?"

"No, I can't stay. I have to get Gran's prescription filled before the drugstore closes." She gathered up the books and glanced through the titles. "These look great. Thanks."

"Keep them. I'm not going to need them anymore."

"Oh, yeah?" she said, grinning. "I thought Max was going for six."

"Not with me, he's not. Oh, here's something else for you." She took a business card from one of the desk's pigeonholes and handed it to Erin.

Erin studied the card, that of a Seattle medical clinic. "I've already got an OB-GYN—Oh!" Underneath the doctor's name was a list of the services in which he specialized. "Termination!"

"This guy is supposed to be good," Kelly said. "One of my clients went to him."

Erin handed the card back to her and dropped into the wicker love seat. "I'm surprised you would even *suggest* termination. You love kids."

"Being a parent is hard enough when you're married. If you're alone and not ready for children it can be really tough. If you're not thinking about terminating," Kelly added, "why aren't you telling anyone?"

Erin stared out the window to the lawn, where Beth was throwing a ball for their golden retriever. She could just imagine Kelly's reaction if she told her John had asked her not to name him as the father, and why. But there were other reasons she wasn't comfortable telling people she was pregnant. "Do you remember when we were in high school and I was voted most likely girl of my graduating class to succeed?"

"Yes, and they were right—you *have* succeeded."

Erin made a face. "That's just the problem. Everyone has these high expectations for me—a big career, fame, fortune, et cetera, et cetera. Now look at me. I'm back in my hometown about to have a baby, with no father in sight. It's…embarrassing."

"Erin, everyone in this town adores you. Why are you worried about what they'll think?"

"Wouldn't you?"

"Well," she said slowly, "I suppose if Max and I were to get a divorce, for instance, I wouldn't like people talking about us."

Something about the way she said it made Erin sit up. "You two aren't really in danger of splitting up, are you?"

"Nah," Kelly said, laughing. "Just because Max and I have been together for nearly fifteen years and he's the only man I've ever known, why should I feel I've missed out?"

Erin smiled, uncertain whether or not her sister was joking. "You and Max are my ideal couple. I've always thought you were so lucky to have found each other so young."

Kelly gave her a sad smile. Then she reached across and tucked the Seattle doctor's card into the side pocket of Erin's purse. "Just in case you change your mind. I know it's a difficult decision, but at this point it wouldn't hurt to keep your options open."

Erin shook her head and let the matter drop. "I'd better go."

Kelly walked her to the front door. "Have you heard from Nick?"

"Not since he found out I was pregnant."

"He'll come around."

"If he does, I won't be waiting." When Kelly skeptically raised an eyebrow, Erin added, "Face it, the romance was over before it started." She hugged her sister. "See you soon."

Erin drove back to town and parked not far from Blackwell's Drugstore. As she got out of the car she noticed Miranda come out of Bernie's Confectionery, eating from a small white paper bag.

Miranda sashayed along the sidewalk in one of the worst of her old outfits, a tight midriff-baring T-shirt and low-slung flared black pants. She attracted the interest of a group of senior high school boys lounging outside the drugstore, and as she passed them to go inside her wiggle became more pronounced. The boys whistled and made catcalls and she tossed her head, flicking her colorfully streaked hair.

Good grief. No wonder Nick was worried about her.

Erin entered the drugstore and went straight to the back, where Mr. Blackwell, in his white coat and wire-rimmed glasses, presided over his dispensary. Miranda had disappeared down one of the aisles.

A display of baby paraphernalia—formula, baby shampoo and lotion, bottles and teething gel—caught Erin's eye. She pictured herself using these items on her own baby, pictured herself with a suckling baby nestled against her breast. The image was *so* not her, and yet was infinitely compelling.

Erin dragged her gaze away from the baby items. "Hi, Mr. Blackwell. Busy today?"

"Moderately so. How's Ruth?" His voice boomed with reassuring familiarity, but even as he spoke, his eyes shifted past her head and his graying brows pulled together in a deep frown.

"She's getting better all the time." Erin glanced over her shoulder and realized he was watching Miranda midway down the center aisle. "Is there a problem?" she asked as she handed over the prescription covered with Dr. Cameron's illegible scrawl.

"That girl came into the store yesterday and hung around for twenty minutes without buying a thing. She won't accept help and won't tell me what she wants. I don't want to accuse her without proof, but I won't tolerate shoplifting even if she is the fire chief's daughter."

"I'm sure she wouldn't..." Erin trailed off.

Mr. Blackwell studied the prescription. "This'll take five or ten minutes." He moved toward rows of shelves lined with bottles.

Erin wandered down the center aisle, one side of which was devoted to feminine hygiene products. "Hi, Miranda."

The girl started guiltily, then in a flash her expression turned belligerent. "I wasn't doing anything wrong."

"I didn't think you were," Erin said mildly.

"That old buzzard in the white coat thinks I'm stealing." She popped a jawbreaker into her mouth and a small bulge appeared in one cheek. Her anxious gaze roved the shelves. "There's a lot of different stuff here."

"Do you need some help?"

Miranda tossed her hair. "I can handle it."

Erin shrugged and started to move away, a little hurt that the rapport she'd thought she'd built with Miranda during their shopping trip didn't seem to have stuck. Then she heard the girl say her name. Erin turned back. "Yes?"

Miranda held a box of tampons in each hand, a pink stain spreading beneath her makeup. "What do you think—the blue or the cream-colored? I...I want to try a new brand."

Poor Miranda. She was obviously embarrassed about buying feminine hygiene products and, with no mother or female relatives living locally, had no one to give her guidance. She probably hadn't had time to make close girlfriends, and somehow Erin couldn't see Miranda going to a school counselor for advice.

Erin took the boxes from Miranda and examined them. "These are regular and these are super. Are your periods very heavy?

The color in Miranda's cheeks deepened to brick red. "I...I don't know."

"What were you using before?" Erin asked gently.

Miranda ducked her head and mumbled something unintelligible. Erin heard the brittle crunch of the jawbreaker crumbling.

"Pardon me? I couldn't hear you."

"Tissues. I've been using tissues."

In the embarrassed silence that followed, Erin

could hear the faint hum of the overhead fluorescent lights. "I see. How long have you been having your period?"

Miranda still wouldn't meet her gaze. "This is only the second time. The first was in L.A. We were in the middle of packing up the house to come here."

"Didn't you tell your dad?"

Miranda shook her head uncomfortably. "He's a guy." She paused, then added, "What do you use?"

Without thinking, Erin said, "Actually, I've stopped for a while, but I used to use—"

"Why'd you stop?" Miranda popped another jaw-breaker into her mouth.

Distracted, Erin drew her eyes from the shelf where she'd been searching for her old brand of tampons. "Pardon?"

"Why did you stop using tampons?" Miranda repeated with avid curiosity. "Our Life Ed teacher said that only happened when you got old or got anorexic or were pregnant."

Erin felt her cheeks heat and glanced around. Luckily no one was within earshot. Damn, how could she have slipped up like that? "This is a good brand," she said, grabbing a package off the shelf. "You should also get some sanitary napkins, in case of spotting." She picked up a box of those, too, and handed both to Miranda.

By this time Miranda had worked out the answer to her own question. "You're not old, and you're not anorexic. You must be pregnant."

"Shh." Erin stared at her. Miranda wasn't stupid,

nor would she be easily brushed off. "Yes, okay, I'm pregnant."

"With my dad?" The words were a startled squeak.

"No! No, of course not. We hardly know each other." Erin spoke urgently in a lowered voice. "Only a couple of people know about this and I don't want it spread around. At least until I figure out how I'm going to handle it. I wasn't planning to have a baby at this point in my life."

Erin frowned, regretting having said so much, and hoped Miranda had more important things on her young mind than Erin's condition.

And so it would seem, for just then the person in the next aisle caught Miranda's attention. "Oh, shit."

Erin curbed the desire to reprimand her for swearing. "What is it?"

"Oliver, a dude from my class."

A tall boy with sandy hair and intelligent blue eyes was strolling toward them. Miranda quickly shoved the boxes into Erin's hands.

"Hi, Miranda," the boy said, giving her a shy smile over the top shelf.

Miranda put her nose in the air.

His cheeks flaming, Oliver moved on.

"He's cute," Erin said, looking after him.

Miranda dismissed that with a scornful wave of her hand. "He's a nerd. Runs the student newspaper or something dorky like that." She hesitated, then added uncertainly, "If I give you the money, will you pay for those things for me?"

"All right. I'll just pick up my grandmother's prescription and meet you up front."

Miranda was leafing through the latest issue of *Rolling Stone* magazine when Erin joined her at the checkout counter. "Hi, Sally," she said to the clerk, and handed over her credit card.

Oliver got in line behind them, carrying a ream of computer paper and assorted pens. He glanced at the cover of the magazine Miranda held. "Smashing Pumpkins is a pretty cool band."

"Yeah," Miranda mumbled and put the magazine back.

"I hear you're from L.A."

"So?"

Erin cringed for her as she signed the receipt. The boy was only trying to be nice.

Oliver pushed a hand through his thick hair. "I was wondering if you'd do an interview for the high school newspaper. You know, what it's like going from La La Land to a small town in Washington."

"I can sum it up in two words," Miranda replied scathingly. *"It sucks."*

Oliver pulled out a notepad from his breast pocket. "Can I quote you on that?"

"Uh, sure." Looking disconcerted at his imperturbability, she tried to glance at what he was writing—far more than her two words—but he flipped the notebook shut.

"I'll be in room twelve tomorrow at lunch if you want to add anything." With another smile, he placed his purchases on the counter.

"Why do you do that?" Erin demanded when she and Miranda were outside the store.

"What?"

"Flirt with guys who ogle you sexually but act rude toward a boy who treats you like a person."

Miranda shrugged, her mouth sullen. "I'm not a Goody Two-shoes, so don't expect me to act like one."

Erin sighed. The senior boys were still hanging around, possibly waiting for Miranda to come by again. "I'll give you a ride home, if you want. You must have missed your usual bus by now. And I'm going past the marina, anyway, to the farmers' market at the end of River Road."

"Well, okay," Miranda said grudgingly.

As they walked to the car, Erin pulled her car keys out of her purse. A business card fluttered to the sidewalk. Miranda bent to pick it up, glancing at the front. She handed the card back to Erin, a puzzled light in her clear green eyes.

"Thanks." Erin absently tucked the card back in her purse. "Is something wrong?"

"No. Nothing's wrong."

On the drive down River Road, Miranda crossed one foot over her knee and began rubbing a scuff mark off her new red shoes with the heel of her hand.

"A good leather cleaner will take that out," Erin said. With a jolt, she remembered belatedly what was on the card. "Er, is there anything else on your mind?"

"No, of course not." But Erin sensed she was

stewing over something. Sure enough, a few minutes later, Miranda blurted, "Could there be something wrong with me? You know, like in my female parts."

At first Erin was relieved it wasn't about *her,* then she felt a little panicky; she wasn't qualified to answer these kinds of questions. "Why would you think that?"

"I'm almost thirteen and I only just started my period. All my friends started ages ago. Am I a freak, or what?"

"Oh, Miranda, you're not a freak," Erin said, thankful the problem was simple. "You're well within the range of what's considered normal. Some girls start as late as sixteen."

"They do? Whew." Her shoulders slumped into a more relaxed position.

"Your mother probably started late, too."

Miranda went very still, then stared out the window. "I wouldn't know about that. She died when I was ten."

Erin had felt the pain of being without a mother most of her life. "I'm sorry it isn't her you're having this conversation with," she said quietly.

Miranda shrugged, as if she couldn't care less, but the tension was back in her shoulders. Then she sat up straighter, looking ahead. "Here's the marina."

Erin turned into the steep lane that led to a road on top of the dike and pulled to a stop above the ramp down to the wharf where the houseboats were moored. "How do you like living on the houseboat?"

"I hate it," Miranda said automatically. "We're so

far from town. Not that there's anything worth going in there for.'' She paused and added unexpectedly, ''Nighttime is nice, though. You can see the stars.''

''There's a waterfowl refuge just down the road that's worth a visit. Right about now it'll be full of migrating birds.''

''I'm not exactly into wildlife, but you should mention it to Dad next time you see him.'' Miranda now took Erin's relationship with her father with a grudging acceptance Erin would have welcomed a few weeks ago.

''Yes, well, I don't know when that will be, so you can tell him about it. Will you be all right using those sanitary products?''

''I'll figure it out. Thanks for the ride.'' She got out of the car.

Erin put the gearshift into reverse and was about to back around when Miranda stuck her head in the window. ''Uh, Erin...''

''Yes?''

''I saw the notice up at school about the basketball team. Maybe I'll come to the practice next Thursday.''

Delighted, but not wanting to frighten her off by appearing too eager, Erin matched her neutral tone. ''That'll be good.''

''And thanks for...you know.'' She held up her drugstore bag by way of explanation, and offered her rare but beautiful smile.

''I was glad I could help,'' Erin said with more

warmth, and returned her smile. "I'll look forward to seeing you on Thursday."

She drove on to the fruit and vegetable market feeling good about the bond that was slowly forming between her and Miranda. For a while in the drugstore, she'd almost felt like a mother helping her daughter. Not even the queasy rumblings in her stomach could detract from the pleasure of chipping away a little more at the girl's protective shell.

Too bad the same couldn't be said about the father.

THE NEXT DAY, ERIN CAME back from lunch to find a breezy message from Nick on her voice mail. "Whatever you did to talk Miranda into joining the basketball team, I thank you from the bottom of my heart."

From the bottom of his heart. *Sure,* Erin thought. Then why had he called when he knew she'd be at lunch?

She played the message over twice more just to hear his deep California drawl. And allowed herself a private moment to dream of what might have been.

AN INSISTENT BEEPING PULLED Nick from sleep. As he reached for his pager to turn it off, he glanced at the glowing red digits of the bedside clock. Friday, 1:25 a.m.

The report from the county dispatcher, crackling with static, sent ice into his veins. "Structure fire...visible flames...25 Linden Street."

He rolled out of bed and stepped into his bunker

pants and boots. Moving quickly and quietly through the houseboat, he peeked in on Miranda, who lay sleeping peacefully, double-checked that all doors and windows were locked and paused in the galley kitchen long enough to scribble her a note. With luck, he would be back home before she woke up. If not, or if anything happened, help was just a shout away at a neighboring houseboat.

He grabbed his bunker coat from the hook by the door and jogged up the wooden dock, his boots echoing hollowly. Mist swirled over the water and fogged the yellow security lights illuminating the marina. The siren mounted atop the fire station wailed in the distance, calling the volunteers out of the bars and out of their beds.

Nick clapped the emergency light onto the roof of the Suburban and skidded down the steep drive off the dike. Linden Street. What the hell was Erin's house number? Twenty-something; he knew that much. He ground the FWD up through the gears and tore down River Road, tortured by visions of Erin trapped on the top floor of the burning house or succumbing to smoke inhalation while she tried to save her grandmother.

The siren stopped after five minutes and the sudden silence seemed ominous, but he knew it meant Steve or one of the volunteers had reached the station and turned the device off. Sure enough, moments later, he heard a different siren start up—that of the fire engine. Nick sped through a four-way stop on the outskirts of town, his spinning red light bleeding onto darkened houses. Listening over the truck radio, he heard units responding from Hainesville and farther afield in Simcoe. He waited, muscles tensed, for the units first in to confirm the fire's location.

Past the fire hall he raced, noting the open doors of the main bay and the absent pumper engine and ladder truck. Half a mile away orange flames leaped against the black sky above the peaked roofs of the houses.

At last he heard Steve's voice over the radio. "Engine One at 25 Linden. We have a fully involved barn fire, flames visible from the roof and west end."

Nick could breathe again. A barn fire meant the place next door to Erin's.

He pulled into the driveway at number twenty-five, guided by the fluorescent markers the first unit on the scene had dropped. Some of his tension flooded back when he saw Erin in a white nightgown, restraining a young girl struggling to break free and run toward the flame-enshrouded barn. The roar and snap of the fire drowned out the girl's cries. In the field behind the barn a mare galloped back and forth, neighing and tossing her head, her eyes white with terror.

Frank and Angela were laying a two-and-a-half-inch hose from the hydrant on the street. Dave was operating the pump controls. An emergency aid unit was parked next to the ladder truck, and inside the lit vehicle EMT personnel were readying their equipment. Steve came around the side of the ladder truck, buckling on breathing apparatus.

Nick noted the flames licking the boughs of the fir

trees between the barn and the house. "Is the house occupied?" he asked Steve.

"Mother and three kids," Steve said. "They've been told to evacuate."

"Dave," Nick shouted. "When the Simcoe unit shows up, get them to lay another line and start wetting down those trees." He turned back to Steve. "Where's the father?"

"In the barn. I'm going in after him."

Rick and Rob pulled into the yard in a Ford station wagon and hurried over. Nick gave them their orders. "You two ladder the barn and cut some holes in the roof to ventilate the smoke and gases."

Goddamn it, he needed backup. He needed more fully trained firefighters. Steve couldn't go in the barn alone, and Nick didn't trust any of the volunteers. Making a tough decision, he reached for a set of breathing apparatus for himself. For the fire chief to be doing anything other than directing the fire was a cardinal sin. But what choice did he have when a life was at stake?

"Okay, Steve, let's go." He ran for the barn, yelling to Erin, "Keep that girl away."

Inside the barn, he inched along the wall, through the smoky gloom. The beam from his flashlight penetrated only a few feet, and his breath rasped through his apparatus. He sensed rather than heard Steve close behind him. From the depths of the darkness came the high-pitched, terrified scream of an animal and sharp thuds as hooves met wood.

He came to a corner and turned, and abruptly the

wall gave way to air. Fumbling, he found the top of
a stall door. Another step and his boot struck something solid and inert. He crouched to find a man lying
prone on the straw-strewn wood floor. Nick ripped
off a glove and felt for a pulse, then breathed out in
relief when he found it, faint but steady. Together, he
and Steve lifted the man in a fireman's hold and felt
their way back along the wall to the exit.

More vehicles were arriving, another pumper and
a ladder truck from Simcoe. Signaling to the driver
of the aid unit, he and Steve carried the farmer across
the yard and deposited him in the paramedics' care.
The sobbing girl, whom Erin had taken to a safe spot
by the fence, broke free and raced over.

"Your dad's going to be all right," Nick said, leading her away from her father, who was being hooked
up to oxygen.

"He's not moving." The girl was terrified, her face
white.

"What's your name?"

"Chrissie."

"He'll be okay, Chrissie. I promise." He started
toward Engine Two.

Chrissie tugged on his coat. "Blackie is still in the
barn."

"Who?"

"My colt. Dad went in to get him."

Nick remembered the screams. And the silence as
he'd left the barn with Chrissie's father. "It's probably too late, honey. I'm sorry."

Tears streamed down her face. "Please save him. Please, you've got to save him."

Nick assessed the blazing barn, the additional fire-fighters. He put a hand on the girl's shoulder. "I'll do my best. Steve," he called. "Get a hose and give me backup. I'm going in again."

CHAPTER EIGHT

NICK STEPPED INSIDE the barn, with Steve hauling line. Since their last foray, the crew had ventilated the building. This had cleared the smoke but fed oxygen to the fire. Flames licked the wooden beams overhead and the hayloft was ablaze. Burning swatches of hay flew sparking through the air, and black smoke turned to billowing white clouds of steam as the water from Steve's line hit the blaze.

"Give me a mist," Nick shouted, and Steve adjusted the nozzle to form a protective umbrella of fine spray.

Nick found the stall again, and precious seconds passed as he struggled with the metal latch. Finally, the bolt slid back and the door swung open with a bang against the wall. He got on his knees and crawled through straw bedding, turning two corners before he came across a hoof. He moved his hand up the leg to the body. The colt was still.

The wall above his head blossomed into orange flame, beautiful and deadly. In the flare of light Nick saw the glazed eyes and lolling tongue of the colt. Then Steve directed a stream at the burning wall and water rained down.

Soaking wet inside and out, Nick gathered up the colt tight against his chest. Using the strength in his thighs, he staggered to his feet and with another heave threw the colt around his neck, its legs dangling over his shoulders.

The bells on his air pack sounded. Exertion had depleted his air supply quickly. Five minutes left.

Bent double under his load, he followed the hose out, while burning embers and straw swirled down from the loft. Lungs straining, heart pumping, he shuffled the last few steps to open air and safety.

Firefighters from Simcoe rushed past him, bringing in another line. Nick dropped to one knee and laid the colt in the grass next to the aid car. He ripped off his mask and gulped for air. Then called to the EMT attendant. "Can we have some oxygen over here?"

The girl fell upon her colt, arms twined around its neck, face buried in its sodden fur. "Blackie, Blackie."

Nick gently pulled her aside so the attendant could fit an oxygen mask over the colt's muzzle. At the fence, the mare whickered anxiously. After a minute or two of breathing pure oxygen, the colt jerked its neck and heaved itself to its knees, coughing and trembling all over.

"He should be okay," Nick told Chrissie. "But get a vet to look at him in the morning."

"Hear that, Blackie?" Chrissie told her pet as she stroked its wet neck. "You're going to be all right." The girl gazed up at Nick gratefully, her eyes glistening with tears. "Thank you, mister."

Nick wiped a hand across his soot-smeared face. "No problem."

His radio crackled and the voice of the Simcoe chief came on. "We've tapped the seat of the fire on the west side. Looks like an incinerator left smoldering sent up sparks that ignited the straw in the loft."

"Good work," Nick said. Crews were fighting the flames from three sides; the fire was under control. He clicked off the radio, walked to the engine for a blanket and took it to Erin, who was standing by the fence. She had her arms wrapped around her waist and was shivering in her flimsy nightdress.

"You were brave to go in after that colt," she said.

"You shouldn't be out here in the cold." He wrapped the blanket around her shoulders. Through the acrid scent of smoke and burning wood, he could swear he smelled Erin's clean floral perfume.

"I couldn't leave until—"

"Blackie's going to be fine." He chafed her arms through the blanket.

"Until I saw you come out safely."

He returned her gaze in silence while he dealt with the lump in his throat. "Do you think I'm a rookie?" he said gruffly. "Of course I'd come out all right. How have you been? You look tired."

She stood quite still, unsmiling. "Do you care?"

Nick pushed back his helmet and felt the night air cool his scalp. Beneath his heavy bunker gear, he was soaked with sweat and water. "That day, I was... shocked. I reacted badly. Considering the situation,

I don't think it's good for us to get involved. But I do care how you are."

She averted her head, but he saw a tear trickle loose and zigzag down her cheek. He reached to wipe it away, tempted to take her in his arms, pregnant or not.

"Don't worry," she said, shaking off his hand. "This baby won't be a problem for you, or anyone else."

"What do you mean?" Before she could answer, Steve called to him from the pumper truck. Nick waved to acknowledge he'd heard, then turned back to Erin. "What do you mean?" he repeated. Something in her tone put him on alert.

"Never mind. You should be worrying about Miranda. You need to keep the lines of communication open. I know it's not always easy for a man to raise a daughter—"

Under his heavy bunker jacket his shoulders stiffened. "I *do* talk to Miranda. It's more a question of her not listening."

Her hand jerked upward with impatience. "You don't understand—"

Steve called again. Nick could hear Rick and Rob arguing about whose turn it was to coil the hose. "I've got to go."

Through the smoke and swirling ash, he crossed the yard to organize cleanup. He had enough problems with Miranda without interference from Erin.

ERIN BLEW A SHORT BLAST on the whistle around her neck. "Okay, girls, that's all for tonight. Before you leave, put away the basketballs on the shelf in the equipment room, please."

Ten pairs of adolescent girls' feet pounded across the polished hardwood floor. Their laughter bounced from the high ceiling of the YWCA gymnasium as they headed first for the equipment room, then the locker room. Miranda, in her long baggy purple shorts and fluorescent yellow crop top, looked out of place among the others with their more conventional sport shorts and T-shirts. But her ball skills were excellent and she could shoot with the best of them. Erin was sure it was just a matter of time before the other girls accepted Miranda—and she accepted them.

Erin caught up with Miranda as she put her ball away. "Want to come to the Burger Shack with the team tonight?"

Miranda eyed her watch with a wistful twist of her mouth. "I'm supposed to go straight home."

"That's too bad. Talk to your father, and maybe you can join us next week. I can always give you a ride back."

In the locker room, Miranda kept to herself. Once or twice, Erin caught her covertly watching the clusters of chattering and laughing girls, and realized that Miranda wasn't so much disdainful as fundamentally shy. Not that the average preteen could tell the difference.

Miranda sat on the bench to remove her black-and-white hightops, and Rita, a gawky girl with long brown braids and glasses, sidled over. "You sank some awesome baskets tonight."

Erin held her breath. Rita was the kind of girl Miranda ate for breakfast. *Don't shut her out.*

But although seemingly taken aback by the praise, Miranda smiled. "Thanks."

"Are you coming to the Shack with us?" Rita asked.

"Um…" Miranda hesitated, glanced at Rita's eager face, then at the group she clearly longed to be part of, and said, "Yeah. Yeah, I will."

Erin caught her eye and cast her a questioning look.

Miranda tossed her hair back. "I'll call Dad from the Burger Shack. He'll understand."

Erin and the girls walked the two blocks over to the fast-food joint known as the Shack since Erin's high school days. The bright yellow exterior was unsullied by graffiti, and every booth was outfitted with a miniature jukebox. The Thursday night movie at the Ridge Theater hadn't yet let out, so the Shack was practically empty when the team jostled its way up to the counter to order.

Almost empty, but not quite. In a corner booth with Limp Bizkit blasting from the jukebox sat Oliver, on the point of sinking his teeth into a HumungoBurger. Milkshake, fries and onion rings awaited his attention, but when Miranda walked in the door, he shifted his focus to her.

Erin leaned over to Miranda. "Isn't that your friend Oliver? I think he waved at you."

Miranda glanced over and blushed. "What's he doing here?"

"Looks to me as though he's preparing for seven years of famine. Did you ever do the interview he wanted for the school paper?"

"Yeah. He turned out to be not as much of a creep as he looks," she added grudgingly.

"I think he's a babe," Rita said. "Go over and say hi."

"No way," Miranda replied.

"You're right," Erin said. "Your dad might not approve." The words were barely out of her mouth when she realized her mistake.

"My father is, like, totally out of touch," Miranda said, grabbing her milkshake. "Come on, Rita. Let's sit over there."

"Don't forget to phone Nick," Erin called after Miranda as she sauntered in Oliver's direction with Rita in tow.

Without turning around, Miranda lifted a hand and dismissed Erin's injunction.

"WHERE HAVE YOU BEEN?" Nick demanded when Miranda walked through the door. He glanced pointedly at his watch. "Practice was over an hour ago."

"The team went to the Burger Shack for a milkshake afterward." She dropped her kit bag in the middle of the entry hall and headed for the kitchen. "It's no big deal."

Fuming, Nick followed her. "I happen to think it *is* a big deal, young lady. We have an agreement—"

"Agreement?" she scoffed, reaching for a glass from the cupboard. "You dictate the rules and I'm supposed to obey."

"Exactly. So why didn't you?"

She got herself a glass of water, took a sip, then stared at him. "I'm trying to get a life. Why don't you?"

Nick controlled his anger and thought about what Erin had said about keeping up communication. But how was he supposed to communicate with a girl who countered his legitimate concerns with dumb insolence? He took a breath and started again. "What was so important about going that you disobeyed my orders? You've never wanted to go out with the team before."

Miranda turned back to the tap, mumbling something.

"Pardon?"

Her shoulders rigid, she said it a fraction louder. "I've never been asked before."

"Oh, sweetheart," he said helplessly. "I'm glad you're making friends. Anyone in particular? What's her name?"

"Rita." She paused. "A guy from school was there, too. Oliver."

Nick tried to stay loose, but he felt the tension knotting his neck and shoulders. "What's this Oliver character like?"

"He's kind of cute. Interesting to talk to."

"Does he go in for body piercing? Tattoos?"

Miranda flung him a pitying glance. "Come on, Dad. This is Hicksville, remember?"

Thank God for that. He recalled the night of the fire. Had Erin been trying to warn him about something—Oliver, perhaps? Did she know something he didn't? "How old is this boy?"

"Fourteen."

Not as threatening as the sixteen-year-olds Miranda had taken up with in L.A., but still… "I want you to promise that next time if you can't get hold of me, you'll come home."

"Aw, Dad. Why don't you trust me?"

"After sneaking out of the house to go to a party I'd forbidden you to attend, you ask why I don't trust you?"

"That was ages ago. I don't see what you're worried about."

"I'm just trying to protect you. In spite of what you think, you're too young to get involved with boys." Ignoring her scathing expression, he went on. "I *know* what teenage boys are like. The last thing you want is to wind up pregnant."

"Oh, please, not the birds and bees talk again. Anyway, aren't you being a little hypocritical? I mean, look at your girlfriend—she's pregnant and single."

Nick froze, his chest tightening. "Who are you talking about? I don't have a girlfriend."

"Come on, Dad, don't play dumb. You know who I mean—Erin."

Nick went into the living room and put another log

in the slow-combustion heater to ward off the damp river air. "How do you know she's pregnant?"

"She told me." Miranda refilled her glass and walked around the kitchen counter to sink into a chair at the dining table. She regarded Nick sternly. "No one's supposed to know."

"I'm surprised she told you."

Miranda twirled her glass between her palms, not looking at him. "I don't think she meant to. I saw her in the drugstore one day and we got talking."

Nick crouched before the heater, watching the flames. Miranda seemed to talk to everyone but him. "Erin's a grown woman. Unlike you, her life is nobody's business but hers."

Miranda frowned down at the streaks her fingers had traced through the condensation on her glass. "I guess it won't matter soon, anyway."

Her tone made him glance up. "What do you mean?"

"She's getting an abortion."

Nick wasn't sure what shocked him more—the news that Erin was going to terminate her pregnancy or the casual way in which Miranda mentioned it. "Abortion! What makes you think she's having an abortion? Did she tell you that, too?"

"No. A business card fell out of her purse. When I handed it back to her, I noticed the address of an abortion clinic on it."

He rose and paced to the sliding glass doors to stare at the lights winking on the water. Erin's words the night of the fire fell into place with horrifying clarity.

This baby won't be a problem for you—or anybody else. She must feel terribly alone to even contemplate such a course of action. He wanted to go to her, reassure her...

"You really like her, don't you?"

Nick snapped out of his trance. "That is none of your business. It's time for bed, young lady. You've got school tomorrow."

Miranda rose, dragging her heels, and moved toward the corridor that led to the bedroom. "I'm going to Oliver's house tomorrow after school to study for our math test, okay?"

He'd grounded her for the whole summer. In spite of what had happened tonight, maybe it was time to loosen the strings. "Will his parents be there?"

"His mom will. His father's Dr. Cameron, the local doctor."

Still he hesitated.

"Come on, Dad. Please. Unless you give me another chance I'll never be able to prove I'm trustworthy."

"Well, all right. If you promise that in the future you won't stay out late without my permission."

"I promise." She backtracked to throw her arms around his waist. "Thanks, Dad. You're the best."

Nick clasped her to him, cherishing an embrace that was all the more precious because Miranda initiated hugging less and less. "I...I've got something to do in town after work tomorrow," he said. "Meet me at five-thirty under the clock tower and we'll go home together."

She gave him her cheekiest grin. "Make it six?"

"Okay, six," he growled. "Don't be late."

Miranda nodded and started to leave. "Dad?"

Her plaintive tone made him hang on to her hands. "What?"

"You will try to change her mind, won't you?"

Nick blinked. He would never, if he lived to be a hundred and two, figure out his daughter. Brushing a strand of hair out of her eyes, he said, "I'll do my best."

The next afternoon, Nick's black brogues crunched through orange and red maple leaves littering the path to Erin's front door. The sun was already low in the sky. When daylight savings ended in a couple of weeks it would be dark at this time. He pressed the doorbell, then shifted the object cooling his fingers into his other hand.

The door swung open. Erin, in dark gray sweats with Washington State University emblazoned across the chest and her hair pulled back in a frayed ponytail, stood with a mop in her hand. She looked tired.

"Is anything wrong with Miranda?" she asked, alarm chasing the fatigue from her face.

"Aside from getting chewed out for getting home late last night, Miranda's fine."

"She tried to call you from the pay phone at the Burger Shack. I saw her. Didn't she get through?"

"She did not," he said, only now remembering how he'd tied up the phone that night trying to re-recruit volunteers who'd dropped out under his predecessor's regime. "May I come in?" He held up the carton in his hand. "I brought you this."

"Milk?"

"Pregnant women need extra calcium."

"I know, but...milk?" Her wide mouth made a delicate moue of distaste.

"If you were expecting flowers or something—"

She propped the mop against the wall and crossed her arms over her chest. "Maybe it's not a good idea for you to be here if we're just going to fight."

She seemed so vulnerable, her face free of makeup, her eyes wide, her uncombed hair in need of smoothing back. If he knew what was good for him, he'd say what he had to from the doorstep and leave. But try as he might, he couldn't *not* care what happened to her.

"I won't fight if you won't."

She scrutinized him in silence, then finally stepped back and allowed him inside. He handed the milk to her and shrugged out of his navy jacket.

She hung his coat in the hall closet, then led the way to the kitchen. "Want some?" she asked, holding up the carton of milk.

"If you'll join me." He stopped in the doorway. Erin gave him the milk to hold and padded across the damp linoleum in thick socks. Flowers filled a glass vase on the breakfast table and the New Haven shelf clock ticked quietly. "Where's Ruth?"

"Having a nap before dinner." Erin took glasses from the cupboard and picked up a ceramic cookie jar shaped like a big ripe tomato. She paused before disappearing through the sliding doors into the adjacent dining room. "Go around," she instructed.

Nick backtracked and entered the dining room from the hall. There, a wall clock caught his attention. Below the clock face was a circle, about six inches in diameter, that showed the date. Inside the circle were two more circles, showing the months and the days of the week.

"That's a lawyer's clock," Erin said, placing the glasses and cookie jar on the table before joining him in front of the clock. Chloe meowed at her feet and she bent to pick up the kitten and cradled it in her arms.

"Nice." He glanced at her. "What is it about clocks that fascinates you so much?"

"There are many reasons," she enthused. "Fine clocks are functional as well as attractive. I think it's marvelous that they don't use batteries or electricity, yet can last virtually forever. The mantel clock in the living room, for example, is two hundred years old and still keeps perfect time."

"They're like the human body in some ways," he mused, looking for a way to lead into his mission. "Works of art and science. Take reproduction—"

"John gave me this clock," she said a little sadly, her fingertips touching the cherry wood casing. "To remind me of all the good times we spent together." She dropped the kitten gently back to the floor, where it wound around her ankles.

This John character was a real Good Time Charlie, all right. Nick watched Erin fill their glasses with milk, noting the dark circles marring the delicate skin below her eyes. Where *was* that bastard of an ex-boyfriend when she needed him? No wonder she felt pressured to take drastic action. Erin needed support, emotional and practical.

She lifted the lid off the cookie jar and out wafted the spicy aroma of ginger and nutmeg. "Have a cookie."

He shook his head, too agitated to eat. Suddenly all his carefully planned speeches flew out the window and he was pleading with her. "Don't do it, Erin. No matter how bad things seem now it's not worth it."

"What on earth are you talking about?" Erin leaned back in her chair, eyebrows rising.

"Abortion. I'm begging you not to do it. I know you don't want a baby, but you've got a responsibility, and I feel sure that someday you'd have regrets. I've seen too many children die in fires and accidents to take the precious gift of life lightly—"

Understanding dawned on her face, quickly replaced by fury. Erin jumped to her feet, nearly knocking over her glass of milk. "Don't you dare lecture me on responsibility! And what do you mean by suggesting that I'm going to abort my baby? I would never do such a thing."

Nick stopped short. "You wouldn't?"

"Of course not."

Thank God. "Then why are you carrying around the name of a doctor who specializes in terminations?"

"I am not!" she began indignantly, then broke off. "Oh! You must be talking about that card Kelly gave me. How did you know about that?"

"Miranda told me. She's worried about you, too." He narrowed his gaze at her. "You're really not going to abort?"

"*No.*"

"Good." He grabbed a cookie from the jar and sank onto a chair. "But you're running yourself ragged, Erin, even I can see that."

"I'm doing what I have to."

"Can't you get some help—a housekeeper or something? This place must be a dog to clean. You're working full-time, plus looking after your grandmother, plus still in the first trimester of pregnancy. I remember Janine was falling down tired at that stage."

"Gran has this thing about strangers in her house. I think she's also concerned about the money. She can't afford a housekeeper and wouldn't be happy allowing me to pay for one."

"Someone ought to let her know that your health is more valuable than your bank balance. I don't understand. She obviously dotes on you, yet she lets you knock yourself out when you should be getting extra rest."

"It's not her fault," Erin began hotly, then subsided in her chair, twisting her glass in her hands, "She doesn't know I'm pregnant."

Nick stared. "What!"

From the doorway came a quavery voice. "I do now."

Erin leaped to her feet. "Gran! What are you doing up?"

"I heard raised voices." The elderly woman clung to the door frame with one wrinkled hand. She'd put her gray wig on in haste and it was slightly askew.

"Come, sit down." Erin took Gran's arm—how fragile and thin she felt beneath the flannel dressing gown—and guided her to a chair. "I'm sorry you had to find out like this, Gran."

"I suppose the baby is John's?" she said, patting her wig into place.

Erin nodded. "We're not getting married. I'm sorry."

"Sorry for what, child? That you didn't tell me sooner?" Her voice turned sorrowful. "Why, Erin?"

"I didn't want to worry you. You're still recovering from your heart attack. The doctor said not to let you get upset about anything."

"And...?"

Erin glanced at Nick, embarrassed to admit she was embarrassed at being pregnant. "That's all."

Ruth clasped Erin's hand, her grip surprisingly strong. "Did John offer to marry you?"

Erin glanced away. "We haven't resumed our relationship. I agreed not to tell anyone he's the father of my baby until the election is over."

"Well, that's between you and him." Gran shook her head sadly. "I would like to see you settled before I die, but more than that I've been hoping for another great-grandchild—yours.'' A shaky smile creased her face. ''Now I've got a reason to hang on.''

Erin leaned forward to hug her. ''Gosh, Gran, of course you're going to hang on—for many years yet,'' she scolded, her voice husky. ''Although I would have hoped that the love Kelly and Geena and I have for you is reason enough to live, if your own interests aren't.''

''Oh, that's important, but a baby...a baby is something special.''

Erin drew back to bask in her grandmother's loving gaze. Suddenly she was filled with gratitude that this woman, who had been a mother to her, would also know and love her baby. ''Yes, a baby is special,'' she said, feeling her eyes grow moist.

''When is the baby due?'' Ruth asked, getting down to practical matters.

Nick had been sitting quietly throughout the exchange, but Erin sensed his attention as he waited for an answer to one of the many questions he hadn't asked. And likely never would ask because he simply didn't want to know.

''April 6,'' she said. ''I'm eight weeks along.''

''You've been pushing yourself too hard—working at the bank, then cooking and cleaning till all hours here,'' Gran said, clucking in disapproval.

''That's what I've just been telling her,'' Nick pointed out.

''I'm fine,'' Erin mumbled.

''Nonsense. You need to take care of my grand-child. We'll get someone in to clean the house once a week. And we'll pay the Mitchell boy from across the street to mow the lawn and do the yardwork. I've got a little money set aside. If you can contribute some, we'll manage just fine. Now, don't you tell me different."

"Yes, Gran," Erin said meekly before her smile burst forth. What a huge relief that Gran knew her secret. Then she visualized everyone else in Hainesville knowing, too. "Don't tell anyone, okay? It's just until the situation with John is sorted out. He's running for Congress—"

Gran's mouth tightened. "Seems to me that man ought to be more concerned about you and his child than an election."

"Hear, hear," Nick said.

Ruth leaned on the table and slowly pushed herself back to her feet. "I'm going to check my knitting patterns to see what I've got in the way of baby garments. Nice to see you again, Nick. Don't be a stranger."

"Yes, ma'am." Nick started to stand, but she waved him down.

At the door Gran paused and spoke to Nick. "*We'll* see that she's taken care of, won't we?" It wasn't an observation, but an order.

"I can take care of myself," Erin said firmly before Nick could open his mouth. No way was Gran going to bully Nick into getting involved. She helped Gran to the sewing room down the hall. When she returned, Nick had his jacket on and was waiting by the front door.

"I told Miranda I'd meet her under the clock tower at six."

Throughout the house, clocks began to chime the half hour—five-thirty. Unable to talk, Nick smiled, showing white teeth that contrasted against a darkly stubbled jaw. Erin felt her attraction to him blossom all over again. He couldn't handle a relationship with a pregnant woman, but he'd cared enough to come over here to talk her out of aborting.

"It only takes two minutes to drive downtown," she said persuasively. "Stay and have another cookie." When he hesitated, she added, "Did Miranda tell you about the long shot she made last night?"

Nick's eyes lit at the mention of his daughter's achievement. "No, she didn't. What happened?"

MIRANDA GLANCED AT her red-and-black Swatch and slammed the math textbook shut. "Gotta go, dude," she said, rolling off Oliver's bed.

Oliver glanced up from his computer. "Already? We haven't even looked at integers."

"I have to meet Dad at six and it's quarter to now." Miranda piled her books into her backpack, careful not to squash her good flat shoes, which she'd changed out of for the walk home from school. "My father's, like, totally anal about time. If I'm not there on the dot, he's liable to ground me till Thanksgiving." She pulled on her black leather jacket. "If you want to study again tomorrow, you could come to my house."

"Cool." Oliver clicked off the computer calculator. "Thanks for your help today. Mr. Wilkinson is going to flip his furry little hairpiece when I ace the test."

Miranda grinned. "Fair's fair. You're gonna help me with my English assignment so that old witch Vogler won't give me a failing grade."

"No sweat." Oliver led the way downstairs, his long legs taking the stairs two at a time.

"Bye, Mrs. Cameron," Miranda called to Oliver's mother in the kitchen.

"Goodbye, dear." Oliver's mother, short, cheerful and plump, appeared in the doorway, wiping her hands on a dish towel. "Come again. Next time, stay for dinner."

"Thanks. I'd like that."

Miranda faced Oliver on the front porch and gazed awkwardly at her black hightops. Some guys would have tried to kiss her by now, but not Oliver. She wasn't sure if she was offended or gratified.

His fists were thrust deep in his pockets so he couldn't even hold her hand. "Did it hurt when you got your eyebrow pierced?"

"No worse than getting my ears done. The navel was a bit harder." She lifted the hem on her sweater and was amused when Oliver quickly averted his eyes. Darn, the skin around the hole was still red. Since the weather had turned cooler and she'd been wearing more clothes, the ring got infected easily. "Are you thinking of getting something pierced?"

His cheeks turned dark and he shook his head. "No way."

Miranda shrugged. Oliver might be a nerd, but he had brains and was a lot more interesting than the guys she'd hung with in L.A. "Well, I'll see you tomorrow."

She walked down Oliver's street and turned onto Linden Street. Parked outside Erin's house was her father's Suburban. Good, he was trying to help. Miranda turned in the walk and climbed the steps to the front door, her running shoes soundless on the painted wooden porch. The murmur of voices, Erin's and her father's, came to her through the open window. She was about to knock, when she heard Erin speak her name.

"Miranda will play center for our first game in a few weeks," Erin was saying. "I hope you'll come along."

"I wouldn't miss it. How is she getting along with her teammates? She doesn't say much at home."

"She's making friends. It helps that she's a good player."

"I appreciate you taking an interest in her." Her father paused. "It's getting late. I'd better go."

Miranda realized she'd better get out of there before they caught her eavesdropping. She was about to sneak down the stairs, when the change in Erin's tone stopped her.

"Nick," Erin began. "We had a false start, but now that the boundaries are drawn, could we be friends?"

Miranda flattened herself against the outer wall and

held her breath during the long pause that followed. *Please say yes,* she implored her father silently.

"Friendship isn't what I'd hoped for," Nick said at last. "In the beginning."

"What do you want now?" Although Erin spoke matter-of-factly, Miranda could hear hope mingled with caution.

"It's complicated—"

"Don't worry about it, then," Erin said quickly, sounding hurt. "I've got other friends."

Nick heaved a deep sigh, and Miranda could picture him running his hand through his short hair. "Of course you do. You've got your sister and your grandmother and friends in this town you've known all your life," he said. "Probably men stacked up to the ceiling who wouldn't care whose baby you were carrying just as long as they could be with you."

"But you're not one of them. Fine, Nick. I'm glad we had this talk. I don't need someone around who thinks I'm a bad influence on his daughter."

Miranda winced. Sheesh! Surely Dad wasn't that stupid.

"I don't think you're a bad influence," he said quietly. "Part of me *would* like to be friends...."

Thank heaven!

"Maybe I should explain my reluctance to get involved. You see, Miranda's mother..."

Miranda's ears pricked. While Nick didn't discourage Miranda from talking about her mother, he hardly ever mentioned her himself.

"Are you still in love with her?" Erin's voice had softened.

"No, it's not that at all."

"Let's sit down," Erin said. "Tell me, what connection can there possibly be between me and your late wife?"

CHAPTER NINE

"I'M LATE, BUT, WHAT the hell...maybe it'll do Miranda good to find out what it's like to be kept waiting."

Miranda heard the scrape of their chairs, and slid down the wall until she was crouched on the porch below the window. The strangled quality to her father's voice when he mentioned her mother tipped her off that something big was coming, but nothing could have prepared her for what she heard next.

"About thirteen years ago Janine had an affair—she admitted to it the day before she died," Nick said. "There's a strong possibility I'm not Miranda's biological father."

Shock hit Miranda like a wave of ice, leaving her shivering and gasping for breath. Dizzy, she dropped her head between her knees. Nick wasn't her father? How could that be?

Dimly, she heard Erin murmur compassionately, "Oh, Nick. I'm sorry. Did you ever have a paternity test to find out if she *is* your biological daughter?"

Miranda risked a peek through the window. Erin had a hand on his arm. Nick was shaking his bent head.

"What good would testing have done?" he said. Miranda heard every bitter nuance in his voice as if through a loudspeaker. "She was my daughter in every other way. I had to look after her. She had no one else. And of course I loved her as if she were mine."

Thanks a bunch, *Dad.* Fancy words that sounded good to strangers, but to her they added up to nothing more than obligation.

"Does Miranda know?" Erin asked.

"No," he said sharply. "And she never will, if I can help it."

"Are you sure that's wise? She might find out accidentally someday. The trauma would be worse for the secrecy and delay in telling her."

"When Janine died, I decided to keep her secret," he said. "Wise or not, I'm sticking to that."

"But if another man is Miranda's father, both he and she have a right to know," Erin said gently.

"Not if knowing destroys all our lives."

Miranda's fingers curled inward, her nails biting into the flesh of her palms. He meant *his* life, the selfish jerk.

"Doesn't the uncertainty bother you?"

"Of course. Some days it's almost impossible to believe she's my child. She's so like her mother, and so unlike me."

Tears spilled down Miranda's cheek; she wiped them angrily away. If she was like her mother who'd cheated on him, he must hate her. No wonder he treated her so mean.

"I was working a lot of shifts in those days, trying to get us established," Nick continued. "I guess Janine felt justified in seeing another man." His acrid tone said he didn't agree.

Pain tore Miranda's heart in two. Her mother had been good and beautiful and kind. She wouldn't have done anything wrong unless she had a reason. Unless Dad had driven her to it. He was never at home; he'd just admitted as much.

"So because Miranda may be the progeny of your late wife's affair, you don't want to get involved with a woman pregnant by another man," Erin said slowly.

Nick's silence acknowledged the truth of her words.

"I understand, I guess, but Nick, don't take Janine's behavior out on Miranda."

The clocks striking six all but drowned out Erin's warning. "Damn," Nick exclaimed. "She'll be waiting."

Miranda heard him get up, and she bolted down the path to the sidewalk. She felt like running all the way home, except that the residence she shared with *that man* suddenly didn't feel like home. Instead she hurried back up the street in the direction she'd come and ducked behind a hedge. When the Suburban started up, she stepped out as though she'd just come from Oliver's, and casually walked toward the truck.

Nick must have seen her in the rearview mirror because he reversed up the street and threw open the door. "You're late."

Head down, she mumbled something.

He looked at her more closely and his voice gentled. "Have you been crying?"

"*No*. Why would I be crying?" She slouched in the corner and kept her head averted. "Let's go ho—" She swallowed. "Back to the houseboat."

AT THE SOUND OF NICK backing up his truck, Erin pushed aside the lace curtain, to see Miranda climb into the passenger seat. Her hand went to her abdomen. Even if John asked her to marry him, she wasn't at all certain she would say yes. And if she said no, how would her child react when he or she was old enough to realize Erin had deliberately decided not to marry the father? Erin knew only one thing for certain; she would try to explain the situation as soon as her child was old enough to understand.

As Nick and Miranda drove off, Erin thought back over their conversation. He'd said he would like to be friends, but his feelings about his late wife interfered. Well, maybe it was time he got over that. For Miranda's sake and for his own. On the other hand, Erin wasn't sure being friends with Nick would be good for *her*. Even now she wondered what had prompted her to make the suggestion. But the alternative was *not* seeing him and that had been making her unhappy.

She let a week go by before making her move. Then on Thursday, when she passed the fire station as she did every day at five o'clock, she paused. From the heavy *kachunk* of metal upon metal she guessed

Nick was working out with weights. She turned into the driveway and walked into the bay.

Nick was lying on his back on the bench press, his legs straddling the narrow bench. He hadn't noticed her yet, so she stopped and watched. With a grunt he lifted a barbell off the rack and raised it above his chest. Sweat beaded on his forehead and his damp white T-shirt clung to his chest as his muscles flexed and stretched. John used to play squash and jog, but he never looked so...masculine.

She was starting to feel like a voyeur, so she cleared her throat. "I hope I'm not disturbing you." He glanced sideways, the barbell frozen midair. "I was passing and...well, I wanted to make sure we parted on good terms. It got a little confusing toward the end. I've been thinking about you and Miranda. If I can do anything to help..."

He replaced the barbell in the rack, sat up and reached for a towel on the chair next to him, still silent.

"I didn't want you to think I'm interfering," she continued, horribly afraid she was talking too much. "I'm certainly no expert on child-raising and I wouldn't presume to tell you what you should do with Miranda. Anyway—" she fiddled with the leather strap of her handbag "—I just wanted to touch base, so to speak, and make sure there were no hard feelings."

Nick began mopping his chest and back.

"So, is everything fine?" She searched his impassive face.

He gave her a brief smile. "Sure, fine."

"You don't sound like you really mean it."

"I'm still thinking about the situation. Don't worry about it." There was an awkward pause. He glanced at her briefcase. "Just get off work?"

"Yes. I was just going home." Lord help them. This conversation had gone from humiliating to inane.

"Have you got a cleaning lady yet?"

"Yes," she said, brightening. "Actually, we've got a cleaning *guy*. His name is Dave, from California. I was going to mention it to you because you must know him."

Nick grimaced. "Don't tell me—he's a volunteer fireman."

"Yes! He's very chatty."

Nick laughed and shook his head. "That's Dave."

"He did a great job on the bathrooms." Another silence fell. "Well, I guess I'd better get back. Gran will be expecting me. I've got her started on a daily walk."

"How's she doing?"

"She can make it around the block now." There didn't seem to be anything more to say. She was about to leave, when she paused. "Did you notice there's a new movie in town?"

"Another chick flick."

A few weeks ago he'd sworn he'd happily sit through one; now he'd dismissed it with a macho grunt. "It's a romantic comedy. *I'm* going."

"I'm taking Miranda bowling. You know, a little quality time. Since she's been studying with this guy

Oliver, I see less of her than ever. I mean, I want her to have friends, but..."

She couldn't compete with his daughter, nor did she want to. "That sounds like a great idea. I hope you two have a good time."

"Thanks. Enjoy your movie."

SATURDAY NIGHT ERIN SETTLED Gran in front of the TV with her yarn and a new pattern for a bunting bag. "You sure you'll be okay? Why don't you come with me? I could take the car."

Smiling up at her, Gran shook her head. "I'm happy right here. I thought Laura was going with you."

"She canceled this morning. Her little girl broke out in measles."

"That's too bad." Gran started casting on stitches. "You could have asked Nick."

She hadn't mentioned to Gran that she had asked Nick and he'd refused, albeit for an excellent reason. She'd been too disappointed to talk about it. "I'll be fine on my own. See you later."

Drizzle misted the streets as she walked the six blocks to the cinema, but she didn't mind the damp; it felt refreshing after the overheated warmth of Gran's house. The ticket office was open and a lineup of people stretched down the sidewalk. At the end of the line, his dark hair pearled with droplets, stood Nick.

Alone.

Her steps faltered briefly, then he saw her and their

gazes held until she came to a halt beside him. "I thought you had a date with Miranda."

"She got a better offer—the school dance with Oliver."

"He seems like a nice boy."

"Could be a lot worse, believe me. I dropped her off at his house and met his parents. I guess it'll be okay."

They bought tickets and walked into the darkened theater together, and by tacit agreement found seats near the back.

"I'm going to buy popcorn," Erin said, getting up again almost immediately. These days she was perpetually hungry.

"What is that—family size?" Nick said when she came back with the biggest carton of popcorn available.

"Be nice or I won't give you any." Then, with Nick's forearm snug against hers on the armrest, Erin settled into the plush seat and stretched her legs under the chair in front.

The movie was Erin's favorite kind—lighthearted, funny and warm. George Clooney made a clever remark and the theater audience chuckled appreciatively along with Michelle Pfeiffer. Erin turned to smile at Nick. She saw his glowing grin and felt the vibration of his low laugh clear through to her breastbone. They weren't on a date, but it felt darn close.

"More popcorn?" Erin whispered, tipping the container toward him.

"Thanks." Nick's hand disappeared into the box

as he gathered popcorn from the bottom. "Remind me never to compete for food with a pregnant woman. Have you got a tapeworm inside you or a baby?"

"Shh," Erin said, suppressing a giggle, aware of the spicy scent of his aftershave as he leaned close.

"Shh," someone admonished from the row behind.

Erin turned back to the screen, then glanced sideways to find Nick eyeing her. Their gazes held, their smiles solely for each other.

Erin looked away, her heart beating a little faster.

"DUDE, YOU LOOK COOL," Miranda crowed to Oliver, who peered at himself in his bedroom mirror. She'd streaked his sandy hair purple and green using hair mascara, then molded it into spikes using gel.

"My mom's going to freak," he said above the Metallica CD blaring in the background. His stereo system, set up on one end of the table that served as a desk, was all but obscured by stacks of books and magazines. Posters of racing cars hung on the wall, interspersed with maps of the galaxy and Oliver's pen-and-ink drawings of titanic battles between supernatural creatures.

"Big deal. Defy and conquer!" Miranda felt a pang as she remembered her father's disappointment when she'd turned down his offer of bowling. If he *was* her father. She spared a sigh for the fun they used to have together, then she tossed sentimentality out the window. "Let's get on the Net."

"We've already used up all my dad's blank CDs

downloading stuff off Napster.'' Frowning into the mirror, Nick pulled at his hair.

"Stop. You'll ruin it.'' She crossed to his desk, pushed aside a draft of the school newsletter and turned on the computer. "I don't mean Napster. I want to check out DNA testing.''

Oliver's hands fell away from his head and he turned from the mirror to stare at her. "DNA testing. What for?''

Conscious of the drama of her situation, she paused for a beat. "Nick isn't my real father.''

Oliver's eyes widened. "Are you kidding! How d'you know?''

"Swear you won't tell anyone? I mean, *no one?*''

"Pinky promise,'' Oliver said solemnly, crooking his baby finger through Miranda's.

While Oliver connected to the Internet, Miranda told him what she'd overheard on Erin's porch. Then she nudged him aside and typed *DNA testing* in the search line and pressed Go. "He says it's only a possibility we're not related, but he secretly hopes it's true.''

"Oh, Miranda, I don't think so.''

"Why else would he be so mean to me all the time? The principal called him when she caught me smoking in the girls' washroom yesterday. He cut my allowance for a month without even letting me tell my side of the story.''

"But you *were* smoking.''

Righteously, she lifted her chin. "I didn't inhale.

But that's not the point. The point is, he doesn't listen.''

"So you're going to test his DNA?"

"And mine.'' Her eyes on the screen, she added, "If we're not related, it's time the truth came out.''

"Then what?''

She stared up at him. "I don't know.''

The computer search engine did its job and a list of DNA testing agencies and their URLs came up on the screen. Oliver leaned over Miranda's shoulder. "There's an awful lot of them. How're you going to choose?''

"Whichever's cheapest and quickest. Have you got any money you can lend me? I've only saved seventy dollars.''

"My aunt in Boston sent me fifty dollars for my birthday. But you have to pay it back. I'm saving up for the two-volume set of the *Compact Oxford Dictionary.*''

Miranda clicked the mouse on the URL of a testing facility. "You're joking, right?''

"It's got this cool magnifying glass because the print is so small.''

She swiveled the chair to gaze incredulously at him while the Web site downloaded. "You want this dictionary because the print is small?''

Oliver rolled his eyes. "Because there are so many words!''

"Oh.'' She turned to the computer once more. "Well, if he's not my father I'll be going back to L.A. Once I get a job I'll be able to repay you.''

"You're only twelve. You can't get a real job, much less an apartment."

"You can do anything in L.A.," she said flippantly. "I'll be thirteen next month and everyone says I look sixteen. When he thinks I'm not listening, even Dad—I mean, Nick, says I'm twelve going on twenty. Aha! Here we go."

She scanned the Web site, decided this particular testing agency was too pricey and asked too many questions, then went on to the next.

"We should leave," Oliver said, looking at his watch. "The dance is starting."

"Arriving on time for a school dance is *so* uncool," Miranda said. "We have to wait at least an hour. Anyway, I told Rita to meet us outside the front door at nine."

"Okay. I'll go wash my hair."

Miranda dragged her gaze away from the monitor. "But it looks good."

Oliver shrugged. "It's not me."

"You want to go back to looking like a nerd?"

"Are you saying you won't like me with ordinary hair?"

"Oh. Well. I didn't mean *that*." She'd never had anyone challenge her with the right to be uncool before. She kind of admired him for it. With an offhand smile, she said, "I'd like you any way you are."

Oliver's face lit. He bent as if to kiss her on the cheek, ended up punching her lightly on the arm, then spun on his heel and left the room.

Smiling to herself, Miranda spun her chair back to

face the computer. After a dozen more tries, she found a DNA testing facility that fit her budget. Oliver returned, drying his hair with a towel, as she was tapping in the details.

Oliver saw the return address Miranda was inserting. "Hey, you can't have the kit sent here. My father's the town doctor."

"So?"

"So it wouldn't look good. Plus, Mom picks up the mail while I'm at school. She'd find it."

"Well, I can't have it sent to the houseboat and I don't know anyone else— Wait a minute. Yes, I do. Erin."

"Your basketball coach?" Oliver appeared skeptical.

"She's cool. She'll understand."

NICK STRETCHED HIS ARMS over his head as the closing credits rolled across the screen. And resisted the impulse to let his arm drop around Erin's shoulder. Instead, he rose and stepped into the aisle, creating a pocket of space in the flow of people exiting so she could get out.

"Wasn't the movie good?" Erin said, smiling over her shoulder at him as they moved slowly out of the theater. When he didn't respond immediately, she nudged his arm. "Admit it, Nick. You enjoyed it."

"Not bad for a chick flick." He'd chuckled all the way through, but he wasn't sure if that was due to the film or because Erin's laugh was so infectious.

They reached the lobby. Outside, the drizzle had

become a steady rain. He helped Erin on with her coat. Her hair was tangled in the collar and Nick pulled it free—an innocent gesture that became intimate when his fingers encountered the warm skin at the back of her neck. Damn it, he wanted to touch her.

Instead, he stepped away to get the door. "Next time *I* pick the movie."

Erin groaned. "Just as long as it's not Charles Bronson."

"You're on." Caught up in the pleasure of her company, he realized too late that he'd just issued an invitation and she'd accepted. "Could you go for a coffee?" he said, issuing another.

"I could go for a triple cheeseburger and fries." Her eyes glowed. "Now that the morning sickness has gone my appetite is back."

"Burger Shack's just down the road."

"Hey, girlfriend. Hey, Chief," Tracy said from behind them. She winked at Erin. "You sly thing. You got yourself a date for Saturday night and you didn't even tell ol' Tracy."

Oh, boy. Nick looked at the ceiling. He should have known better than to think they'd get away with a simple thing like seeing a movie together.

"It's not a date, Tracy," Erin said, throwing Nick an apologetic glance. "We just happened to turn up to see the same movie."

"Sure thing, sister. Tell it to the judge." She gazed from Erin to Nick, shaking her head and smiling. "You two look damn fine together. Don't they,

Rocky? This here's Rocky." Proudly, she dragged forward a slightly built, gentle man who stood a good three inches shorter than she did.

"Hi, Rocky," Erin said. Nick leaned down and shook his hand.

"Nice to meet you," Rocky said, with a charismatic smile that gave a hint of what Tracy saw in him.

"See you all later." Tracy linked her arm with Rocky's and strolled away, still chuckling.

"Sorry about that," Erin said.

"It's not your fault. Do you still want to go to the Shack?"

"Do you?"

Frankly, he was having second thoughts. "We're not going to let a little gossip stop us from having a good time, are we? I mean, as long as we're clear on the limits of our relationship." Her smile began to fade. "Just friends, that is," he added, and her smile disappeared altogether.

"I think I'll go home after all," she said. "Gran might need me for something."

"Fine. I'll drive you."

"I can walk."

"It's raining. Come on, my truck's just across the street." Without waiting for her to protest again, he grabbed her hand as the traffic light turned green.

The drive to Erin's house took all of three minutes. One hundred and eighty seconds of uncomfortable silence. Nick glanced at Erin, wondering what was going through her head. Why did everything have to be so complicated? He wanted to see her again, but he couldn't accept the whole package, woman and baby. And she knew that.

She was fumbling with her seat belt even before he came to a complete stop at the curb in front of her house. "Thanks for the ride. Please don't bother getting out."

Nick pretended not to hear. He exited, then rounded the truck to support her elbow as she stepped down. At the door he waited while she dug out her key. If they'd been on a real date, this was where he'd kiss her. But they weren't on a date. They were tiptoeing around each other, trying to find the new limits of their friendship.

"I'll see you...soon," he said.

"Sure." Her smile was determinedly cheerful.

He didn't want to leave it at that so he held out his hand. "Pals?"

She placed her hand, cool and slim, in his. "Pals. Sure, why not?"

With a final nod, she twisted the key in the lock and slipped through the door, sliding the dead bolt firmly shut behind her.

Nick shoved his hands in his pockets and walked swiftly through the rain to his truck. Friendship wasn't what *he* wanted, either, but ever since he'd learned of her pregnancy, it seemed the only path to take.

Except that after tonight, he wasn't sure even friendship was possible.

"PANCAKE BREAKFAST THIS Sunday at the firehall," Erin said, reading from the notice Nick had just handed her. He stood on the other side of the teller's cage in his white shirt with the blue-and-gold bugles on the collar, looking good enough to eat.

"Whoo-wee, I *love* pancakes," Tracy said, reading over Erin's shoulder. She gave Nick a huge smile. "*I'll* be there."

"Great." Nick's dark eyes flicked to Erin. "What about you? It's a good cause. We're trying to raise the profile of the fire department and attract more volunteers."

Erin had thought a lot about the previous Saturday night and come to the conclusion she'd allowed herself to be too easily put off Nick's company. She wasn't responsible for other people's opinions and there was no percentage in second-guessing the Greta Voglers of the town. Her feelings were complicated by disappointment that he seemed content to be just friends, but she would have to get over that.

"Gran and I will come, too," she told him with a smile. "How's Miranda? I didn't see her at the last practice."

"She's got a cold. Been away from school for a few days. I left her tucked up on the couch with Neocitran and a stack of videos." He tapped the pile of leaflets into a square on the counter. "I'd better finish delivering these. See you Sunday."

Tracy leaned on the counter and watched every long stride until the glass door swung shut behind his broad shoulders. She sighed. "That is some man. You and he got a date this Saturday?"

Erin, who'd also been watching Nick's exit, drew herself up smartly. "No. I told you—we met by chance at the theater."

Tracy's full lips, as red as her silk blouse, tilted slyly. In a singsong voice she said, "Ah, but he knew you were going to be there. And he drove you home!"

Erin stared. "Who told you all that?"

"I was in the grocery store checkout behind Greta Vogler. I overheard her telling Kathy all about it."

Okay, Erin could understand how his driving her home might be common knowledge, but how in the world did Greta know Nick knew she would be at the movie? Greta obviously had even greater powers than Erin had previously given her credit for.

At least she could be grateful that, so far, nobody seemed to suspect she was pregnant. She wished now she hadn't promised John she wouldn't reveal the identity of her baby's father. What would she say to people when she started to show? How would Gran feel when she realized the whole town was talking about her granddaughter?

Least said, soonest mended, she decided. And that applied to the conversation she was having with Tracy about last Saturday night. "I need to leave a little early today. Gran has an appointment at the physiotherapist. Mr. Haines is in if you need anything."

"Sure thing, boss," Tracy said good-humoredly.

A light rain was falling when Erin left the bank.

She hurried toward home, head bowed under her umbrella as the wind whisked brown leaves across the
sidewalk to collect in the gutter. Wisps of smoke from
a fireplace somewhere scented the autumn air.

As she neared her corner she glanced up. A slight,
hooded figure was at Gran's front gate, peering into
the mailbox. A hand went out to poke through the
contents.

Erin frowned, quickening her footsteps. "Excuse
me. Can I help you?"

The figure straightened with a startled glance,
snatched her hand away and thrust it into a pocket,
paper clutched between her fingers.

"Miranda?" Erin said incredulously. "What are
you doing? Did you take something out of my mailbox?"

"N-nothing," Miranda stammered, and showed
Erin that her hand contained only a crumpled flyer
from the hardware store. "I was passing and I saw
this blow out of your mailbox. I was just putting it
back in."

And Erin was a monkey's uncle. Miranda was lying, but Erin couldn't see that she'd actually done
anything very wrong. "Your dad said you had a bad
cold and were off school."

"I do have a cold." As if to prove it, she sneezed
noisily, then pulled out a wad of used tissues and
mopped up. "But I got bored and I needed to pick
up some homework from Oliver, so I caught a bus
into town."

"Okay," Erin said, allowing herself to be convinced. She removed the contents of the mailbox, aware of Miranda watching her every move. The girl seemed to relax when she saw the slim pile of bills and letters.

"Take care of that cold," Erin said. "Will you be at practice this week?"

"I think so. I'm getting better." With a quick wave, she started walking toward Oliver's house.

Erin moved up the path to the house and paused at the steps to observe Miranda turn the corner. What on earth had the girl been looking for?

TWO DAYS LATER, a package arrived in the mail addressed to Erin, listing the return address as a P.O. box in Santa Monica, California. Puzzled because she knew no one in Santa Monica, Erin ripped open the brown paper wrapping. Inside was a testing kit of some sort, complete with swabs and vials for collecting samples. She scanned the accompanying literature and learned that the swabs were for scraping cells from the inner cheek and the vials for holding specimens of hair follicles.

She held in her hands a DNA testing kit.

For a moment Erin just stared at the kit in astonishment.

John! He hadn't believed her when she'd told him the baby was his, and he was determined to find out for sure before paying child support. Fuming, she dialed the first three digits of his phone number, ready to tell him where he could stick his money. Then a chilling thought struck her.

Miranda peering into her mailbox, searching for something.

Slowly lowering the telephone receiver, Erin cast her mind back to the day Nick had stopped by with the jug of milk. He'd told her of his wife's infidelity and that Miranda might not be his child. What if Miranda had overheard? The window was open. She'd been just down the street when Nick had left. She could have easily run from the porch to the corner in the time that Nick had taken to leave.

Miranda wouldn't have had the testing kit sent to her own home, and Oliver would have refused on the grounds that his parents would inform Nick if they found it.

Miranda obviously thought Erin would keep her secret. Part of her was touched that the girl trusted her. Part of her was angry at being used. And part of her was just plain scared at what Miranda might find out. Scared for Nick if his suspicions were confirmed. Scared for Miranda if she learned that the man she thought was her father wasn't after all.

Erin dialed John's number. Better she should eliminate him as a suspect before accusing Miranda. His secretary answered and put her right through. John's genuine surprise quickly convinced Erin he'd had nothing to do with ordering a DNA testing kit.

"How is your election campaign going, Congressman?" she asked.

"I figure I have just one opponent worthy of the name," he said. "But don't worry. I'll find a way to defeat him."

"I'm sure you will." They chatted for a few more minutes about mutual Seattle friends Erin was gradually losing contact with. When she hung up, she felt as though she'd been talking to a mere acquaintance.

Miranda's phone number was on the corkboard beside the phone, along with those of the other girls on the basketball team. But Nick would be home by now and she wanted to talk to Miranda privately before she said anything to him.

She could hardly drop by the houseboat in the evening to chat to Miranda without arousing Nick's curiosity. And Miranda was back at school; Erin had seen her and Oliver walking past with books in their arms. Walking *slowly* past, casting glances at her mailbox. So many little things made sense now.

Erin pushed herself away from the kitchen table and went in search of her grandmother. She found the older woman on her knees in the garden, planting bulbs. Ruth looked up guiltily, then noticed the package still in Erin's hands. "Hello, dear. Anything interesting in the mail?"

"It's nothing." Erin tucked the small parcel behind her back. "Do you want to go to the pancake breakfast this Sunday?"

"Oh, I don't know…"

"The firefighters are putting it on down at the station."

Gran's face brightened. "Will that nice Nick Dalton be there? I'd love to go."

CHAPTER TEN

SUNDAY MORNING, GRAN was waiting for her on the parson's bench in the hall, her best wig in place and her eyes shining behind her plastic-rimmed glasses. As Erin came down the stairs, Gran used her cane to push herself to a standing position. "Let's see if Nick can cook pancakes as well as he barbecues fish."

Erin could smell the pancakes and maple syrup from half a block away. Her arm linked with Gran's, they moved slowly through the milling crowd inside the engine bay. Gran paused now and then to chat with friends and neighbors. Erin's gaze roved over the crowd, in a futile search for Miranda, but it always ended up back on Nick, who stood behind one of several camp stoves set on trestle tables. He wore a navy apron over his white shirt and black pants and sported a white chef's hat atop his dark hair, managing to look both authoritative and approachable.

And deliciously masculine.

At another cookstove, Dave, his protruding stomach spattered with batter, stuffed a pancake into his mouth with his fingers when he thought no one was looking. Frank had noticed, though, and chewed Dave out. With a hangdog expression, Dave went off to wash his hands. Steve and Angela manned a third stove, Angela cooking while Steve hovered, holding the bowl of batter and handing her implements.

Once again, Erin's eyes were drawn back to Nick. His grin flashed frequently as he flirted casually with the women and joked with the men. Everyone seemed to like and admire him.

Including her.

Someone called her name. "Laura, hi," she said, refocusing as a brunette appeared out of the crowd with a toddler in her arms. "How've you been? Where's Ted?"

"Sleeping in, the rat," Laura said cheerfully, shifting her little girl to the other hip. Kylie's mouth was rimmed with buttery syrup and her pudgy fingers left dark smudges on her mom's red corduroy jacket.

"Gosh, she's grown since I last saw her," Erin said, tickling the child under the chin until she giggled. Erin's hand dropped to her abdomen. Someday *she* would be walking around with a child on her hip. The thought filled her with gladness and fear.

"I swear she grows every time I turn around. I wish I could stay and visit with you, but I've got to get Kylie home." Laura touched Erin's arm. "Our old friends are complaining that since you've been back in town we've hardly seen you."

"I've been pretty busy with Gran."

"I know. I'm having some of our girlfriends over for lunch next Friday. Can you make it?"

"Sounds great. I'll see if I can get away."

"I warn you, though, with everyone's kids running around, it's not like the old days," Laura said apologetically.

"That's all right. I'll love it. See you then."

As much as Erin wanted to see her friends, she knew it would be hard being with women preoccupied with nursing babies and wiping grubby faces and not be able to mention her own pregnancy. But then, she didn't really want to. All the women had husbands. She didn't want anyone feeling sorry for her or looking at her as if she were less than whole because she was on her own. Or asking questions she couldn't answer, like who the father was.

Gran tugged on her arm. "Do you see any place to sit down?"

"Over there," Erin said, guiding her to more trestle tables and folding chairs set up along the back of the bay. She left Gran saving her a seat and went to join the lineup for pancakes.

As she drew closer, she saw Miranda behind the camp stoves, measuring pancake mix into a big stainless steel bowl. Good, she was here. But how was Erin going to talk to her with Nick around?

Miranda turned to grab the measuring cup from the table, saw Erin, and red flooded her cheeks. Her movements became awkward and she spilled the cup of water she was transporting to the mixing bowl.

The line moved ahead and took Erin with it. Suddenly she was face-to-face with Nick. His twinkling eyes and crooked smile blocked thought and she stared stupidly, forgetting for a moment why she was there.

"What's your pleasure, ma'am?" Nick rumbled.

"Two orders of pancakes, please."

"Coming right up." Nick scraped off the griddle and started to pour batter onto the black cast iron. "How many would you like? Three, four?"

"Two each is plenty, thank you."

He waggled the spatula at her. "Ah, ah, ah. You're eating for—"

"Ahem!" Erin cleared her throat, cutting him off.

While they'd been talking, Greta Vogler had pushed in between Erin and the woman next in line to waggle her fingers at Nick.

"'Morning, Greta," Nick said. "What can I do for you?"

"We're all out of blueberry syrup at our table. Have you any more?"

"I think that can be arranged." He turned to Miranda. "Get out another jug of blueberry syrup, please, honey, and fill the bottles on the tables."

Greta hovered closer, peering over Erin's shoulder at the griddle. "Your pancakes are almost as good as mine," she simpered.

"High praise, I'm sure." He gave her a polite smile, then leaned forward as if to whisper a secret. "I got the recipe from my Aunt Jemima."

Greta tittered, her hand over her mouth. Miranda straightened up from a cardboard box on the concrete floor, holding a gallon jug of syrup against her chest with both hands. Having no other excuse to tarry, Greta followed Miranda back to the tables.

"We should be finished by noon," Nick said. "Can I come by and pick you up?"

"I beg your pardon?" Erin said, distracted. She'd been following Miranda's progress. "What for?"

With deft flicks of his wrist, Nick flipped the pancakes. "I thought we could go fishing."

"Fishing? The salmon runs are over."

"Contrary to what some folks think, *catching* a fish

isn't essential for enjoying fishing. Just sitting in a boat on the water on a beautiful autumn day is good enough for me. What do you say?''

Erin didn't know what to say. Accidentally meeting up with Nick at the movie theater was one thing. Deliberately making a date was quite another. ''I, uh, planned to clean the leaves out of the gutters this afternoon. With all the rain we've been getting lately they're starting to clog.''

Nick's dark brows pulled together. ''You shouldn't be cleaning gutters in your condition.''

Erin gave him a meaningful glare. ''I'm over the *flu*. I'm fine.''

''Nevertheless, I'll help.'' The set of his jaw told her he was equally determined that she not risk a fall from a ladder.

Erin sighed. ''Okay, thanks. Gran will really appreciate it.''

Nick slid pancakes off the griddle and stacked them on two plates. The aroma was making Erin ravenous. ''Enjoy,'' he said, handing the plates to Erin.

Her eyes locked with his and only a discreet cough from the man behind made her move along. Honestly, she was worse than Greta the way she mooned over Nick. ''I'll just get these over to Gran while they're hot.''

He winked. ''See you later.''

When she got back to the table, Erin set Gran's plate in front of her, told her she'd be back in a moment and went in pursuit of Miranda. The girl was standing with her back to Erin at the next table, pouring syrup into plastic squeeze bottles.

Erin put a hand on her shoulder. "I'd like to talk to you."

Miranda jumped. Her guilty expression was a marked change in demeanor from her defiance of less than a week ago. "I…I'm pretty busy helping Nick."

"This will only take a minute."

Erin walked with Miranda to the far side of the bay. She glanced around, making sure no one was nearby and listening. "I got a package in the mail the other day."

"You did?" Miranda blurted eagerly. Then, as if recollecting she had an image to maintain, she adopted her familiar slouch. "I mean, *so?*"

Erin had no doubt Miranda knew what she was talking about. "The package was from a company that tests DNA samples for paternity. You ordered the kit and had it sent to my house so your father wouldn't find out."

"What if I did?" In spite of her bold words, Miranda's lower lip began to tremble and her fingers twisted the ends of her apron strings.

Suddenly Erin felt sorry for her, sorry enough to want to hug her. But she didn't want Nick to see and wonder what was going on, nor did she want Miranda to think what she'd done was okay, even though she empathized with the girl. "What would your father say if he knew?"

"He's not my father," Miranda said in a fierce whisper.

"You don't know that."

"I'm going to find out—with or without your help. If you don't give me the kit I'll order another one and have it sent somewhere else."

Erin sensed she was bluffing. The kits had to be expensive. "Where did you get it, anyway?"

"Off the Internet. It was easy."

"You used me without my knowledge. I don't like that. Why should I help you?"

Miranda was silent. When she raised her face, the tough act had disappeared and her eyes were shiny with unshed tears. "Because no one else will."

Oh, Lord. "Don't you think you should talk this over with Nick?" she said, more gently.

"He's lied to me all these years. How can I trust him?" Miranda ducked her head and Erin saw two plump tears drop onto her apron.

"He just wanted to protect you," Erin said desperately, wishing she didn't have to defend Nick, yet certain he wouldn't deliberately hurt his daughter.

"I'm not telling him," Miranda said stubbornly. "If you do, I'll deny everything."

Erin was pretty sure the evidence, circumstantial though it was, would be enough to convince Nick that Miranda had ordered the kit. On the other hand, Miranda was intensely unhappy. That wouldn't go away unless the issue was resolved. Moreover, she deserved to know who her father was. What if Nick refused to take the test?

"Okay, I'll give you the kit," Erin said reluctantly. "But if he ever asks me, I won't lie to him about it."

"Oh, thank you, thank you." Miranda forgot her cool image and threw her arms around Erin's waist.

The girl was so vulnerable Erin hurt for her. "Hang on. There's a condition."

Miranda pulled away, drying her eyes with the heel of her hand. "What?"

"Should you find out that Nick isn't your father, you will come to me, if not to him, and we'll arrange for counseling."

Miranda looked at her as though she'd suggested double amputation. "No way."

"You have to agree or we don't have a deal," Erin insisted.

Miranda's face smoothed into acquiescence. "Whatever you say."

Her about-face seemed a little too quick to be true. Nevertheless, Erin expelled a relieved breath. Deep down, Miranda was intelligent and sensible, qualities that would come through in a crisis. "I'll bring the kit to the next basketball practice."

Miranda immediately appeared worried again. "You won't let the other kids see it, will you?"

"Of course not. I'll put it in a paper bag."

Miranda gave her a rare and radiant smile. "It'll be our secret."

But as the girl strolled away, humming happily, misgivings assailed Erin. How could she pretend to be Nick's friend if she lied to him?

"YOU REALLY DIDN'T HAVE to clean our gutters, but thank you," Erin reiterated, handing Nick a roast beef sandwich and a cold beer. Miranda had declined the offer of a gutter-cleaning party and had gotten a ride to the houseboat with Oliver and his parents.

Nick leaned back in the kitchen chair, the sandwich poised near his mouth. "You don't need to sound so apologetic. Or so grateful. Friends help each other out. It's no big deal."

"I know, but..." Guilt rode her like a highwayman, urging her to confess her part in Miranda's deception. Desire for Nick's good opinion kept her mouth shut. "I haven't done anything for you."

"Friendship isn't tit for tat. Anyway, you have done something for me. You've helped Miranda." He bit into his sandwich.

Erin pushed away from the table. She went to the sink, discovered nothing she had to do there and moved across the room to the Regulator clock on the wall. Opening the glass front, she took the key off the wooden ledge below the pendulum and wound the mechanism, remembering too late that she'd wound the eight-day clocks the previous day.

"Something the matter, Erin?" The chair legs came back to the floor with a thump.

"No," she said suddenly, turning to him. "Just wondering why we're keeping those fish waiting."

Nick's boat was a sixteen-foot aluminum runabout with a collapsible canvas-and-plastic Bimini top and a fifty-horsepower Evinrude motor. Erin got in and sat on one of the padded seats at the front.

Clad in hip waders and his fishing vest, Nick handed her his tackle box and the fishing rods, and a daypack to stow beneath the seats. Then he untied the painter and cast off, leaping into the boat as he pushed away from the wharf. He primed the fuel pump, before coming forward to turn the key to start the engine. A shout from the deck of the houseboat made him kill the spluttering engine before it properly caught.

Nick shaded his face with a hand and looked back at Miranda standing at the rail. The boat floated gently downstream. "What is it?"

"Where are you going?"

"To the channel off Coot Island. I told you I was going fishing."

"I didn't know you were going with *her*."

Nick glanced back at Erin, puzzled and apologetic. "She blows hot and cold all the time."

Erin knew exactly where the girl's querulousness stemmed from. She was afraid Erin would tell Nick in spite of having promised not to. "It's okay." Lifting her head, she repeated the words louder, to Miranda. "It's okay."

The tension seemed to go out of Miranda's taut shoulders and she stepped back from the railing of the houseboat. Nick's frown deepened, and for a moment Erin worried that he'd ask what she meant. Then he shrugged, waved goodbye to Miranda and turned the key again. The motor roared to life, and with a spin of the wheel Nick swept across the river in a broad curve and headed upstream.

The faint saltiness in the few drops that came over the windscreen tasted good to Erin, and the cool fresh air was like the first bite of a crisp apple. As they chugged against the current, crabs scuttled into their burrows in the mud banks. Farther up, past the tidal influence, mallards and coots swam through the marshy grasses in the shallows. Shining in the distance, the Olympic Mountains wore the first frosting of new snow on their peaks.

The strange, wild excitement that bright autumn days sometimes brought surged through her. She'd experienced such feeligs since childhood, moments when she was fully conscious of being alive, of wanting to seize the day with both fists and hang on tight. Right now, Nick was part of the moment.

He drove the boat half standing, one knee resting on the seat, his eyes narrowed against the wind and trained on the river for snags.

"Are you warm enough?"

Despite the sunshine, his question was reasonable. The breeze was cool and the season late; the branches of the alders that grew profusely along the riverbanks were bare. But Erin had on one of Gran's thick hand-knit fisherman sweaters, jeans and a red Gore-Tex jacket. "I'm fine."

"You are at that." Nick's smile, casual yet warm, lifted her heart.

"Why the hip waders?" Erin asked. "Do you plan to fish from the river?"

"No. Miranda was right, I don't like getting wet." In response to her puzzled glance, he elaborated. "As a young firefighter I spent too much time getting soaked inside my bunker gear from perspiration and because of water raining down from the hoses. Nowadays I prefer to stay dry."

"So you came to the Pacific Northwest. Good move."

His mouth curved in a smile. "I *can* swim."

"Why did Miranda say you couldn't?"

He shrugged. "To cause a scene, embarrass me, who knows. I've learned that when it comes to arguing with Miranda, you don't sweat the small stuff. That girl would swear black is white without blinking."

Erin grew quiet, trailing her fingers in the water.

He was so caring of Miranda. And all the time, she was bent on proving he wasn't her father.

Half an hour later they came to a section of the river Erin remembered well from her youth. Nick steered to the left of a small island and pulled back the throttle to motor slowly through the shallows, where most boaters wouldn't venture. Unless they knew of the deep hole just around the bend where trout lurked. In a cove on the far bank where the water was deep and slow moving, he dropped the anchor.

"Doesn't get better than this," he said, stretching his arms over his head, his feet so steady the boat barely moved. Then he moved past her to the wooden bench in the stern and opened his tackle box.

Erin swiveled her seat around to watch him select a lure. "Do you ever miss L.A.?"

"Nah. I only stayed because Janine had grown up in Orange County and she didn't want to leave." He threw her a wry glance. "She loved the shopping."

Erin grinned. "I can relate to that."

Nick attached lures to both lines, baited the hooks and handed one rod to her. They cast on opposite sides of the boat and settled into a companionable silence. Twenty minutes passed without a word or a bite.

"So why did it take you two years to move?" Erin said at last.

"It seemed logical to wait until Miranda started high school." Nick reeled in his line to check his bait. "As it turned out, we left not a moment too soon. She'd gotten mixed up with kids several years older. Bunch of losers."

Erin knew that story. What she didn't know was much about *his* personal life. "Were you involved with anyone there?"

"You mean, did I leave a woman behind?" he said casually as he recast his line. "Nobody's pining for me. And I'm not pining for anyone, either."

She shouldn't feel relieved, but she did.

"What about you? Do you miss that blockhead who let you go?"

She had to think about that. She missed some of the things they did together, but it was strange how quickly and completely John had dropped out of her life. If not for her pregnancy she might not even think of him.

"Does he call?" Nick said when she still hadn't answered. "Ask how you and the baby are doing?"

She shook her head. "He sent a check. I tore it up."

"You should have banked it—money is the least the bastard can give—but I guess in your position I'd have done the same."

"You must understand. We broke up before I knew about the baby."

"What was the problem? If that's not too painful or personal a question."

It was both, but somehow she didn't mind telling Nick. "We met nearly three years ago at a party. He was smart, ambitious and knew a lot of interesting and powerful people. He swept me off my feet, as the saying goes. It wasn't long before we were engaged."

Nick reached into the daypack and pulled out a thermos of coffee and two mugs. He filled one and handed it to Erin. "Go on."

"When he became prosecuting attorney, things started to go wrong. His ambition, which I'd admired so much, suddenly came between us. First he put off our wedding date until after he was appointed, then he was too busy. Something always came up that was more important than our life together. Finally we set another date, only for him to announce he was running for Congress and we'd have to delay again. That was the last straw."

"So why are you protecting him?"

She shrugged. "A lingering sense of loyalty. He *is* my baby's father."

"Yeah." Abruptly, Nick tossed the dregs of his coffee overboard.

Conversation ceased again, so Erin reeled in her line to check the bait. The hook was empty. Leaving her seat to sit beside Nick, she got another worm from the plastic container and threaded it onto her hook.

"You're the only woman I've seen do that without being squeamish," Nick said, watching her.

"My grandfather trained me well." She leaned across to replace the worm container and her thigh pressed against his, the warm physical contact making her gaze rise involuntarily. She was pretty sure he didn't mean to look at her all dark and hungry, yet something electric passed between them, and Erin retreated to her own seat so quickly the boat rocked, water slapping at the aluminum hull.

Nick gazed at his fishing line as though nothing had happened and she wished she could bring back the easy camaraderie they'd shared earlier. But as long as they were attracted to each other and determined not to show it, they were going to have this problem.

Minutes passed. When Nick spoke again, his voice sounded almost too casual to be natural. "What were you and Miranda talking about this morning at the fire hall?"

"Uh, something about basketball practice. Why?"

"She's been a little tense the past few weeks." He glanced at her, his eyes opaque. "I thought maybe she'd confided in you."

Erin studied the angle of her fishing line where it intersected the water and the concentric ripples that emanated from the point of contact. At one time Miranda had brought them together; now she formed a barrier to honesty. Not a good situation when two people were trying to be friends.

"No," she said at last, aware the atmosphere between them was cooling further and helpless to prevent it.

"This morning she called me 'Nick' and I realized she hadn't called me 'Dad' in ages." Pain salted his voice, made it rough. "You didn't tell her what I told you about Janine, did you?"

"No! I wouldn't do that."

He sighed. "I didn't think so."

"Miranda needs to hear the truth about Janine from *you*."

"What *is* the truth?" he said bitterly. "I wish I knew."

"She's growing up—"

"I came across tampons in her bathroom. I wasn't even aware she'd started having periods." Nick grimaced. "Do you think that's why she's acting weird?"

"Partly, maybe." Erin gripped her rod and swiveled to face him. "You need to close the distance between you. You can only do that with honesty." *Oh, God, who was she to talk?* "She needs to know who she is."

"What if she isn't my biological daughter?" Nick's voice hardened. "What if the other guy doesn't accept her? Or supposing she is my daughter and I get her all worried and worked up for nothing?"

Miranda was worried *now* but Erin couldn't tell Nick that. "You can't protect her forever. She's a resourceful kid. She'll find out on her own someday."

He shook his head and lapsed into stony silence.

Defeated, Erin drew her jacket around her and did up the zipper. While they'd been arguing, a cold front had moved in from the west and now clouds blocked the sun. Erin felt the coming winter through the layers of clothing. "Nick, I think I've had enough fishing for today if you don't mind."

He glanced at the sky. "It's getting late, anyway. Looks like we're in for more rain."

They reeled in their lines, stowed the fishing gear and motored back downriver, neither talking. Erin hunched into herself, feeling as bleak as the dark clouds that lined the horizon.

"HEY, NICK, ARE YOU ASLEEP?" Miranda slid over the back of the couch on which Nick was stretched out, dozing. She was still in the shorts and crop top she wore to basketball practice. Her hair was damp at the temples and she smelled faintly of perspiration.

"Not anymore." He eased himself up the cushions. He'd attended two call-outs last night, one a structure fire and the other a highway accident—a busy night for Hainesville, and all the more hassle to deal with due to heavy rainfall for the past two weeks. "By the way, I'm *Dad* to you."

Miranda glanced sideways at him from beneath her long bangs, an odd look in her eyes. "*Are* you?"

The back of his neck chilled. She almost sounded as if she *knew*. Surely Erin hadn't lied when she'd said she hadn't told Miranda about Janine's confession. "What do you mean by that?"

"Nothing." Miranda examined her fingernails and began peeling away a broken one.

He forced himself not to tell her to use a nail file. They'd had so little interaction lately he didn't want to lecture her the one time she voluntarily sat with him. Keeping his voice light, he asked, "How was practice?"

"Good."

"Sink any more amazing baskets?"

"No."

"How's Erin?"

"Fine."

Miranda, master of the monosyllable. Somedays, a conversation with her was like squeezing water from a nearly dry sponge—drop by drop. He studied her. She'd left the first nail and was busy chipping another down to the skin. "Nervous about something?"

Her startled gaze flew to meet his. She laughed, the sound high-pitched and strained. "Me, nervous? Why would I be nervous?"

"I don't know. You've been acting kind of strange

the past couple of weeks. Anything you want to talk
about?''

Dumb insolence replaced her tense smile. ''*No.
Anything you want to tell* me?''

That stare of hers pushed his buttons. Jaw tight, he
counted to ten, forcing himself to relax. Exasperating
as she was, she was just a kid, vulnerable and basi-
cally unsure of herself. He squeezed her shoulder.
''Well, there's something I haven't said for a while.
I love you. I'm proud of you.''

In a blink her face froze. Thinking she was about
to burst into tears, Nick tried to pull her into a hug.
She pushed against his chest, refusing to be cuddled.

''Did you know you have some gray hairs?'' she
said jovially, as if she'd rehearsed a joke. Her tone
contrasted badly with the anguish in her eyes.

Hurt by her rejection, Nick loosened his hold. She
would say anything these days to avoid getting close.
''Not that I'm aware of.''

''No, seriously, I can see gray hairs.'' She got on
her knees and started pawing through the hair on top
of his head. ''Don't worry, I'll take care of them.''

''No… *Miranda.* Ouch!'' Rubbing his crown, he
glared at her. Her innocent gaze seemed too good to
be true. ''What are you trying to do, scalp me?''

''Just helping you maintain a youthful appear-
ance.'' She glanced down at the clump of hairs between her fingers. ''My mistake. They're not gray after all,'' she said cheerfully. ''Oh, look, I got the
roots.''

'''Oh, look, I got the roots,''' he mimicked. She
scrambled off the couch. ''Where are you going?''

''To bed.'' She yawned elaborately, a hand over

her mouth. "I'll just get rid of these," she said, holding up his hair. "Unless you want to make a locket for your lady love."

Despite his irritation, Nick had to laugh at her simpering expression. "Get outta here."

Yes! Miranda crowed silently. *Got 'em.* She departed via the kitchen, making a show of stepping on the foot pedal that opened the trash can. It closed with a bang, and she glanced across the open-plan dining area to the couch. Nick was getting to his feet.

Gripping the hairs, she hurried out of the kitchen and down the hall to her bedroom. Once inside, she shut the door and locked it. Not even her posters of Ricky Martin and Britney Spears, her CDs and her stuffed animal collection that she knew was babyish but wasn't ready to give up could make this room feel like home to her.

She paused in front of the dresser and spoke to a framed photo of herself and her mother. "You understand why I'm doing this, don't you, Mom?"

Then, before the sudden prickle in her nose could lead to tears, she went to her closet. On the top shelf below her folded clothes she'd hidden the DNA testing kit. One-handed, she pulled it out, sending sweaters tumbling.

A noise outside her door made her freeze. *Don't come in. Don't even knock.* Heart racing, she waited what seemed like an eternity before she heard the water running in the bathroom. *Thank God.*

She tiptoed over to the desk. The hand holding the hairs was beginning to sweat, but she didn't dare put them down in case the roots, which was the part they tested, got contaminated or something. Fumbling a little, she got the box open and the little plastic sample bag out. Only when she had the hairs safely inside and the top sealed did she breathe easier.

One sample down, one to go.

CHAPTER ELEVEN

"COME ON IN, KEL," Erin said, hustling her sister through the front door a mere thirty minutes after she'd called with the news that a box had arrived from Geena. "It's in the living room. Be quiet, though, Gran's fallen asleep in her rocker."

Kelly, having a rare day off, wore jeans and a navy pullover under her jacket, and her chin-length brown hair was pulled back in a stubby ponytail. "Thank goodness Geena finally made contact," she whispered. "I was beginning to think she'd vanished off the face of the planet. Where's the postmark from?"

"Italy, I think." Erin sat on the couch in front of the battered cardboard box and studied the colorful foreign stamps. "Amalfi," she read. "Isn't that on the coast?"

"Beats me. You're the one who traveled around Europe between high school and college. *I've* never been anywhere."

Erin tore her gaze from the postmark to stare at Kelly, whose voice held a bitterness she'd never heard before. All these years she'd thought Kelly had been totally content to stay in Hainesville with Max and raise kids. "You got married straight out of high school."

"Tell me something I *don't* know. Let's get this open." Kelly pulled at the layers of twine binding the box.

"I hope she included a letter," Erin said, reaching across to the side table for Gran's sewing scissors.

"Or at least a note explaining why she hasn't contacted us for so long." Kelly gave up trying to open the tightly wrapped package and bounced impatiently on the footstool. "Man, she tied this sucker up like a Thanksgiving turkey."

"Is that from Geena?" Gran said suddenly from her rocker by the window. She sat up, blinking and rubbing her eyes behind her glasses.

"Yes, from Italy." Erin cut methodically through the twine and the tape that sealed the flaps and sides. Gran joined her on the couch, and soon the click of knitting needles merged with the steady snip of the scissors. Finally Erin pushed back the flaps and reached inside through rustling layers of tissue paper.

After a minute's fruitless search, she slumped back against the couch. "No note."

"She probably met some gorgeous Italian count and is cruising the Mediterranean on his yacht," Kelly said. Leaning over the box, she started removing carefully folded clothes. "Let's see what she sent. Since you're pregnant, I'm perfectly justified in cutting the clothes down to my size."

"I won't always be pregnant," Erin replied absently, her worries over Geena still at the forefront of her mind. She tried to tell herself that Kelly's version was probably right; Geena never stayed in one spot for long and never refused an offer for luxury and travel, especially from a rich, handsome man.

Erin held up a sheer blouse of gossamer pink, trimmed with purple and silver beads. "This silk is so soft and fine. I don't think it'll fit me, though."

Kelly blinked in surprise. "How small is *that?* It wouldn't fit *anybody.*" She rose and let the evening dress she'd removed from the box fall against her own slender body. "And this! Geena's always been the thinnest of us three, but this is ridiculous."

Erin set aside the blouse and picked out a cream-and-blue jumpsuit that any other time she would have leaped at owning. Now she stared down at the tiny garment in shock and dismay. True, her own middle had thickened somewhat, but the waist of Geena's jumpsuit was barely as wide as her handspan. "Only a beanpole could wear these clothes."

Kelly sank onto her footstool and gazed at the pile of designer clothing, not one article of which would fit either her or Erin. "Maybe she made a mistake and sent us a box of children's clothing."

Gran snorted. "What child wears evening dresses? Besides, even the daywear is too long to be children's clothing."

"You're right." Erin's worried gaze met Kelly's. "But if Geena fits these clothes, that means she's lost a lot of weight."

"She's *anorexic.*"

"Kelly, don't say that. There must be some explanation. Maybe they're samples and the agency was getting rid of them so Geena sent them to us. You know how she hates to waste anything.''

Gran paused in her knitting to shake her head. ''No grown woman should be that thin. I think it's time we tried harder to contact her.''

Erin began to refold the clothes and pack them back in the box. ''You're right, Gran. She practically lives on her cell phone and we're used to her calling us. I've tried to reach her a number of times, but her phone's always shut off or is busy. First thing Monday morning I'll contact her New York modeling agency.''

MIRANDA WAITED TWO DAYS after the hair-pulling incident before she cornered Nick at the breakfast table.

''Dad,'' she began on a winsome note that she hoped didn't sound false, ''would you help me with my science project?''

Smiling, Nick set aside his newspaper. ''Sure, honey, what do you need?''

''Just a cheek swab.'' She held up the small wooden spatula that had come with the DNA testing kit.

''What is this for, microbiology?''

''Uh, yeah. We're growing cultures from different sources—soil, moldy cheese, the inside of human cheeks....''

''Just don't sample the bathroom sink or we'll have the health department out here.''

Cleaning the bathroom was her job and he was only

half joking. "I promise I'll scrub it out today. Right after school."

"Fine." His expression turned wary as she advanced on him brandishing the wooden spatula. "Maybe I should brush my teeth first."

It would make no difference for the DNA test, but for her ruse to work the scenario had to appear authentic. "That might destroy some of the bacteria." She stood over him, spatula poised. "Open wide."

"Ever think of becoming a dentist?"

"Ha, ha." Peering into his mouth, she scraped hard down one side. He groaned in protest, but she ignored him, turned the spatula over and ran it down the other side just for good measure.

"Man, these projects are brutal," Nick said, rubbing his jaw. "I hope we get an A on this."

"Thanks, Nick," she said, backing away. Now that she had what she wanted, she could revert to his given name.

He didn't seem to notice. "What are you going to do with that? Don't you need to put it in a petri dish or something?"

"I, uh, I left it in my bedroom. But you're right. I've got to store it properly."

That night she lay in bed, running over how she'd obtained and stored the samples of hair and skin cells. She'd done everything according to instructions, including collecting samples of her own hair and mouth. She'd put more than enough postage on the package to send it back to California.

Everything was done. Now all she had to do was

wait for the results. Then she'd know one way or another if the man she'd grown up calling Daddy was her biological father. If he was, life went on as usual. If he wasn't... Her skin went cold. She didn't want to think about that.

He'd said he loved her.

Tears pressed on the backs of her eyelids. No matter what he said or did, she couldn't let it stop her from doing what she had to do. She tried to harden her heart, to not care what he felt about her. But no matter how hard she tried, she *did* care.

Set on her course of action and hating it, she pulled her ancient and love-worn stuffed panda into her arms, turned her face to the wall and cried.

"HELP! FIRE!"

Tracy's hysterical cry brought Erin rushing out of her office. She collided with Tracy coming from the back room, trailed by smoke. Mr. Haines appeared in his doorway, a new spin-caster reel in his hand.

"Quick, Bobby!" Erin shouted. "Call the fire department."

Bobby lunged for the phone while Erin wrestled the extinguisher out of its case on the wall behind the counter. Her arms sagged with the weight and she wondered belatedly if she could injure the baby by lifting heavy objects. Edna Thompson, who was on her way in through the heavy glass doors, saw the smoke and backed out again in such a hurry her cane caught in the door.

"How did it start, Tracy?" Erin, coughing from the

smoke and squinting through burning eyes, scanned the instructions on the side of the extinguisher.

"We got another leak in the roof," Tracy squealed, looking anxiously at the smoke billowing from the back room. "Ohmigod, I think I left the vault door open."

The thought of bills going up in smoke, of paychecks and pension checks going unpaid, of people left without money for groceries over the Thanksgiving weekend, galvanized Erin. She pulled the safety pin from the nozzle of the extinguisher, hoisted the heavy cylinder into her arms and charged blindly through the smoke-shrouded door into the back room. A siren wailed in the background.

Orange flames licked their way along the wall from the computer station toward the open bank vault. Through the smoke she heard loud voices, feet thumping, a barked order to clear the building. She pumped the extinguisher to prime it and aimed the thin hose at the fire. Just then a jet of water was let loose from a fire hose behind her. The splash back hit her in the face and soaked her hair and clothing.

Erin shrieked as a pair of strong arms in a yellow bunker jacket hoisted her. The fire extinguisher fell from her hands with a heavy thud. "Put me down!"

Ignoring her demand, Nick marched out of the bank with her, leaving Steve to subdue the flames. Erin raised her head as he pushed through the front door onto the sidewalk, where Tracy, Bobby and Mr. Haines stood watching the action from a safe distance.

"Put me down!" she ordered again.

He set her back on her feet, flipped the mask off his face and proceeded to give her a tongue-lashing.

Great. More than two weeks had passed since the ruined fishing trip and he had to see her in a soggy suit with her hair wet and straggly. It was a new suit, too; she'd been forced into buying clothes the next size up.

"If you *ever* risk your life again," he began. "Or the life of your ba—"

"Stop it!" Damn. She was going to cry. Damn him. She couldn't look at him for fear she'd either punch him or fall into his arms sobbing. He was right, but he didn't have to be so vocally, so *publicly,* right.

She gazed in dismay at the Manolo Blahnik pumps Geena had picked up especially for her in England, twisting an ankle to one side to inspect the stained blue suede. "They're ruined!"

"Did you get hit in the head?" Nick asked, peering at her.

"I'm fine. My shoes aren't." Why hadn't he called her?

Steve came out of the building, trailing the slack inch-and-a-half hose behind him. "Fire's tapped, Chief. Looks like water shorted out the wiring on a computer."

"Good work." Nick turned to her. "I thought you had that roof fixed."

She started to wring out the hem of her skirt. "It's a new leak."

"I'll just have a word with Jonah. Don't go away."

The instant he left, Tracy and Bobby hurried over.

"You okay, girlfriend?" Tracy said. "Oh, your *poor shoes!*"

"I'll get your coat from your office," Bobby offered.

Minutes later, Bobby handed Erin her coat and Tracy helped her on with it. Nick returned, his helmet under his arm, and Tracy took Bobby by the arm and pulled him away.

He rubbed his jaw with long, blunt fingers. "Can I buy you lunch to make up for the damage to your shoes?"

"Lunch in *New York* wouldn't make up for these shoes."

The atmosphere was as chill as the November rain still falling. Maddeningly, Nick appeared not to notice. "How about a movie?"

Erin saw Tracy watching them through the bank windows. Steve was winding the hose back onto the fire truck. Nick was waiting for her decision. "What's playing?"

"You'll see. My choice, remember?" Nick tucked a strand of curling wet hair behind her ear. "I'll pick you up Saturday. Seven o'clock."

God, she was hopeless at staying away from him. But suddenly the gray sky looked less gloomy and the end-of-month accounts less daunting.

SATURDAY NIGHT, ERIN couldn't do up the button on her favorite pair of gray wool slacks. Staring at her reflection in the mirror with dismay, she sucked in her belly and tried again. This time she was able to fasten the button, but when she let out her breath the waistband cut into her skin painfully.

She tried on another pair. They, too, were tight. Panicking, she ransacked her closet for her fat clothes. Although wearing sweatpants, even ones with a designer label, was no way to impress Nick, defiantly she pulled them on, anyway. Just because she and Nick were going to a movie didn't mean he'd changed his mind about getting involved with a pregnant woman. And she had enough on her plate taking care of Gran and herself without the complication of a romance. Erin donned a matching sweatshirt and turned sideways to look at herself in the mirror. She might not look like a fashion plate, but no one would suspect she was pregnant.

Three hours later, the house lights came on after the movie. Nick rose and stretched his cramped legs, then lent Erin a hand. She drew her coat up around her shoulders, releasing the faint floral scent that had intrigued and tantalized him throughout the movie.

He'd been a little surprised to see her in sweats on a night out, but he figured that meant she was getting comfortable with him. He, on the other hand, was less comfortable in some ways. With pregnancy, her delicate femininity had taken on a lushness. As a "friend" he knew he shouldn't be aware of the swell of her breasts or the curve of her hips. He could deny his attraction all he liked, but it was growing stronger all the time.

She turned to him, smiling, and reached up to wipe her thumb across his chin, just brushing his lower lip.

"You had a fragment of popcorn caught in your beard."

He rasped his hand over the stubble to wipe away the tingle left behind by her touch. She must not have any idea what she did to him or she wouldn't be putting her hands on him. "Did you enjoy the movie?"

"If you'd told me beforehand we were seeing a Jackie Chan picture I would have run, screaming. But *Shanghai Noon* wasn't bad," she said, then grinned at his expression. "Okay, I admit I laughed the whole way through. Chan's no Mel Gibson, but he's kind of cute."

"How about that triple cheeseburger at the Shack?" he suggested, determined not to let the evening end too soon. To his delight, Erin agreed. "Wait here," he said. "I'll get my truck."

"Let's walk. It's such a beautiful evening."

"Excuse me? It's raining."

"Just a sprinkle." Erin tucked her arm through his and tugged him toward the brightly lit Burger Shack two blocks away. "What's Miranda doing tonight?"

"She went to Oliver's for pizza and videos."

"I'm glad Miranda's made a real friend. She's chummy with Rita, but she and Oliver really seem to get along well."

"As long as they don't get along *too* well, if you know what I mean."

"Underneath that tough facade she's pretty level-headed."

"I hope so." Nick hunched into his parka and tried

to ignore the steady "sprinkle" that was rapidly soaking his hair and shoulders. "And Ruth? Will she be okay on her own?"

"She went to bed early. We went on an extra-long walk today. Tired her right out." Erin fell quiet, her forehead faintly creased. "I finally talked to Geena."

"Your fashion model sister? Is something wrong?" Nick asked.

Erin bit her lip. "She sounded weird...hyped... strung out. She said she was jet-lagged from going back and forth from Paris to New York twice in the past week, but I don't know... I'm worried about her."

Nick recalled a TV program Miranda had watched one night about the modeling industry and the disturbing methods models used to stay thin—bulimia, anorexia, cigarettes and drugs. Nick folded his hand over hers. "Wouldn't she have told you if she was ill?"

"I guess so...." Erin said doubtfully. "It's hard when she's so far away. I was hoping she'd get home for Thanksgiving, but she has a cosmetics contract. And over Christmas she'll be doing a fashion shoot in the Caribbean."

"Some people have all the luck. What are your plans for Thanksgiving?"

"Kelly always puts on a feast. Would you and Miranda like to come? I know you'd be more than welcome."

"Thanks, but the Camerons have invited us already. Did I tell you we got ten new volunteers following the pancake breakfast?''

"That's great."

"I'm still lobbying town council for another paid firefighter, but it's a start. Ah, here we are," he added as they came under the neon sign illuminating the Burger Shack.

Nick brushed the water from his head and held the door to let Erin precede him. Warm air brought the smell of grilling burgers and the Shack's speciality—onion rings in a spicy batter. "Ah," he said, as his stomach started to rumble. "Heart attack heaven."

Erin nudged him in the ribs before removing her arm from his. "Like you need to worry. I'm going to have to lengthen my daily walk if we make a habit of this. Kelly warned me about the dangers of putting on too much weight."

During pregnancy. Words Erin was careful never to utter in public. Nick didn't like to admit it, but he was glad. Just as he was pleased that she'd accompanied him tonight. His conflicting feelings about her played hell with his sleep most nights, but for the moment he simply enjoyed watching the way her eyes lit up when she smiled.

"Let me take your coat," he said when they'd found an empty booth near the back. He liked playing the gentleman with her because she was so feminine. More than that, he enjoyed the physical closeness that such gestures afforded. Erin seemed to like it, too, and leaned in closer as she dropped her coat into his waiting hands. Pretending they were nothing more than friends while taking opportunities to touch was like playing a dangerous and exciting game.

"Just a cheeseburger and diet Coke, please," she said after he offered to get their order.

When he returned to the booth with a laden tray, Erin reached eagerly for her burger and drink. She lifted the top half of her bun, removed the pickle and handed it to Nick. "I signed up for prenatal classes today. They start in January over in Simcoe."

"I went to those with Janine. Who's your partner—Kelly?" He added the extra pickle to his Humungo-Burger and took a big bite.

"She can't do it. Robyn has piano lessons the same night and Kelly has to drive her because Max also has something on."

"Will you ask one of your girlfriends, then?"

She shook her head. "I still haven't told anyone. But not to worry, I'm sure I'll find someone. Or I'll just do it on my own."

Nick nodded. He was finished with all that baby stuff. Nevertheless, he fell into a gloomy silence, feeling as though he'd let her down.

"Hello, Chief Dalton, Erin." Greta Vogler stood over their table. "Did you enjoy the movie? You look nice, Erin, dear. Have you put on weight?" Before Erin could respond, Greta patted her on the arm and winked at Nick. "I'll go and let you two lovebirds alone."

Erin stared after her, astonished and appalled in equal measures. "Lovebirds!" Hurriedly she slid out of the booth. "Excuse me, Ms. Vogler."

Greta paused, and regarded Erin avidly. "Yes, my dear?"

Nick watched Erin earnestly inform the older woman that she and Nick weren't a couple. They were friends—*good friends*—but that was all.

Greta smiled indulgently and patted Erin's arm again. "Yes, dear. That's what Jennifer Anniston and Brad Pitt said, too."

"She didn't believe me," Erin stated when she'd returned to her seat.

Nick pushed an onion ring into his mouth. "Methinks thou didst protest too much."

"I hate that woman." Tears welled unexpectedly, darkening her blue eyes and reminding Nick of lake water under a cloudy sky.

Surprised, Nick put a hand over hers. "Why does she upset you so much? She's just a harmless old bat."

"She's not harmless. When my parents died in a car crash coming home from a party, Greta Vogler started a rumor that my father drove off the road because he was drunk." Erin blew her nose with a napkin. "It wasn't true," she said fiercely. "Gran told me he never drank when he was driving. Never."

Nick glanced over his shoulder to where Greta was sitting with another woman. "I didn't think she'd be malicious."

"Oh, she didn't go up to people and say outright that he'd been drunk. She'd just say things like, 'Did anyone at the party notice how many drinks he'd had?

No? Then no one would have realized that maybe he shouldn't have driven home.'''

Nick swore. "It's absurd that anyone would take her seriously."

"Enough people did that my sisters and I grew up with whispered comments about our irresponsible parents. As if it wasn't enough to lose them when we were so young." She pushed aside her half-eaten burger. "I hate gossip. People's lives are nobody's business but their own."

"You're right." Nick paused. "What night are your prenatal classes?"

"Tuesday. Why?"

"I'll partner you."

"Nick, it's sweet of you to offer, but I can't accept. If *Greta* thinks we're—" she broke off as pink suffused her cheeks "—lovers, you can bet the rest of the town does, too. Attending prenatal classes as my birthing partner would confirm it in everyone's mind."

"I don't care."

"Don't you? This is a small town, with small-town values." Her next words came slowly, as if they caused her pain. "You might find it difficult to get another woman to go out with you on a real date."

Nick dropped the onion ring he was about to bite into. He didn't want some other woman. He wanted Erin. But he wanted her without someone else's baby inside her. He was a jerk for feeling that way, but he couldn't help it. Maybe he wasn't doing her any favors by being her friend. Maybe he was preventing her from meeting someone who might see her in an entirely different light.

On the other hand, he refused to allow small-town minds to dictate to him. And at the moment he was the only one who could partner her.

"I'll take my chances," he said, squeezing her hand. "As you said, friends don't drop someone at the first sign of difficulty."

"Thank you." Her curving lips broke into a smile shining with gratitude.

Nick had trouble swallowing, much less speaking. Erin had a heart ready and deserving of love. A heart he might break if he gave in to his baser feelings and didn't follow through. His own heart felt it was being torn in two.

"YOU DIDN'T TELL ME when I offered to partner you that the prenatal classes included water exercises." Nick gazed with trepidation at the rippling water in the Simcoe aquatic center.

A month and a half had passed since the Jackie Chan movie. Thanksgiving had come and gone. There'd been other movies, dinners, bicycle rides and walks along the dike when the weather permitted. At Christmas they'd exchanged small, thoughtful, yet strictly friendly gifts over a drink on Christmas Eve before Nick and Miranda headed south to Nick's parents' home in Pasadena. Now January was here, Erin was six months along and it was time for Nick to put his money where his mouth was, so to speak.

"Surely you're not bothered by a swimming pool."

Erin dropped her towel on the bleachers, shed her white cover-up and proceeded to pin up her hair.

"Water is water, in my book." He unloaded a couple of his biggest towels from his kit bag, then glanced back at Erin. Her long, lithe body was still sleek in a sea blue bathing suit. "Are you sure you're pregnant?"

Arching her back, she ran her palms down her ribs and cupped the gentle bulge of her abdomen, which was just prominent enough to look like another of her sexy curves. "My doctor says I'm carrying the baby next to my spine, which is why I hardly show."

More couples wandered in. "Uh-oh," Erin said, noticing another pregnant woman entering the pool area. "That's Kathy from the grocery store." Erin waved, but worry crept into her voice as she added, "I didn't realize she'd be in this class. She's a worse gossip than Greta Vogler."

"Don't worry about it." He dipped his big toe in the water and suppressed a shudder. "Kathy's big mouth is small potatoes compared with leaping into the deep end."

"Oh, don't be a baby," Erin teased. She dropped to the edge of the pool and slipped in up to her waist. "Ready?"

Nick set his jaw in determination. "As I'll ever be."

Once the session began and Nick was holding Erin in the water he forgot his discomfort. He supported her from behind while she floated on her back and did her exercises to the sound of gentle music and the instructor's soothing voice. With his head close to Erin's and his hands loosely around her ribs, he learned to breathe in rhythm with her.

After months of being close but rarely touching, and then only in the most innocent manner, Nick was bursting with sexual tension. He was agonizingly aware of Erin both as a woman and as a mother-to-be. Swelling above her swimsuit top, her ivory-toned breasts were faintly veined with blue, and the dome of her abdomen rose and fell above the surface of the water like a playful newborn dolphin.

She was sexier than any woman he'd ever known.

But what the hell was he going to do about it?

"HI, OLIVER." MIRANDA SAT cross-legged on her bed and spoke into the phone. On her lap lay the unopened manila envelope Erin had slipped to her at basketball practice. Miranda's chest felt tight and her next words sounded squeaky and breathless. "The DNA test results are here. Nick's gone to Simcoe with Erin. Want to come over?"

Twenty minutes later she heard Oliver's boots clumping down the wharf and she hurried to the door. Outside, remnants of a light snowfall crusted the riverbank and frosted the deck. Oliver's cheeks were red and his breath emerged in white puffs of condensation.

"Brr, it's cold out there," he said, removing his down jacket and kicking off his lined boots. "Have you got anything to eat? I was just about to have a snack when you called."

"I'll see what's in the pantry."

She found a bag of Doritos and cans of Coke and they shut themselves in Miranda's bedroom. When Nick was home, Oliver wasn't even allowed in her room, much less with the door shut. But Nick wasn't home. Not that his presence or absence made any difference to their behavior. She and Oliver had never even kissed. That was fine with her, she'd decided; it kept things simple.

Miranda climbed back on her bed and picked up the envelope. She stared at it and swallowed. This was even harder than she'd expected.

"Go on, open it," Oliver urged. He leaned back on her desk chair and munched on Doritos while she ripped across the top of the envelope. A single sheet of paper formed the entire contents. Miranda read it over twice before she could take in the meaning.

"What's the verdict?" Oliver demanded. "Is he your father, or not?"

Miranda lifted her gaze. Oliver's worried frown and blue plaid flannel shirt blurred behind a film of moisture.

"*Not.*"

CHAPTER TWELVE

"GOD, MIRANDA." Oliver transferred himself to the bed and awkwardly circled her with his long arms. "What are you going to do? Are you going to L.A.?"

Miranda hunched into herself, unable to accept his comfort. She'd never felt so scared in her life. Or so alone. Oliver was doing his best and she was grateful, but her overwhelming longing was to climb into her daddy's lap and hear him say that everything was all right.

But everything was not all right, and it never would be again. She still didn't know who her father was; she only knew it wasn't Nick.

Oliver liked her because she was tough, so tough she would be. Even though the thought of being on her own in L.A. made her want to throw up, she lifted her chin and blinked back her tears. "I said I would, didn't I?"

With trembling hands, she slipped the paper into the envelope, then rose and tucked it back into the bottom drawer of her dresser.

Oliver remained on the bed, leaning against the wall. "I don't know, Miranda. Maybe you should talk to your father."

"I will when I find him," she snapped, fighting back tears.

"I meant Nick."

"Forget Nick." She spun around. "Are you going to help me or not?"

"Yeah, 'course I will. But we need a plan. I know, when we go to the Seattle Aquarium for our field trip on Friday, you can slip away and catch a bus to California. Or would Amtrak be better?"

"No!" Miranda almost shouted. Things were moving too fast. She'd talked big about running away, but deep down she'd never expected to have to do it. "I...I don't have enough money."

"You can have my Christmas money. I'll go to the bank tomorrow at lunch and withdraw my savings."

Miranda crossed her arms tightly, her hands tucked beneath her armpits, and paced the narrow space between her bed and her dresser. "I'm not ready. I'd be stupid to just charge off without knowing what I'm going to do when I get to L.A. Plus, I can't take all your money. I already owe you too much and who knows when I'll be able to pay you back."

"You don't have to pay me back," he said quietly.

"You want that dictionary set, don't you?"

"I got it for Christmas." From across the room his gaze bored into hers. "I'm going to miss you."

Eyes burning, she turned her back to him. Goddamn it, did he have to say stuff like that? "I'm not going yet. I'll stay until I earn some money and the weather's warmer in case..." She gulped. In case she had to spend some nights on the street. Oh, man, she could end up as a prostitute or a drug addict. Her overactive imagination tortured her with visions of her funeral and everyone weeping.

"Your dad will miss you, too. He'll go ballistic."

Nick had said he loved her. Was it enough?

"Would you mind going now, Oliver? I need to be alone."

AFTER THE PRENATAL CLASS, Erin waited for Nick outside the change rooms. "Thanks for coming along," she said. "I hope it wasn't too awful for you."

"Not awful. You could even say I enjoyed it." He held the door for her and they left the steamy warmth of the aquatic center for the icy chill of the outdoors.

"Do you want to stop at the house for a hot drink?" Erin asked as they crossed the parking lot to the Suburban.

"I'd rather go back to the houseboat, if it's all the same to you. Miranda said she was going to ask Oliver over and I don't like to leave them unchaperoned for too long."

Back at the houseboat, Erin removed her coat. She waited at the end of the hall, watching as Nick tapped on Miranda's door.

"Miranda?" he said. "Is Oliver still here?"

"He went home" was the muffled reply.

"Erin's here, if you want to say hello."

"Later."

Shaking his head in puzzlement, Nick retraced his steps. "Could you hear?" he asked in a low voice. "Did her voice sound odd to you?"

"It's hard to tell," Erin equivocated. To her, Miranda's voice had sounded thin and wobbly, like the aftermath of a crying jag. What dreadful news had that manila envelope contained? It had arrived just after New Year's, delayed by the Christmas mail. She'd hesitated before handing it to Miranda to open on her own, but she'd agreed to help and had to stick to their plan. She only hoped Miranda would keep *her* promise.

In the living room, Nick put a thick wedge of yellow cedar into the slow-combustion fireplace and levered the door shut. Behind the thick glass, smoldering embers burst into flame.

Erin warmed her hands above the fireplace, her gaze roaming over the mementos of Miranda's childhood that decorated the room—the handprint in clay, an imaginative portrait of the Tooth Fairy, a bronzed baby shoe on the mantel. Evidence of Nick's love for his daughter was everywhere. How could either of them doubt it?

"Have you got any photos of Miranda as a baby?" she asked.

"In the bookshelf," he said, going to the kitchen. "The red album on the left."

Erin took the album to the chocolate-brown sofa opposite the sliding glass doors that looked onto the deck. "She was a cute baby," Erin said, referring to a photograph of Miranda at about six months with a big cheesy grin on her face.

"She wasn't born with a ring through her nose, either, as I remind her now and again." Nick came around the kitchen divider with a glass of red wine for himself and a hot lemon drink for Erin. He set them on coasters on the coffee table and sat beside her, putting his arm along the back of the sofa in a manner that had become familiar over the months.

Erin had thought time would dull her sexual awareness, but Nick's smile, his most innocent touch, caused stirrings deep within her and imparted a heavy ache to her womb that had nothing to do with her pregnancy. She could no more divest herself of these feelings than she could divide herself from the baby that grew inside her.

Even now, she was aware of the soft fabric of his chamois shirt brushing her hand as he leaned close to turn the page, and of the wine-scented warmth of his breath on her cheek. The rich timbre of his laughter penetrated to the hollow of her bones. Laughter her baby undoubtedly heard. Did the little one think Nick was its father?

"She seems to like the turquoise stud I gave her for Christmas." Erin held back the fullness of her dress to lean forward to pick up her steaming mug. So far she'd been able to avoid buying maternity dresses, though she'd gone up two sizes in women's clothing.

"I wasn't too happy with you when I saw that," Nick admitted. "Then she put it in and I realized that a tiny dot of colored crystal was preferable to something you could lead a bull around with."

Erin smiled at the image—as if anyone could lead Miranda around by the nose. "She won't stop wearing a nose ring just because you say so. Might as well minimize the damage."

Erin inhaled tangy heat as she sipped her drink. If she moved her other hand a mere inch, she could touch Nick's thigh. She sighed, knowing she wouldn't.

She and Nick confined their touches to utilitarian movements like helping each other on with coats. It was only at night that Erin drifted into half-waking, half-dreaming fantasies of kisses and caresses, heat and skin.

In her fantasies her stomach was always flat.

She was pretty sure Nick's fantasies, whatever they were, would involve flat-stomached women, too.

Nick leaned back against the sofa. "Have you thought of a name for your baby?"

"Elizabeth for a girl," Erin said promptly. "That was my mother's name. If it's a boy, maybe John. Maybe Erik, after my father."

She turned another page. And came upon a newspaper photo of Nick's late wife holding the newborn Miranda. Janine had been a small-boned woman with wild hair, large, deep-set eyes and a sensual mouth.

"This could be Miranda in ten years," Erin blurted, startled by the close resemblance.

"God, I hope not." Nick rose abruptly and stalked across the room.

"Nick? What's wrong? Where are you going?"

Without answering, he went out through the sliding doors onto the deck, letting in an icy blast of air from off the water.

Erin took a last look at the photo and closed the album. Janine's infidelity still bothered him. *Raising another man's child bothered him.* Awkwardly she pushed herself up off the couch and started toward the sliding glass doors.

Miranda came into the room, her eyes red-rimmed. When she saw Erin, she stopped, startled. "I heard the door slide shut. I thought no one was in here."

"Your father went outside." Erin paused, studying her. "Ready for the game against Redmond High on Saturday?"

"Yeah," she mumbled, retreating to the kitchen to pour a glass of orange juice.

Erin glanced out at Nick. He'd picked up a snow shovel and was vigorously scraping snow off the deck. Turning back to Miranda, she asked, "What did you find out with the DNA testing?"

"Nothing very interesting." Miranda's smile was quick and false; her knuckles white where they gripped the glass.

"What do you mean? Did testing prove he's your biological father?"

Miranda's eyes betrayed a desperate desire to speak, but her mouth was clamped shut. For an instant she wavered, then hardened. "You're my basketball coach, not my mom. I don't have to tell you anything."

"I'm your *friend*," Erin stressed quietly. "And no, you don't *have* to tell me anything. But you did promise to talk to me if—"

"If I wanted to talk, it wouldn't be to you," she said rudely. "Whatever I said, you'd tell Nick."

"That's not fair. I haven't mentioned a word to him about all this."

"Yeah, well, life's not fair." She thunked her empty glass on the benchtop, stomped down the hall to her bedroom and slammed the door.

Beneath her surface irritation, Erin felt her heart ache for Miranda. The results couldn't be good for the girl to behave so obnoxiously.

Outside, her breath rose before her face in puffs

and she trod carefully on the icy deck, gripping the rail for balance as she approached Nick.

"Was that Miranda's door I heard slam?" Nick's cheeks were ruddy with cold and his hair looked black against the silver-blue sky.

Should she tell him all she knew and the little more she suspected? All her instincts screamed *yes*. But the poor girl seemed to have so few people she could turn to. Once Miranda calmed down she might trust Erin again, but not if Erin broke *her* promise.

"Why did you run away when Janine's name was mentioned?" she chided him lightly.

Nick moved away, the harsh sound of the metal shovel against the deck nearly drowning out his words. "I'm trying to forget her."

"Why?" Erin rubbed her arms to keep warm as she followed him across the frosty deck.

Nick stabbed at a chunk of ice. "Our entire marriage was a lie. All those years after Miranda was born, she kept the truth from me."

"How do you know what the truth is? Maybe she regretted her affair. Maybe she didn't want to lose you."

"She made a fool out of me." His face had frozen into a mask of pain and anger. "I never cheated on *her,* not once."

Erin grasped him by the arm, determined to make him see past his own hurt. "Would you have been happier if she'd told you about the other guy when she was pregnant with Miranda? If you'd split up back then, you might not have had a daughter at all. Is that what you want?"

His defiant glare faded, and his shoulders sagged

as he leaned on the shovel. "I can't imagine life without Miranda."

"I'm glad to hear it." Drawn by a powerful urge to comfort him, Erin broke their unspoken agreement and slipped her arms around his waist. She wanted to urge him to let go of the bitter memories, to tell him that DNA alone didn't determine who a child belonged to, but she was afraid he'd feel she was making a case for herself and her baby. She didn't want him to think her needy or that he had any obligation to her. So she just held him, as a friend would. After a moment's hesitation he relaxed a little and wrapped his arms around her. They stood together, her head resting on his chest, his chin resting on her head, warming each other where they touched.

Being in his arms felt good. Too good. She began to withdraw, only to feel his mouth brush her cheek as she pulled back. His palm cupped her jaw; his fingers pressed against her cheek, stripes of warmth across her cool skin. His eyes reflected the longing she felt. His face came near, nearer. He was going to kiss her.

"Are you sure about this?" she murmured against his mouth, her breath mingling with his. Their lips were tantalizingly close, barely touching yet sparking currents of desire. Straining to be closer, she pressed her swollen stomach against his swollen groin, and heat flooded through her.

Suddenly he was stepping backward, the kiss unconsummated, his passion rapidly cooling. Frigid wind off the water blew through her hair and Erin felt her longing congeal into loneliness.

They went inside. When Nick held her coat, she

was conscious of him deliberately not getting close. Her arms were halfway in when she felt the baby kick. "Oh!"

"What is it?"

"The baby's awake." Forgetting the constraint between them, she grabbed his hand and pressed it against her abdomen, laughing with delight. "Did you feel that?"

A smile spread across his face as, eyes riveted to hers, he moved his hand over her belly, following the rapidly shifting bumps. "I think he's dribbling a basketball around your rib cage."

Erin glanced down at his long fingers splayed across her belly. This was the first time Nick had felt her baby move, and his pleasure in it meant the world to her.

Slowly, he withdrew his hand, and his eyes softened, as if he was regretful that his interest couldn't mean more. He drew her into a hug. "I'm sorry."

"It's okay," she whispered, forgiving him his sorrows.

Stepping back, she shrugged into her coat and tugged on a felt hat. "See you next week?"

He nodded, and walked her out to her car.

FOR MANY WEEKS, bulky winter clothing had helped conceal Erin's burgeoning figure, and by some quirk of fate, she was indeed one of those lucky women who don't show until the pregnancy is well advanced. She might have gotten away a little longer with not publicizing her condition but after Kathy had seen her at the prenatal class Erin knew it was time to come out of the closet, so to speak.

But not in standard maternity wear. Ugh.

She went shopping in Seattle and picked up some stylish maternity outfits she wouldn't be ashamed to be seen in. The shoe situation was a little more desperate. Her feet had a tendency to swell and no longer slid comfortably into the narrow toes of her Prada slingbacks. The Dolce & Gabana spike heels made her feel as though she might topple off balance in a stiff breeze, and the Mollini ankle boots she couldn't even get on her feet. None of her beloved shoes fit, yet she couldn't justify buying expensive replacements for a temporary problem. The only solution was…shudder…sensible shoes.

So it was with a sense of having come down in the world that Erin entered the bank in her new getup. That everyone would soon know she was pregnant seemed almost secondary to her present humiliation. Tracy was the first to notice Erin had taken leave of her fashion sense, at least in the footwear department.

"What have you got on your feet, girlfriend?" she demanded, hands on her hips.

Erin glanced around, then whispered sheepishly, "Loafers."

"Loafers!" Tracy screeched. "What's wrong with you!"

Erin removed her coat, revealing to Tracy's astonished gaze the stylish wool knit dress that molded her small rounded belly like a watch cap on a bald sailor.

Tracy gasped. "Good Lord, woman, you're pregnant!"

Bobby, his eyes wide and his jaw slack, fumbled the stack of twenties he was paging through and lost count.

Jonah Haines appeared in his doorway, blinking like an owl. "Well, this is a surprise." He peered first through his glasses at her, then over them. "Who's the lucky father?"

Erin had spent days preparing for this moment. Calmly, she folded her coat over her arm and strode toward her office. Marvelous, really, how easy loafers were to walk in. At the door she faced her employer and co-workers. "I'm afraid I can't tell you who the father is. He doesn't wish to be identified."

For a week or so after that, Erin felt pretty pleased with how well folks in Hainesville accepted her pregnancy and her silence on the subject of her baby's father—until the day she ran into Greta Vogler.

She'd just said goodbye to Nick after having lunch with him and was walking down Main Street on her way back to the bank when she met Greta coming the other way.

"Why, hello, Erin," Greta said, her gaze glued to Erin's stomach. "I hear you're pregnant."

No amount of preparation was adequate to deflect Greta's determined nosiness. Declining to answer, Erin fixed her smile and edged around the other woman. "Excuse me."

Oblivious to the snub, Greta turned and walked with Erin. She leaned close enough for Erin to smell the onions she'd had at lunch and said in a sing-song voice, "You've been keeping se-crets."

"If I have, it's because they're mine to keep. Nice seeing you, Greta."

She was so anxious to escape that she entered the next store without looking where she was headed. Or-ville Johannson, his scissors and comb poised above

Herbert Gribble's gray head, seemed surprised to see her.

"Hi, Orville, Mr. Gribble. Lovely day, isn't it?" Hastily, she backed out of the barbershop. Greta was waiting for her.

"So tell me all about your baby," Greta said conversationally as they walked. "Kathy says you're nearly seven months along."

Erin stared straight ahead. Maybe if she ignored Greta, she would go away.

"Aren't you a sly one, not telling anyone you're pregnant," Greta rattled on. "You look more like four months along than seven. Just like your mother, poor thing. No one could believe she was having a baby that first time, then out you popped. And now here you are, having one of your own." Greta beamed. "You and Nick must be so excited."

Erin stopped dead and swiveled to face her. "Nick?"

"Are you two getting married soon, or waiting until after the baby's born? I must confess, I don't understand young people these days, being so casual about these things. In my day, we got married first so the child would have a name."

"My child will have a name," Erin growled.

"Of course it will, my dear." Greta patted her arm. "Have you and Nick settled on anything yet? Now, let's see…what will go with Dalton?"

"The baby's last name won't be Dalton." Erin hated giving the old busybody *any* information but she had to get this straightened out before Greta spread the rumor around town. "Nick and I aren't marrying."

Greta looked nonplussed. "I just assumed…"

Erin felt like snapping that she ought not assume anything, but ingrained courtesy prevented her from being rude, even to Greta. Even when Greta's own behavior was the epitome of rudeness. "I'm not marrying *anyone*."

Greta blinked. "I don't understand."

She sounded so bewildered Erin might have felt sorry for her, except that would have been like the minnow feeling sorry for the barracuda just before it was devoured. "I've really got to rush, Greta. Goodbye."

"That Nick Dalton seemed like such a nice man," Greta said, shaking her head as Erin moved away.

Erin stopped and let out a long-suffering sigh. "The baby isn't his."

"Who else's could it be? You're nearly seven months along. You and Nick both arrived in August and you've been seen around town together ever since. He's attending prenatal classes with you—Kathy told me so." Greta clasped her hands, her old-fashioned handbag dangling from her wrist, and waited, head tilted, for Erin to tell her she was right.

Erin opened her mouth, not to speak but because she was flabbergasted at the woman's audacity. She was damned if she owed anyone, least of all, Greta Vogler, an explanation.

"*Goodbye,* Ms. Vogler. Have a nice day."

IF NICK WAS THE SUBJECT of gossip over Erin, his air of authority defied anybody to say it to his face. When he was out with her in public, he behaved toward her with his usual courtesy and respect, doing nothing that could be construed as having any greater meaning than friendship. Yet at times he would enter a store and conversation would abruptly stop. On other occasions he'd catch people looking at him and Erin with a speculative glint in their eyes.

The fact that he'd invited no other woman on a date in all the time he'd been in Hainesville, even though he'd received plenty of encouragement, only added, he was certain, fuel to the gossip bonfire. He didn't care. If people wanted to make something out of nothing, let them. Only the prenatal class worried him, as his attendance could seem a tacit admission of responsibility. He might have made a mistake there, but if he had, it was too late.

Toward the end of February, Nick was in his office writing up a report of a fire in the hardware store. Steve popped in and dropped a stack of envelopes on his desk.

"Mail call." The lieutenant lounged against the door frame. "Did you hear? Angela is engaged to that guy over in Simcoe."

"Is that so?" Nick searched the younger man's face. "You okay, buddy?"

Steve shrugged. "I guess. I'd sure like to find someone like her someday, though. Really fit and strong. Did you know she can press one-fifty, no sweat?"

Nick chuckled. "Whatever turns you on." He signed his name at the bottom of the report and set it aside. "Those new volunteers seem to be shaping up okay."

"You've trained them so well they're almost as

good as paid firefighters.'' Steve sipped from an oversize mug of coffee.

"Almost. I'd still like to have another paid man aboard.''

"Or woman.''

"Or woman,'' Nick agreed. "I'm meeting with the town council next month to ask for one.''

"A woman?''

Nick grinned. "A paid firefighter.'' He leaned back in his chair. "What do you think my chances are?''

Steve stroked his lean jaw and considered the question. "Ordinarily I think you'd get Greta Vogler's vote, but I hear she's lobbying for a new maternity wing for the Hainesville Hospital. She claims we're about to have a population explosion. Jonah Haines is awfully tight with money, even when it's not his, and Mayor Gribble opposes Jonah on principle.''

"I thought they were fishing buddies.''

Steve shook his head. "Rivals from way back. They fish together to make sure there aren't any tall stories about the one that got away. I'm not as familiar with the other council members, but with those three involved it'll be a crapshoot.''

"Surely council is concerned about the safety of the citizens,'' Nick said. "Personalities shouldn't play a role.''

"You haven't spent enough time in a small town yet, Chief. You'll learn.'' Steve pushed himself off the door frame. "I'll be washing down the ladder truck if you need me.''

Nick picked up the sheaf of envelopes and flyers,

glancing over the Washington State Association of
Fire Chiefs' newsletter before setting it aside to read
later. A plain white envelope caught his attention. It
was addressed to Chief Dalton and marked Personal.

CHAPTER THIRTEEN

NICK TURNED THE ENVELOPE over. No return address. He slipped a finger beneath the flap, ripped open the envelope and pulled out a single sheet of plain white paper. The typewritten lines stood out stark and black:

Chief Dalton,
It's time you owned up to your responsibility as
a father—

What! How did whoever wrote this know about Miranda?

He read on and discovered it wasn't about his daughter at all:

It's not fair for Erin Hanson to bear the sole burden of carrying your bastard. Marry her, or face the consequences!

There was no signature, of course. His first reaction was to laugh. Boy, had they got it wrong if they thought he was the father of Erin's baby. Then, as he read the words again, his amusement turned to disgust. He tore up the paper and threw it into the wastebasket. Then tossed the remains of his lunch—an orange peel and a piece of waxed paper filled with crumbs—on top.

Feeling a little better, he picked up the fire chiefs' newsletter and put the note from his mind. Whoever wrote that message was nothing but a crackpot.

NICK HAD ALL BUT forgotten about the anonymous note by the time he met with the town council the third week in March.

"'Morning all.'' His sweeping glance around the oval table took in Mayor Gribble, Jonah Haines, Dr. Cameron, Hank Lawson and Gary Cleggman, the latter pair a dairy farmer and a fisherman, respectively. And of course, Greta Vogler. Ordinarily Greta favored him with a smile, but today her mouth formed a thin flat line as she scrutinized him in cool silence.

Herbert Gribble cleared his throat. "Good morning, Chief. Glad you could join us.''

"My pleasure.'' All very civil, so far. Nick poured himself a coffee from the carafe on the sideboard and sat down opposite Gribble. Haines and Greta flanked the mayor; the three exchanged stern glances. Nick loosened his tie. He'd hate to get on these people's bad side.

"Have you got something for us?'' Mayor Gribble asked, nodding to the folder Nick had brought and placed on the table. His secretary sat in a chair against the wall with a pen and pad of paper, prepared to take minutes.

Nick passed around copies of his proposal for additional personnel and allowed those gathered a few moments to read the summary at the top. Then he gave a quick spiel about the growth of the community and the coordinated effort the Hainesville Fire Department was expected to play in the county.

"We've been successful in attracting additional volunteers, but Hainesville is in dire need of more paid firefighters. One is essential. Two would be preferable," he concluded, gazing around the table again.

This time, openly disapproving glances passed among Gribble, Haines and Vogler. Brent Cameron had told Nick earlier that he favored Nick's proposal. Lawson and Cleggman were unknown quantities. Things could get interesting when his motion was put to a vote.

"This is a small community with a low revenue base of mainly primary producers and seasonal workers," Jonah Haines said, peering over his wire rimmed glasses at Nick. "We've always relied on volunteer firefighters. I see no reason to expand the paid portion of the department." He smiled genially. "You and your crew did a fine job protecting the bank."

"If you'll turn to the second page of my report," Nick said, undeterred, "you'll see that we're understaffed according to standards set by ISO, the Insurance Service Organization. Hainesville's been given a lower rating this year, which I'm sure you're all aware will result in higher fire insurance premiums unless we do something about staffing."

"I sure as heck don't need higher insurance premiums," Hank Lawson said. "What with the cost of dairy feed these days."

"We never heard anything like this from Chief Roland," the mayor argued. "You've got a whole swag of new volunteers. Why is staffing still a problem?"

"Volunteers don't have the same level of training as professional firefighters," Nick replied. "Without denigrating the previous chief, may I point out that with the new housing developments going up between Hainesville and Simcoe, circumstances have changed. But I'm not only concerned about insurance premiums. I should be directing firefighting activities, not manning a hose, yet occasionally I'm called upon to be actively involved. I take my responsibilities seriously—"

"Perhaps not as seriously as you should," Greta murmured.

"I don't understand what you mean by that remark," he said stiffly. Yet her insinuating tone and the way Haines and Gribble were frowning at him gave him the sneaking suspicion he did. Well, if she was going to get snarly, she'd better be open about her accusations. "We're discussing firefighting, right?"

Wrong.

"Erin Hanson is pregnant and won't say who the baby's father is," Greta said, fixing him with a gimlet-eyed stare. "It's my belief the man has refused to marry her and she's protecting his reputation."

Six pairs of eyes waited for his response. *God Almighty.* This wasn't a council meeting, but a lynch mob. He rose to his feet and leaned forward on his knuckles on the walnut veneer table. Something clicked in his brain. "*You* sent me that anonymous note, didn't you, Greta?"

Silence.

Mayor Gribble cleared his throat. "The position of fire chief is an appointed one. It can be revoked if the holder is guilty of gross negligence. Going into a fire when you should be directing operations might justly be deemed negligent.''

Feeling as though the wind had been knocked out of him, Nick slowly slid back into his chair. The threat to his job was no less real for being outrageous. If they wanted to get rid of him, he was down the road. Oh, he could sue for reinstatement, but the fact was, he had gone against regulations when he'd saved Mr. Contafio from the burning barn. That he'd had to do it because of the very reason he was before council today was galling, but no defense.

This was the downside of small towns, which Erin had talked about. Yet part of him had to admire the way they protected their own. A big-city council wouldn't give a damn about a single mom as long the job got done.

He held the trump hand—the truth—but he couldn't play it. If he told them who had fathered Erin's baby, he'd force Erin to break her promise to the scumbag who'd gotten her pregnant. If he lied and said he was the father, he could kiss his job goodbye. Either that or he'd have to marry Erin. Neither of them wanted that. And anyway, he refused to be blackmailed.

Grimly, he gathered up his papers and crammed them into the folder. ''I'll see you at the town meeting. We'll let the people of Hainesville decide.''

SPRING PERFUMED the evening air flowing through Gran's open kitchen window, beckoning Erin out into the lengthening dusk. Quickly she cleared away the dinner dishes and she and Gran set out for their walk through the quiet residential streets of Hainesville.

"You've come a long way since August," Erin said to her grandmother as they turned the last corner for home thirty minutes later.

"I'm my old self," Ruth agreed, jauntily lifting her cane to show she didn't really need it. "Better in fact, now that I'm exercising regularly."

A little boy passed them on his tricycle, bell tinkling, legs pumping. The child's pregnant mother and father strolled along behind. Erin smiled at the mother, then she glanced at the father, whose protective hand rested on his wife's back as Erin and Gran maneuvered around them. Her smile dimmed. Would she and her baby ever be part of a happy young family?

"You don't need to stay once your baby's born, Erin," Ruth said. "If you want to get back to your life in Seattle, don't feel you have to stick around here on my account. Though of course I'd love it if you did."

In the silence that followed, Ruth's cane tapped the concrete, and two pairs of loafers made soft shushing sounds with each step. Erin daily was torn between wanting to give birth so she could cuddle her baby and wanting to keep it inside forever, protected.

"I haven't decided yet what I want to do."

"Well, don't worry about it now, honey. There's no rush. I just wanted you to know you're free to leave if you want."

Free to leave. Was she, though? Her reliance on Nick scared her. Not the practical things he did for her, like cleaning gutters or fixing the screen door.

You could pay someone to do that. No, it was the emotional connection, the sympathetic ear when her back ached, the hours they spent dissecting movies and books, the way he always made her laugh when she was feeling glum.

She'd quit work a week ago, but she still walked down to the fire station at noon to have lunch with Nick. Her whole day seemed to revolve around him and the time they spent together. She needed him as much as she wanted him. But he would never love her. Maybe she *should* go back to Seattle when the baby was born.

Erin's hand supported the rounded bulk of her belly. She felt enormous and ungainly. A few days earlier the baby had dropped and its head was pressing down on her groin like a ten-pound coconut. "Not long now."

"Have you got a bag packed?"

Erin nodded. "Nick said he'd take me to the birth center unless he's on a call. Kelly's my backup, then Laura."

The phone could be heard ringing through the open window when they turned into the yard. Gran chuckled. "Race you to the door."

"You're on." Erin put on a burst of speed, which was to say, she went from a snail's pace to that of a fast-moving turtle.

Laughing at their slow progress, Erin just beat Ruth to the door and, breathless, burst inside on the tenth ring. A few more steps took her into the kitchen, where she clutched the receiver to her ear, eager to hear Nick's voice. "Hello?"

"Erin. It's John."

"John?" she repeated, as stunned as if she'd never heard the name before. Months had passed since she'd last talked with him. "What...what's happening?"

"The election's next month, in case you don't get Seattle newspapers out in there in the sticks." His brisk tone was evocative of his life—people to see, places to go, things to do. A life she'd left behind. "I've got a damn good chance of getting elected."

"Congratulations." Had he called just to crow?

"Erin, I've been thinking—soul-searching, if you like. I want to marry you."

Erin dragged out a chair and collapsed onto it. "Marry me?"

"Yes, as soon as possible. Next week if you can." He paused. "Er, have you had the baby yet?"

"No." She pressed thumb and fingers to her temples. "It's not due for two more weeks."

"Good. So what do you say?"

She'd waited more than two years for John to be eager for them to marry. The trouble was, it was too late. She didn't love him. Maybe she never had, because what she used to feel for him didn't begin to match what she felt for Nick. Sometime during the past months her liking for Nick had turned to love, infatuation to deep desire.

"We'll have to concoct some story about why we haven't been together," John continued without waiting for her answer. "I know, we could use your sick grandmother. Always best to stick close to the truth—"

"What are you talking about? Why are you suddenly proposing?"

"I have a slight disadvantage with respect to my opponent, Anderson. He has a wife and three kids." John became persuasive, as if addressing a jury reluctant to convict. "The people want a family man in office. It's idiotic, really. A politician can do a better job without the time constraints imposed by a wife and kids."

Erin couldn't imagine John letting a wife or child constrain his time. Loving Nick might mess up her life, but knowing it made one thing crystal clear—she could never marry John.

"No," she said. "I won't marry you."

"Erin, honey. You've a right to be ticked, but I'll make it up to you. Think of it. You'll be the wife of a Congressman."

"I am thinking of it…and it stinks. *You* stink."

"Erin." He switched to an authoritative tone. "Think of the baby. Think of all I could offer him. Or her. Uh, do you know…?"

"John, you don't give a damn about this baby. Or me. All you care about is yourself and your career. Why don't you ask *Andrea?*"

John snorted. "Come on, Erin, she's a career woman. You know, honey, you don't sound well. Maybe you should go lie down and we'll talk about this later."

"Don't patronize me. And don't call me again, because I'm not going to marry you. Ever. If someday you have a genuine interest in your child for his or her own sake, we can talk about visitation rights. Till then, *goodbye.*"

She slammed down the phone, flushed with victory

at conquering her last niggling feeling that maybe she should be trying to make a life with her baby's father.

A second later, the phone rang again.

"Hello, John," she said wearily.

"Look if you won't marry me, at least don't tell anyone the baby's mine. You haven't, have you? You did promise. Erin? Erin?"

"NICK, CAN I TALK TO YOU?" Miranda rinsed the dinner plates and stacked them in the dishwasher. Two letters lay in the bottom of her dresser drawer. Two letters that preyed on her mind. One contained the DNA results; the other she'd brought home today from the high school principal.

Elbows propped on the cleared table, Nick was going over his speech for the town meeting. Pen in hand, he muttered and gesticulated to an unseen opponent. Greta Vogler, Miranda presumed. She hated Greta Vogler, who always glared at her disapprovingly, and she hoped Nick would whup her ass. But right now she needed his attention.

"Hello, Dad. *Nick.*"

"Huh? Sorry, hon, did you say something?"

"Um, uh…" *Man, he was going to have a fit.* "Something happened at school today."

He was looking straight at her, but she could tell he was taken up with whatever was going on in his head and wasn't listening. "Hang on," he said. "A thought…got to write…it…down." His head was bent; his hand moved rapidly over his notepad.

Miranda sighed heavily. "Never mind." She spooned leftover spaghetti and meatballs into a plastic container and put it into the fridge.

Nick threw down his pen. "What were you saying?"

She twisted the wooden spoon in her hands. "Well, you see…" Would he believe that this time the cigarette Mrs. Jenkins had caught her with in the bathroom hadn't been hers? That she'd been holding it for another girl, a popular girl who had the power to bring Miranda into her circle of friends? Miranda felt her bottom lip tremble. Was she that desperate for friends? She had Oliver and Rita.

While she stalled, Nick's gaze strayed from her to the clock. "Damn. I'm going to be late." He swept his papers together and shoved them into a manila file folder. "Come on. You can tell me on the way to the meeting."

"Oliver's coming over to do homework, remember? I'm not going to the meeting."

He tossed his suit jacket over his shoulder, and came around the benchtop into the kitchen to kiss her absently on the forehead. "Okay, but he's to go home by nine o'clock. Can whatever you were going to tell me wait until tomorrow?"

"It's important," she said sullenly.

"Miranda." In a breath, he'd gone from placating to exasperated. "You sat through dinner without saying a word. Why didn't you tell me then?"

"I didn't want to spoil your meal." She'd been working up her courage. If he cut off her allowance again, she would never save the money she needed to leave.

"First thing in the morning, then. Don't worry about my digestion." He opened the door, and the sound of rain pinging on water and splashing wetly on wood made him reach for his umbrella. "And don't wait up."

HAINESVILLE'S TOWN HALL stood on the corner of First Avenue and Brockley Street, one block off Main, opposite the Anglican Church. For decades the townsfolk had talked about replacing the wooden structure built seventy-five years earlier, but something more important always came up: a public swimming pool, an addition to the library, a memorial erected in the park to Vietnam soldiers. The hall might be old and rundown, Greta Vogler was fond of saying, but it brought the community together. Like Greta herself, was the not-so-subtle implication.

On the evening of the third Saturday in March, less than a week after Nick's disastrous meeting with the town council, the concerned citizens of Hainesville gathered in the hall to vote on whether to spend money on an additional paid firefighter—which Chief Dalton had campaigned for, or to build a maternity wing on the tiny Hainesville hospital, which was Greta's idea.

A table had been set up on the stage, Mayor Gribble presiding. When everyone was seated in folding chairs, Gribble called for order, banging a gavel borrowed from the council chambers.

"Good evening, ladies and gentlemen. If you've read the *Hainesville Herald* and the flyers circulated by both parties, you all know the issues at stake here tonight. I'll call upon Chief Dalton to speak first, followed by Greta. Then we'll open the floor to discussion."

Nick rose and cleared his throat. "I'll keep this

brief because I've already talked to virtually everyone in the room at some point over the past months. First, let me say that I have no problem with a maternity wing, per se. Some of my best friends are pregnant.'' He grinned at Erin, who was sitting in the second row; she smiled up at him encouragingly. ''However, Hainesville badly needs additional professional fire-fighting personnel. Existing services are inadequate, putting lives and property at risk. Besides safety issues, there're the additional insurance costs to consider. Please put your support behind your local fire depart-ment. You never know when you'll be in need of our services. Thank you.''

After he sat down, Greta got up and thanked the mayor effusively. For what, Nick wasn't quite sure, unless it was the opportunity to bend so many people's ears at one time. Her case was fairly simple, too. Why should Hainesville always take a back seat to Simcoe? Their community was growing, about to be increased by at least one in the near future—here *she* glanced at Erin and smiled.

Then she trained her laser-beam gaze on Nick. ''Chief Dalton, you of all people should wish for proper birthing facilities for our children.''

All eyes in the hall turned to him, then to Erin. Talk hummed through the hall as neighbor turned to neighbor, heads shaking, tongues clucking. Oh, for the love of Mike!

Nick got slowly to his feet. ''Ms. Vogler, I don't know what you're referring to, but I doubt it's relevant to this discussion.''

All trace of the flirtatiousness with which Greta had treated him early in their acquaintance vanished.

"You know exactly what I'm referring to—your unborn child, carried by Erin Hanson." She walked to the edge of the stage and pointed a finger straight at Erin. The townsfolk let out a collective gasp. Erin went white, and very still, her gaze fixed.

Greta whirled back to Nick. "You, a stranger, come into our town and despoil our most beautiful and brightest daughter. You ignore your responsibilities as a father and expect us to kowtow to your demands." Of the assembled crowd, she asked, "Do we want a man like this to be in a position of authority, someone the children are taught to look up to?"

Nick could hardly believe what he was hearing. She'd lost her mind. He no longer gave a damn about his job or his own standing in the town. All that mattered was that this twisted old woman should not hurt Erin.

"I would *never* ignore any child I fathered," he vowed, and without thinking, he put a hand over his heart. "Just as you all do, I hold Erin Hanson in the highest esteem."

At this, Erin got awkwardly to her feet and edged past legs to the end of the row before climbing the steps at the side of the stage.

"Erin," he whispered fiercely, reaching for her arm to assist her. "You don't have to say a word to these people."

"I grew up among these people and it's time I did them the courtesy of revealing the truth." Her low voice held gritty determination. "I won't stand by and let them blacken your name. They're small-minded, some of them, but they've got big hearts."

Her jaw set, she marched to center stage. As she gazed at the townsfolk, many of whom she'd known since childhood, Erin's determination faltered. Then she glanced back at Nick and he gave her a thumbs-up. He'd always been there for her, his support lending her the courage to raise her baby on her own, and at the same time, the knowledge that she wasn't alone.

"Good evening, everyone." Her voice cracked. She cleared her throat and started again. "Very few people know the identity of my baby's father. I've kept it a secret to protect the man's reputation."

A triumphant noise, like the trumpeting of a small elephant, erupted from Greta Vogler, and an excited buzz filled the hall.

"But it's not what you think," she continued loudly, striving to be heard. The crowd quieted. "The father of my baby is a public figure. We broke up before I knew I was pregnant. When I found out, he wanted nothing to do with the baby, or me. He made me promise to keep his name out of it. Foolishly, I agreed, but I'm still bound by that promise."

A voice Erin didn't recognize called out, "Would that public figure be John Sneedham, prosecuting attorney for King County and Seattle?"

Oh, dear. She supposed she shouldn't be surprised. Although she'd never talked much about her relationship with John before her breakup, neither had she made it a secret. "Who are *you*, may I ask?"

"Charlie Thirsk, a reporter for the *Hainesville Herald*. I repeat, is the father of your baby John Sneedham?"

When she didn't deny the association, the hubbub

in the hall escalated. No one could have missed John's recent campaign ads on TV. A flashbulb went off in front of the stage and Erin flinched. No doubt John would be reading about this meeting over his Wheaties tomorrow morning.

Erin reached over to the mayor's table and banged the gavel. "Let me continue, please. Yes, my baby's father is John Sneedham. In many ways I wish Nick Dalton was. I know he'd make an excellent parent because I've witnessed the love and attention he's bestowing on his daughter, Miranda. Even though I'm close to giving birth, I'd rather see town funds go to another firefighter for Hainesville. A maternity wing would be nice, but really, Simcoe is just down the road and their maternity ward isn't overcrowded. I suspect Greta's recent push for a new wing on the hospital has been an attempt to thwart Nick. Shame on you, Ms. Vogler."

Facing her nemesis sent a charge of adrenaline through Erin's veins, and she ended on a triumphant note. "Last, I'm raising this baby on my own. Not an ideal situation, but it's the hand I've been dealt and I'm going to make the best of it. Anyone who doesn't like it can just lump it!"

Nick blinked moisture from his eyes. Erin was strong and true and utterly beautiful. He was proud of her, proud to be her friend, and moved by her generous tribute. To the sound of hundreds of hands clapping, he went to her side and put his arm around her. In that moment, Nick forgot all about his objections to being romantically involved with a woman pregnant by another man. This was Erin. He could think of nothing but letting her and the whole world know how much he admired and respected and liked her. How much he *loved* her. Yet even then, he didn't realize what he was going to say until he heard his voice over the applause.

"Erin, will you do me the honor of becoming my wife?"

CHAPTER FOURTEEN

STILL FLUSHED FROM HER impassioned speech, Erin blinked back at Nick. His words might have been uttered in Swahili for all the sense they made to her. "What did you say?"

His confident smile unfaltering, he spoke in a voice that was pitched for her ears alone but, thanks to good acoustics, carried to the back of the hushed auditorium. "I asked you to marry me."

Erin didn't know who was going to expire first— she from embarrassment or he from the severe bashing he was about to receive at her hands. *No,* she mouthed.

"No?" Puzzlement creased his face.

He didn't get it. Mr. Understanding didn't have a clue! Heat started at the base of her neck and spread upward.

"No," she said loudly, thinking volume might aid his understanding.

Nervous laughter rippled through the audience. Erin glanced at the crowd and quickly away, excruciatingly aware that the entire town was watching them make idiots of themselves. No doubt Nick thought he was being gallant, but he should know better than to ask her something so personal in front of all these people. He was still staring at her as if stunned.

"Weren't you listening? I said I was going to raise this baby on my own." Her low-pitched voice was stiff with embarrassment.

A horrible silence fell over the crowd. Hundreds of faces stared expectantly, waiting for the next move. Suddenly Erin couldn't bear to stand there a minute longer.

Pushing Nick aside, she fought her way through the heavy draperies at the back of the stage. Amid dusty stacks of folding tables, she paused to let her eyes adjust to the dim light. A roar of voices reached her from the hall. Her departure had broken the silence. Nick's proposal and her refusal would give the people of Hainesville something to talk about until the next millennium.

She was heading for the backstage exit, when Nick appeared at her side, furious.

"For God's sake, Erin," he said, taking her by the arm. "Why'd you leave me to face that mob alone? I felt like a jackass."

She tugged away. How dared *he* be angry? "*You* made an ass of yourself, not me. How was I to know you'd do something silly like propose marriage?"

Glowering, he backed her against a stack of tables. "In my book that's about the highest honor a man can bestow on a woman, or have bestowed on him. You acted like I'd offered you money for sex."

"Your proposal was gallant but totally inappropriate. I'm a big girl. I can take care of myself." She pushed him away and resumed her progress toward the side door. "Two proposals in one day," she muttered, "and neither based on love."

"What do you mean, *two* proposals?" he demanded, following her to the exit. "Someone else asked to marry you?"

"Surprised?" She stepped outside and let the heavy spring-loaded door swing shut in his face.

He shouldered the door aside to accost her in the parking lot. *"Who?"*

"John," she said, weaving through the parked cars toward the sidewalk. "Being a family man suddenly suits his political aspirations."

"That jerk. I hope you told him where to go."

"If I married John, I could give my child a proper home. With its *biological* father." She was just mad enough to want Nick to squirm.

"That's a hell of a thing to say to me."

"How can I marry you?" she said, throwing up her hands. "You still have unresolved issues with paternity. You've raised Miranda for thirteen years and yet she doubts your love."

"She's going through a stage. Of course I love her."

"I believe you. *She* doesn't. You take out your resentment over your late wife's infidelity by not trusting Miranda."

"Have you seen the way she dresses? The way she acts around boys?"

"She gets a rise out of you, gets the attention she

craves. You don't trust her, Nick, so she feels rejected. And insecure. My baby doesn't have your genes, either. How would you treat him or her?'' Erin knew she wasn't being totally fair. Nick was a caring, conscientious father. He *tried* not to let his doubts show.

Nick kept pace as she began walking down Brockley toward Main, past dark bushes and picket fences, blue TV light flickering in the front windows of the houses of the few people who hadn't witnessed their debacle.

''Would you take the chance if it was just me and you?''

He was asking if she loved him. Life was never that simple. ''I can't answer that.''

''I didn't propose out of gallantry. I love you. I want to marry you.''

In the yellow glow of the streetlight she stopped and searched his face. If his proposal had come at another time, in another place, she might have believed him. ''Would you love my baby?''

Doubt, the merest flicker, swept across his features, but it was enough to convince her she was right to be skeptical. Spinning on her heel, she resumed her homeward journey.

They came to Erin's house. The windows were dark. Nick walked her up to the porch and waited impatiently while she dug through her purse for her key.

''You're not really going to marry John.'' He took

her by both arms, forced her to look at him. His eyes burned with a light she'd never seen in them before.

"What do you care?" she taunted.

"You think I don't care?"

In a flash his hands were tangled in her hair and his lips were seeking hers. Her baby came between them, literally, but Erin forgot the awkwardness as Nick's lips traced a path across her cheek to her mouth. The heat of his lips on hers melted her resistance. Over the months their hearts had grown close, and now the longing and frustration of past months lent fervor to her response. Temporarily, she forgot her baby, thrust the uncertain future aside. All that mattered was Nick's tongue mating with hers.

His hand moved to her breast, squeezing as his thumb brushed an ultrasensitive nipple. He'd never touched her in this way before and her body responded as if she were a young maiden instead of a woman heavy with child. Hormones sped through her body, causing heat to pool and juices to flow.

"What the hell…?" Abruptly Nick broke the kiss and pulled his hand away from her breast. His palm was damp.

Erin touched her fingers to her dress and found the wet circle where milk had leaked. She laughed softly, uncertainly. "I can't help it."

Carried away by the kiss he'd craved for so long, Nick had forgotten for a moment that she was pregnant. Milk from Erin's breast. *Mother's milk.* His head filled with a confusing mix of erotic and maternal images. A baby suckling. Himself sucking. And underlying it all, a kind of atavistic rage because his woman had accepted another man's seed, and was bearing another man's child. She was pregnant and the baby wasn't his.

His woman? Maybe not.

Maybe she was right and he *had* proposed out of misplaced gallantry. Would he still have negative feelings about her baby's paternity if he truly loved her?

"I'm going in now," she said, her ardor clearly cooled by his long silence.

He stared at her, racking his brains for *something* that would salvage the rapport they'd shared a moment ago. Then his beeper went off.

The county dispatcher's voice, crackling with static, dispassionately announced a fire at 257 Southpark Way. "...visible flames. Emergency aid unit requested. Repeat, visible flames."

"I've got to go," Nick said.

One corner of Erin's mouth kicked up in a dry smile. "Saved by the bell."

WHEN NICK GOT HOME the next morning at seven, dead on his feet, with the smell of charred wood permeating his hair and gear, Oliver was standing in his kitchen, inspecting the inside of the fridge.

This was not turning out to be a good twenty-four hours.

"I'll *bet* you have an appetite," he growled, advancing. "What the hell are you doing here?"

Oliver raised his shaggy head, his face turning white. "Uh, hi, Mr. Dalton."

"What are you doing here?"

"Miranda was kind of upset when you didn't get home."

"Where *is* Miranda?"

"I'm right here, and it's not what you think." Miranda stood in the doorway in her pajamas, hugging her panda and holding a sheet of paper.

Nick rounded on her. "What's *he* doing here?"

"He was being a friend. Something you know nothing about. Just as you know nothing about being a father."

She was using that tone again. "I come home, and my daughter, who *promised* me she was trustworthy, is having a sleepover."

"Don't be sarcastic. You're jumping to conclusions."

"I slept on the couch," Oliver put in.

"Do your parents know where you are?" Nick demanded.

"I called my dad last night. He said it was okay to stay until you got back."

"Well, it's not okay. Miranda, you're grounded. Indefinitely."

Miranda's face went white. "You can't do that to me."

"I'm your father. I can do whatever it takes to protect you."

"No, you can't." Her mouth hardened into defiance. "You're not my father."

"What? What are you talking about?"

She thrust the sheet of paper into his hand. The words seemed blurry to his smoke-stung eyes, but the letterhead told the story. *Linfields DNA Testing—For All Your Genetic Analysis Needs.*

"For God's sake, Miranda, what have you done now?"

"Just read the results."

"Wait a minute." Nick turned to Oliver and pointed. "You, go."

"Yessir." He gathered his schoolbooks from the dining table.

Miranda ran and stood in front of the door, barring it. "He's giving me a ride to school. You can't ground me from there. I'll call the Department of Education."

"You're not going anywhere until I find out what this is about." He opened the door for Oliver. "We'll talk about it later. Don't think you're getting away with anything."

"No, sir."

Miranda took his arm. "You don't have to go, Oliver."

He hugged her awkwardly. "I'll call you later."

"*I'll* let you know when you can call," Nick said, and ushered him out the door.

Nick shrugged out of his heavy bunker coat, the sheet of DNA results clenched between his teeth. He dropped the coat on a chair and walked past Miranda into the living room.

A blanket sprawled untidily along the seat and back of the couch.

Okay, so he'd jumped to conclusions. The kid was still a bum.

He turned to Miranda and rattled the paper. "Why did you do this?"

Miranda looked scared but still defiant. "I overheard you tell Erin my mother slept around."

"I said nothing of the sort."

"You think that I'm so much like Mom I must sleep around, too."

"Miranda, I don't think that." Damn, how had he gotten on the defensive?

He sat on the arm of the couch and scanned the document in his hand. Fatigue had dulled his brain, and his head and lungs ached from breathing smoke. "Ninety per cent match of DNA between sample A and sample B." He wondered briefly when she'd obtained a sample of his DNA, then remembered the science experiment and the hair follicles. The significance of the result didn't become clear until he reached the bottom line: "Paternity: unestablished."

Miranda was watching him, tears spilling down her cheeks. "See. You're not my father."

He pushed off the couch and wrapped his arms around her. "Regardless of whether you're my biological child, you're still my daughter. Listen, honey, I've been up for thirty-six hours and I'm about to collapse. I can't be fair or objective or any of the things I need to be to deal with this. So I'm going to grab some sleep, and when I get up, we'll talk about it. Okay?''

"Typical," she said, stiff and miserable. "You're never there when *I* need to talk."

"You know that's unfair. Why don't you get some more sleep, too. You look tired."

"*Oliver* and I talked till late."

He stiffened. "I'm not ready to discuss Oliver. Sleep first. Then talk."

He led her to her room, just as he had when she was little. He wondered suddenly when he'd stopped tucking her in at night. Then he remembered; right after Janine died. As a battalion chief and single father, there had never been enough time.

Oliver had been there for her. That hurt.

She wouldn't kiss Nick and was unresponsive when he hugged her. Her mouth drawn down, she wouldn't meet his eyes. He'd fix it, he thought desperately. Later.

NICK AWOKE TO THE SOUND of seagulls and a fishing trawler chugging past on its way out to sea. Disoriented, he blinked at the sunlight slanting through the gap in his curtains. Then his brain informed him the afternoon was half over.

Erin occupied his first real thought. Then Miranda.

He groaned and rolled onto his stomach, pulling the pillow over his head. Erin thought he was a monster. So did Miranda. Right now, he wasn't sure they weren't right.

Soon he was rolling out of bed. First things first,

and that meant Miranda. Now that his anger had cooled, he remembered his tone when he'd told Erin about Janine—dismissive and hostile—and cringed as he thought about the effect his words must have had on Miranda. Why the hell couldn't she have come and talked to him?

He was never there for her.

Now, that was bull.

He dressed in chinos and a rugby shirt as he considered how best to approach Miranda. She was probably watching *Oprah,* grumpy but not averse to a day off school.

But when he came out to the living room, she wasn't there. Nor was she anywhere on the houseboat. Maybe she'd gone to school, anyway.

To see Oliver.

He shoved a chair out of his path as he headed for the kitchen. It might take another day or two before he got his temper under control on that score. He didn't really think she'd slept with Oliver, but he'd bet they hadn't just been holding hands till the early hours of the morning.

He fried a couple of eggs and a thick slab of ham, jammed them between two slices of toast and ate leaning against the kitchen counter. The clock on the stove read 4:00 p.m. Two cups of coffee and a cursory glance at the *Hainesville Herald,* including the article on the town hall meeting, which made him wince, brought him to four-thirty. Miranda should have been home from school by now. At 4:45, he called Oliver's house.

Oliver's mother answered. "He came home briefly at lunchtime," Melanie Cameron told him. "That was odd, because usually he stays at school to work on the student paper. I haven't seen him since. Is there a problem? I hope he's not making a nuisance of himself."

"No," Nick said slowly. He wondered how she could be so unconcerned that Oliver and Miranda had spent the night together unchaperoned. But the phone wasn't the place to discuss it, nor did he have the time. "I'm looking for Miranda. Was she with him when he came home at lunch?"

"No. If I see her, I'll tell her to phone you."

"Thanks." Nick hung up and stared at the phone. Erin. Was she really the next logical person to call or was he just obsessing over her?

He couldn't worry about that now.

Her voice, when she answered, brought a wave of longing and chagrin that he pushed aside. "Hello, Erin. Have you seen Miranda?"

"Not today." She paused. "What happened? You sound worried."

"We…had a fight this morning. It was serious. She should have been home by now."

"Did you call Oliver's house? The school?"

Why did *she* sound so worried? Why wasn't she reassuring him that Miranda was probably just at a friend's and had forgotten to call? *Did she know something she wasn't telling him?*

"She's not at Oliver's. I'm heading over to the school now. If she's not there, can I stop by?"

In her slight pause he read reluctance to see him. "Sure," she said after a moment. "Come on over."

At the school, the office staff told him Miranda had been recorded as absent. He got clearance to search the building and spent the next half hour walking the halls, peering into empty classrooms. A few students, working on projects, raised mildly curious eyes when he poked his head through the doorway to ask after his daughter.

No one had seen Miranda all day.

On his way to Erin's, he called the Camerons on his cell phone. Oliver had come home, eaten a couple of sandwiches and gone over to a friend's house. He claimed he hadn't seen Miranda since morning.

Nick told himself he was getting worked up over nothing. In her defiant mood, she'd probably skipped school and gone to a movie, maybe even taken the bus to Simcoe and was hanging around the mall. She would turn up at dinner, unrepentant but ready to talk. His watch read 5:30. He phoned home, but the phone just kept on ringing.

He clicked off and pulled into the curb in front of Erin's house. By the time he'd gotten out of the vehicle she was at the door, one of Ruth's handknit sweaters pulled tight over her flowing dress.

She drew him into the house and through to the living room, made him sit in one of the armchairs in front of the fireplace. Without asking if he wanted it, she brought him a cup of black coffee with plenty of sugar. Three cups in two hours; he was going into caffeine overload.

''What did you two fight about?'' she asked. Chloe, padding by on silent paws, saw a lap and leaped up. Erin stroked the kitten's blue-gray fur, leaving her steaming coffee untouched on the mahogany side table between their chairs.

Nick shook his head, set down his coffee, as the shameful incident flooded back. ''She overheard me telling you about Janine and sent away for a DNA testing kit. How she got the money or where she had the test results delivered, I don't know.'' Leaning forward on his elbows, he scrubbed his face with his hands, feeling ridges of fatigue and worry on his forehead and around his mouth. ''The results say we're not genetically related.''

Half a dozen clocks ticked in the silence. He glanced at her and was shocked to see she already knew.

''I'm sorry, Nick. I should have told you.'' Her eyes were rimmed with moisture. ''I promised Miranda I wouldn't.''

''How long have you known about the test results?'' His voice was dull, his fingertips strangely cold.

''Since January.''

Months, in other words. While he'd breathed in unison with her, massaged her back, made her herbal tea, she'd kept secrets. *Betrayed* didn't begin to describe what he felt. Betrayed by his daughter, and now his... What *was* Erin to him?

Nothing. A friend at best, and not a very good one. He could hardly believe now that he'd asked her to marry him. The events of last night and his feelings of love and desire seemed impossibly distant.

Like a robot, he put down his coffee cup and rose to his feet. Only one thing mattered now—finding Miranda.

His cell phone rang before he reached the door. "Yes?"

"Nick, it's Brent Cameron. Oliver's home and we questioned him more thoroughly about Miranda." He paused. "Apparently she went to Seattle to get a bus or a train down to Los Angeles. I'm sorry."

Nick squeezed his eyes shut. *He should have been there for her.*

"Thanks for letting me know," he said. "I'll leave now for the city. If she calls Oliver, try to find out where she is and get her to stay put. I'll keep in touch."

He was turning to say goodbye to Erin when she drew a sharp breath. A spasm crossed her face and she pressed her hands to her ripe belly. His pulse quickened. "Are you going into labor?"

"Braxton-Hicks contractions," she said, her voice tight. Gradually her breathing eased and her features relaxed. "I've been having them on and off all day."

"How can you tell they're not the real thing?"

"It's too soon. The baby's not due for another ten days." She scribbled something on a notepad by the door, then slipped her feet into her loafers. "Wherever you're going now, I'm coming."

"You've done enough damage." Seeing her mouth tremble, he added less harshly, "I don't know where

I'm going, or how long I'll be. You need to take care of yourself. And Ruth.''

"Gran's at Edna Thompson's. I've written her a note. She'll manage. Kelly's around if she needs help. And I'm fine, just moving a little slowly.'' She put a hand on his arm. "Please, Nick, I feel responsible. If Miranda's being stubborn, it might help to have someone objective to mediate.''

Damn it, she had a point. The only thing worse than Miranda running away would be Miranda refusing to come home. Insisting on finding her birth father. His heart constricted painfully. How could he bear to lose her?

"I know Seattle—you don't,'' Erin added, clinching the argument.

"All right, you can come,'' he said, still seething.

"Once she's safely home,'' Erin continued, stoically holding his gaze, "we won't have anything more to do with each other.''

He gazed at her for a long moment. For once, where Erin was concerned, emotion and reason dictated the same conclusion. "Fine by me.''

ERIN ADJUSTED THE SEAT BELT in Nick's Suburban to fit more comfortably over her. Drops of rain splattered the windshield as Nick merged with the stream of freeway traffic heading to Seattle. Thick cloud cover darkened the sky.

"So when were you going to tell me that you helped Miranda obtain DNA testing without my knowledge or consent?'' he said, breaking the silence that had held since they'd left Hainesville.

''I repeatedly asked her to talk to you,'' Erin said, steeling herself for questions and recriminations. ''Failing that, I told her that if the results were negative, she should tell me and I would arrange counseling.''

''Taking rather a lot upon yourself, weren't you?''

Erin sighed. ''She turned to me for help in a matter she clearly couldn't talk to you about. What was I supposed to do, let her fend entirely for herself?''

''You should have told me what she was up to!''

''Then she would have trusted me as little as she trusts you!''

That shut him up, but Erin didn't feel any better for having stemmed his tirade. Their friendship was over and she'd ended it. How could people who cared about each other speak to each other so hurtfully?

''We both failed Miranda,'' she said quietly.

Without warning, the band of muscles circling her belly tightened. As the intensity built, she leaned forward, one hand gripping the dashboard while she tried to catch her breath.

Nick glanced at her, frowning. ''Are you sure you're all right?''

''I'm fine,'' she gasped. Seconds later the contraction eased and she relaxed again. How long were Braxton-Hicks contractions supposed to last? She tried to recall what the baby books said, and couldn't. The irregular intervals between contractions had led her to believe they weren't the real thing. She hoped that was true.

"I should have left you at home," Nick said. He cursed the rain and flipped the wipers onto high. "I hope Miranda's not out in this."

"She wouldn't hitchhike, would she?"

"Not if she values her life." The slap of the wipers punctuated the stark silence. "I meant," Nick added quietly, "I would be very unhappy with her if she hitchhiked."

"I know what you mean." She squeezed his arm. His glance was brief and unfathomable, and she withdrew her hand.

They were quiet after that. Nick's grim profile suggested he, like Erin, was torturing himself with the potential dangers a young girl faced alone in the city or on a dark highway.

Could she have prevented Miranda from running away by telling Nick earlier about the DNA testing? Reluctantly she had to conclude that maybe she could have. If he'd known how serious his daughter's concerns were, he might have worked on their problems sooner. Erin flattened the curling end of her purse strap, blocking out her most grisly thoughts.

"I'm sorry." Her quiet words could hardly be heard above the rain and the noise of the cars whooshing by. She cleared her throat and spoke louder. "Nick, I'm sorry."

He didn't look at her, just shrugged, his mouth a hard line. Erin's heart carried a double burden; if anything happened to Miranda, Nick would never forgive her.

The traffic was thickening on the outskirts of Seattle when the next contraction came. Erin shifted on the seat, trying to get more comfortable as the tightening began across her belly. She crossed her arms to ride it out, glancing at her watch. Forty-two minutes since the last one.

Nick glanced at her. "Are your contractions getting closer together?"

"I can't tell," she prevaricated. When the day had begun, they'd been hours apart. She looked around for a street sign or familiar landmark. "We come to the train station first. Turn off Highway 99 at King Street."

A few minutes later Nick parked and they hurried through the rain to the station. He held the umbrella but kept his distance, protecting her and getting himself wet. Nothing could have made her feel worse than Nick being chivalrous while showing her just how much he couldn't stand to be near her.

Nick and Erin paused inside the entrance to the cavernous main hall of the station to scan the crowd. People were lined up at ticket windows, milling near the doors to the platforms, browsing through newsstands or sitting around tables at fast-food outlets. Nowhere in the throng could they see an auburn-haired girl wearing denim flares and a blue sweater, carrying a black backpack.

They split up, Nick to inquire at the ticket windows and Erin to move through the crowd. They were both armed with a recent photo of Miranda and a description of her clothing, height and approximate weight. Most people were sympathetic, some were dismissive, but no one had seen Miranda.

Erin had just reached the far end of the great room, when a contraction stole her breath and doubled her over. Gripping a bench for support, she forced herself to breathe.

A uniformed station attendant pushing a broom came up to her. "Are you okay, lady?"

"Fine, thank you," she gasped. The attendant scratched his grizzled head and looked around as if for help. The contraction eased and Erin straightened, able to say more firmly, "Really, I'm fine."

"If you say so." With a dubious backward glance, he shuffled off, pushing a mound of paper scraps ahead of his broom.

Erin wiped her damp forehead with a tissue. Thirty-five minutes between contractions. She was glad to see Nick moving toward her, but the grim set of his jaw told her he hadn't had any luck, either.

"She hasn't bought a ticket," he said when he reached Erin. "Where's the bus station?"

"The Greyhound station is on Stewart Street, off Oliver Way." With an effort that she did her best to hide, she pushed herself to her feet.

Nick noticed, anyway. "Good God, you're pale." He touched her forehead with the back of his hand. "And perspiring. Did you just have another contraction?"

"I'm fine," she insisted. "Let's go to the bus station."

"So help me, Erin, if you have your baby on the bus station floor I'll—" He threw his hands in the air with an air of disgust at himself. "What am I saying? I'm taking you to the birthing center."

"*Later.* We have to find Miranda." She dealt with his protests by moving back toward the main door. Between contractions she *was* fine, but she was beginning to think the pains were more than just Braxton-Hicks. If only she'd brought her copy of the *Modern Woman's Guide to Pregnancy and Childbirth,* she might know for sure.

The bus station was even more crowded than the train station. Erin quailed at the prospect of having to push her way through the packed room. The baby's head was pressing down painfully on her groin and every lead-footed step was a major effort. She was digging through her purse for the photo of Miranda when Nick caught her arm.

"I think I saw her!"

CHAPTER FIFTEEN

"WHERE?" ERIN IGNORED her aching pelvis and put a hand on Nick's shoulder to stand on her toes and peer above the sea of heads.

"Over by the vending machines. She looked straight at me." Taking her hand, he strode across the room, weaving in and out of people and piles of luggage. Dragged along, Erin hurried breathlessly in his wake.

When they got to the vending machines, a little boy was repeatedly punching the change button on the cigarette machine and a teenage girl was unwrapping the Hershey's bar she'd just bought. Miranda was nowhere in sight.

"Are you sure it was her?"

"Whoever it was looked exactly like her. How many teenage girls have multicolored hair, a ring through an eyebrow and tight clothes?"

Erin gave him a look. "You've got to be kidding."

Nick glanced around. Two girls within a ten-foot radius answered to that description. "Okay, but I still think it was her. I'm going to ask at the ticket window. Are you able to ask the people waiting? Maybe you should sit and rest."

"I'll ask around. But first I've got to use the bath-room."

"Okay. I'll meet you back here." Nick headed for the ticket office.

Erin trudged toward the ladies' room. Halfway there, another contraction gripped her. This time, not just her midsection but her whole body felt as though it were being squeezed in a giant vise. She couldn't breathe, couldn't move; even her thoughts seemed paralyzed. When the wave of pain and pressure passed, she found herself crouching beside a row of pay phones. Surely that was no Braxton-Hicks.

After a moment, she remembered to look at her watch. Good grief. Could it really only be ten minutes since her last contraction?

Oh, God. This was *it*. She was going into labor. *In a bus station.*

She looked around for Nick and saw the back of his head bobbing a distance away from her. The pay phone. She could call an ambulance.

But she still had to pee—*badly.*

She dragged herself to her feet. Taking one labo-rious step at a time, she formulated a plan. Once she'd gone to the bathroom, she'd phone for an ambulance. Then she'd find Nick and tell him she was going to the birthing center to have her baby. Everything would be fine. Her plan made a lot of sense.

She reached the ladies' room. So far, so good. Oh, no. All the stalls were full. Just when she was about to burst. She went down the line, pushing gently on the doors in case one was only stuck and bending over to check for feet.

A pair of bright red clunky platform shoes stopped her cold. She never forgot a pair of shoes. Above the red shoes were the flared bottoms of denim jeans. Bottoms that weren't folded over the shoes, as they would be if the person had her pants down. Whoever was in there was standing. Hiding.

"Miranda?"

Silence.

"Miranda, if it's you, please come out. Your father is really worried."

"He's not my father."

Relief surged through Erin at the sound of the girl's voice. "You can't run away. You have to talk it out with him."

"I hate him. I never want to see him again. I'm going to look for my real father."

"Miranda, I don't care what the genetic tests say, *Nick* is your real father." Exasperated and increasingly desperate to pee, Erin squeezed her legs together. "Now, *please* get out of there so I can go in—*Oh, my God!*"

A gush of warm liquid poured down her legs. At first she thought she'd wet her pants, but the fluid splashing around her feet and into Miranda's cubicle looked and smelled nothing like urine.

Miranda shrieked. In seconds she was outside the stall, her shocked gaze going from the wetness on the floor to Erin's face.

"My water broke," Erin gasped. "Go find your father. He's at the ticket window."

Miranda hesitated.

"Quickly!" Erin moaned. "I refuse to have my baby in a bus station toilet."

Miranda bolted out the door.

Five minutes and an eternity later, Nick was pushing through the ladies' room door, Miranda right behind him. Erin had never been so glad to see anyone.

"An ambulance is on the way." Calmly, he took her forearm in one hand, his other arm supporting her back. "Are you okay?"

"My dress..." she began, embarrassed about the wet splotch down the front.

Unruffled, he held her gaze with his dark brown eyes. "No one's looking at your dress. They're looking at your beautiful face and thinking what a miracle is about to take place."

Blushing, smiling, she shook her head. "You're full of it, Dalton."

But some of his composure flowed to her, and his words had power. They stayed with her even when the ambulance drivers wouldn't let him ride to the birthing center with her. They stayed with her through increasingly intense contractions. And when she screamed at the admissions nurse that she was having a baby, damn it, she didn't have time to fill in forms, she forgot his exact words, but she remembered the sound of his voice and the memory calmed her.

As an orderly wheeled her toward the labor room, she craned her neck to see back down the corridor.

Where was he? She'd just about resigned herself to having her baby alone, when Nick barreled through the double doors, Miranda in tow.

The midwife's outstretched arm barred Nick's headlong rush to Erin's side. "Are you her husband?"

Erin was fully prepared to lie if that was what it took to have him with her through the birth of her baby. Apparently Nick had the same idea, for he spoke first, loud and clear. "I'm the father."

Nick heard his own words with shock, then a sense of rightness that felt inevitable. Hell, he'd done everything a father was supposed to do except supply the sperm. Why shouldn't he claim father's rights?

He turned to Miranda, who was staring at him with a gaping mouth. "I'm *your* father, too," he said fiercely. "Don't ever try to tell me differently."

"Yessir," Miranda answered meekly. "Are you really going in there?"

"I'm her birthing partner. I've got a job to do."

"Miranda can come in, too, if she likes." Erin's warm smile included her.

"Really?" The midwife nodded and Miranda followed, hesitant but willing. By the time the nurses had prepped Erin, and Miranda and Nick had donned gowns, she was smiling.

Nick stood on Erin's left, one hand holding hers, the other around her shoulder, and coached her through the labor. He slipped ice chips between her parched lips, blotted perspiration from her forehead, panted and blew with her. He even stoically allowed her to dig her nails into his arm when her pain seemed unbearable. Two hours later, when the crown of the baby's head appeared, his eyelashes were wet, and he couldn't have been more proud or thrilled.

"Nearly there, sweetheart," he said, his voice soft and low. "You're strong and beautiful. You're bring ing your baby into the world."

"One more big push, Erin," the midwife coaxed.

"Is the doctor coming?" Nick said as Erin breathed deeply and prepared to push.

"She's been called," the midwife told him.

The baby wasn't going to wait.

Erin bore down. Nick gripped her shoulders and felt her pain and tension as if it were his own. Miranda hovered in the background, fascinated and fearful. With a guttural cry from Erin, the baby's head emerged. Nick couldn't breathe.

His exultant gaze flashed to Erin's. "He's beautiful."

"How do you know...? Ahhh!" Erin cried, as the baby's shoulders pushed through. The rest of the body slithered free and into the midwife's waiting hands.

"It's a boy," the midwife declared.

Nick couldn't take his eyes off the baby. "He blinked. Look at his scrunched-up little nose. And his hands, they're opening and closing."

"Da-a-ad," Miranda said, but she, too, wore a wide grin.

Dad. Nick had never heard such a beautiful word.

Erin's tears trickled into the creases of her smile. Her beautiful smile. Nick hugged her, kissed her, his heart overflowing with love for her and her baby. He longed to speak volumes, compose poetry in her honor, tell her everything that was in his heart.

"You did good" was all he could manage to say.

It seemed to be enough. Erin let loose fresh tears. Laughing and crying at once, she held out her arms. "I want to hold my baby."

A nurse removed the mucus from the baby's mouth, then lifted him, naked, onto Erin's stomach. Erin pushed aside her gown and guided the baby to her nipple. Instinctively, his tiny mouth grasped and suckled, his small fist fluttered at her breast. An unexpected contentment flooded through Nick at the sight of mother and child. His arm went around Miranda and he pulled her to his side. She gave him a smile that lifted his joy onto another plane.

The umbilical cord ceased to pulsate. The midwife held a pair of surgical scissors out to Nick. "Want to do the honors, Dad?"

He really ought to enlighten them.

Erin beamed and nodded, Miranda gave him a nudge and the baby let out a sudden howl of encouragement. Aware of how momentous an occasion it was, Nick stepped forward and cut the cord. The baby was no longer physically connected to Erin; he belonged to both of them.

"What are you going to call him?" the midwife asked.

Nick glanced away; a portion of his happiness evaporated.

"Erik, after my father," Erin said, stroking the

baby's cheek. She glanced up then and met Nick's eyes. "Erik Nicholas."

Nick's vision blurred. His chest swelled with pride and for a moment he was unable to speak. At last he said, "Erik Nicholas. A fine name."

WHEN ERIN WAS SETTLED in the maternity ward, with Erik asleep at her side, Nick and Miranda drove back to Hainesville through the early hours of the morning. They traveled in silence, absorbed in their own thoughts. Gradually the joy of experiencing the birth receded and they were left with the events that had preceded it.

"You know, Miranda, I meant what I said at the hospital. I'm your father and you're my daughter, even if our DNA doesn't match one hundred percent. But I talked to Dr. Cameron before I set out to find you. He told me that a ninety-percent match doesn't prove I'm *not* your father, just that the results don't show conclusive evidence that I am."

Her head came around sharply. "Huh? I don't understand."

"He said sloppy techniques sometimes give results that are hard to read. Maybe the testing facility wasn't as good as it could be."

"It *was* the cheapest." Miranda admitted. "And it asked the fewest questions."

"Never mind. It doesn't matter anymore." He placed a finger under her chin and brought her gaze to meet his. "I know things haven't been great these past couple years, but we can work on our problems. That's what families do. Right?''

She twisted her chin out of his grip.

''What is it?''

Miranda balled her hands into fists in her lap. ''Maybe you *are* my father. I…I hope you are. But maybe you're not. It has nothing to do with us being a family. It's about who I am. Don't you see?'' Her eyes beseeched him to understand. *''I need to know.''*

Nick drove a few miles in silence, trying to come to grips with what she was saying. Painful as it was to admit, she did have a right to know, no matter how afraid he was of losing her. ''We'll go to a proper facility and get tested again.''

''What if…if it turns out we're not related?'' Her chin was held high, but she couldn't hide the tremble that had crept into her voice.

Nick slowed and pulled over to the side of the road through a deep puddle that sent up a muddy spray against the side of the Suburban. With the motor still running, he turned in his seat to face her. ''No father could feel more fear for his child than I felt today when I discovered you were missing. I love you, Miranda. I truly wouldn't care if you *weren't* my biological daughter. You're the child of my heart.''

Erik Nicholas Hanson was another.

''I need to know,'' she repeated.

Nick sighed. He'd misinterpreted the tremor in his daughter's voice. As much as she needed his love and reassurance, she wanted facts. For a long few minutes he stared at the raindrops zigzagging down the windshield like a giant's tears.

"If we're not related," he said at last, "we'll find the man who is your biological father."

Concerns cropped up immediately. Supposing they could even find the guy, would this hypothetical father want to know her? If he didn't, how would Miranda handle that kind of rejection? Nick pushed these thoughts from his mind. He was her father; he would protect her as best he could.

"Thank you." Her eyes shone. "I'm really sorry about running away. I...I thought you wouldn't want me."

"I'll always want you."

"Me, too." She paused. "No matter what."

Meaning, even if he wasn't her biological father. He couldn't ask for more. His eyes burned as he combed his fingers through her curls. "I'm sorry if I ever made you feel unwanted. The truth is, I was angry with your mother and took it out on you. It wasn't fair, and I'm ashamed of myself."

Miranda looked down at her hands. "Did she really...have an affair?"

"Apparently she did."

"But she stayed with you. She must have loved you."

He sighed heavily, reaching back through remembered pain to a happier time. "Yes, I believe she did. I guess I've ignored that fact these past two years. She chose me, even though her child might belong to someone else." He looked back at Miranda. "You might think it's unfair to the other man, but I can't help but be glad she did. Your mom and I had a good life together. She was a good mother, and except for a certain lapse, a good wife. I...I loved her very much.''

The truth of his words lifted a weight he hadn't known he'd been carrying; a weight that had hampered his relationship with Miranda and his ability to move on to new commitments. Unable to forgive, he'd never properly grieved for Janine. In the dark hours of early morning, with the rain beating steadily on the car roof, he felt her loss with fresh sorrow.

A tissue appeared in front of his face, held in Miranda's outstretched hand.

''Hell.'' He took it and blotted his eyes, then turned a tentative smile on his daughter. ''Are we square?''

''Oh, Dad.'' Miranda flung herself across the seat at him.

Nick closed his arms around her. New tears fell into her hair. After a moment, he pulled back a little to speak and was prevented by a yelp from Miranda and something catching in his sweater.

''Don't move!'' she cried. Her forehead was apparently attached to his chest. She frantically fumbled with her eyebrow ring, laboriously unhooking it from a thread.

''For God's sake, Miranda. Get rid of that damn thing.''

''I will.'' She succeeded in releasing herself, and to his surprise, she opened the window and tossed the silver circle into the night.

"Great," Nick said. "Now, how about losing the navel ring?"

"Uh, I got rid of that a while ago," she confessed. "The skin around it got infected." Nick grimaced and she quickly added, "It cleared up. I'm fine now."

"I'm glad to hear it." He gently touched the spot where the brow ring had been, looking forward to the day the hole would grow over. "And the nose ring?"

Miranda could still produce her cheeky grin. "Don't push it, Dad. I'm keeping the nose ring. Otherwise I can't wear the cool stud Erin gave me."

He noticed suddenly that the rain had stopped and the moon glimmered through the clouds, illuminating the dried tears on his daughter's face. "Let's go home."

He'd barely pulled back onto the highway, when Miranda asked, "Are you going to marry Erin?"

He glanced at her in the darkness, trying to gauge her attitude. "Would that be okay with you?"

"*Yeah!* What do you think?"

He thought he must be the slowest, clumsiest suitor in the Pacific Northwest. So slow and clumsy someone else might beat him to the punch if he wasn't careful. If it wasn't already too late. A small smile curved his lips. He might be slow, but he was learning.

"I'll ask her properly this time."

CHAPTER SIXTEEN

"HE'S FINALLY ASLEEP," Erin whispered. Gently she detached baby Erik from her breast and rose slowly, cradling him in her arms.

"Hallelujah," Nick murmured.

Erin glided on stocking feet upstairs to her bedroom. She carefully lowered the sleeping baby to the mattress and eased her hands out from beneath his small, warm body. A little snort, a tiny sigh and he settled deeper into sleep. Erin leaned on the side of the crib to gaze at her child with a rapture that bordered on bliss. He was so sweet, so perfect. How could she ever for one moment have not wanted him? Thanks to Nick...

She smiled to herself. She had a lot to thank Nick for. He'd been so attentive since the birth, so caring, lavishing flowers and gifts upon her and her baby. She loved Nick. She believed he loved her. If only he loved her *and* her baby.

Nick came through the doorway to stand beside her. "He's got your nose," he said, his voice low. "And your coloring."

Erin grinned. "It's too early to be certain, but I think he's got your sense of humor."

"Come on." Nick's arm went around her waist and

he drew her back downstairs to the lamp-lit living room. He'd been restless all evening, almost impatient.

"Do you want coffee?" she asked as he pulled her down onto the couch. Now that the baby was born, she cherished these moments alone with Nick more than ever.

"No." His thigh lay next to hers. In his pocket, something small with sharp corners, pressed into her.

"Tea?"

"No." He took her left hand and placed it between his palms. His skin was slightly damp, as if he was nervous.

"*Me?*" Behind her self-mocking smile she felt hysteria. She'd had her chance. In spite of his caring and kindness she knew he wouldn't easily get over her public rebuke and private rejection.

Maybe when he got the results of his and Miranda's additional DNA testing, absorbed the implications, dealt with reality, put the pain behind him...

Nick, serious, said, "We need to talk."

Oh, God. Not that. She could raise her baby alone. She could survive. But she wanted Nick's love. She'd hoped... Panic would have propelled her to her feet had he not gripped her.

"Where are you going in such a hurry?"

"Um... The clocks. I have to wind the clocks."

"No, you don't." Gently but firmly, he settled her back on the couch beside him. Erin's eyes smarted at the bittersweet pain of wanting him and fearing she was going to lose him. Wild scenarios ran through her mind. He was going back to L.A. He'd met someone else—

"Erin? Are you listening to me?"

She sighed. "Yes."

"Good, because I have something important to ask."

Hope flared, along with a resurgence in belief. If he was dumping her, surely he'd be telling, not asking. "What is it?"

His chest rose on a long breath, and he loosened his tie with a crooked finger. "The night of the town meeting you said John had asked you to marry him...." He took another breath. "But you didn't tell me what your response was."

"I told him no, of course."

Nick shut his eyes on a long exhale. "Good." He opened them again and looked at her. "Will he be a father to your baby?"

She shook her head.

"I think Erik needs a father, don't you?"

"A father who wants him and loves him," she amended firmly.

"I agree absolutely." He put his hand in his pocket and withdrew an envelope. Erin eyed it blankly. "I would like very much, with your permission and blessing—" she raised her gaze to his "—to adopt your son."

"I beg your pardon?"

He swallowed. "I would like to be a father to your son and help raise him."

She could only stare at him in stunned disbelief. Of all the things she'd been hoping and expecting he might say, this wasn't one of them.

"I have here an application for adoption," he continued. "If you agree, we can fill it out together and—"

"Hang on!" She pushed away the adoption form. "If you want to adopt my child, you're going to have to marry me."

"Oh, well..." He pretended to consider her proposal, but his lurking smile widened, and his eyes said, *Gotcha!*

"I'm confused," she complained, smiling. "What happened to 'I don't want any more children'?"

The teasing light in Nick's expression faded. "You were right. Having more children didn't bother me so much as raising another child that wasn't mine."

Erin studied her hands. "So what's changed?"

"My understanding of what it means to be a father. I'm not sure where the change began, with the prospect of losing Miranda or the thought that I would be forever standing on the sidelines as nothing more than a family friend to your child. I knew it wouldn't take long before someone smarter than me came along and you fell in love with him."

He caught her hand in both of his. "When I saw Erik being born, I realized that being a father isn't about genetics. It's about being there on a daily basis, tying shoelaces and drying tears and making sure children know they're loved. I realized I wanted to be a father to that baby I watched grow in your womb, whose heartbeat I heard before it was born." He raised her hand to his lips. "And whose mother I love with all my heart."

"Oh, Nick." Her heart was so full she could barely speak.

"I want us to be a family. Miranda wants it, too."

She laid a hand on his cheek, rasping her fingertips along his beard. "You realize that if you and I get married, Greta will take the credit."

He kissed the tip of her nose. "Greta doesn't bother you anymore because you finally stood up to her."

Erin considered that. "You're right."

"Of course I am." Reaching into his pocket, he brought out a tiny cloisonné clock. "This is for you."

The square-edged something.

"It's lovely!" Enchanted, she held up the antique brass-and-colored-enamel timepiece. Around its base was inscribed a message: *Tempus fugit.* Time flies. "How true."

He took her hand. "Let's not waste any more time. Erin, will you marry me?"

"Oh, yes."

A lifetime seemed to have passed since she'd been in his arms. Her son's lifetime, to be precise. *Their* son, was her last coherent thought before Nick's mouth descended. She raised her lips to his.

A little later, she murmured, "Nick?"

"Mmm?" He pressed soft kisses against her neck.

"It's only been two weeks since I gave birth. I'm not supposed to make love."

"We'll wait until we're married. And then we'll only make love when you're ready. How does a June wedding sound?"

He'd think she was an idiot for crying at that, but she couldn't help it. "Orange blossoms," she said happily.

"Anything you want." He stroked her hair and whispered silly love murmurs in her ear. Kisses and endearments and the closeness of body and soul she'd always dreamed of and never found. Until Nick.

EVERY DAY FOR THE NEXT six weeks, Nick and Miranda, and often Oliver, too, came to Ruth's after work or school to be with Erin and the baby. Nick and Miranda would fight for the right to change the diaper, while Oliver kept a safe distance.

One day Nick and Miranda arrived with huge grins. Grins that looked nearly identical when viewed side by side. Funny, Erin had never noticed that before.

"We got the DNA results from the laboratory in Seattle," Nick began.

"They took blood samples," Miranda broke in.

"It's a 99.99 percent match," Nick said.

"There's no doubt," Miranda finished exuberantly. "Nick's my father."

He chucked her under the chin. "So how about calling me 'Dad'?"

"I've been thinking about that...." Miranda got a teasing look in her eyes. "I've tamed down too much." She tugged her rich auburn hair, which looked so much nicer without the streaks. The eyebrow hole had disappeared and the turquoise stud in her nose looked positively sedate. "I'm thirteen, practically a grown-up. I can call you Nick."

"Miranda." He pretended to be angry, then hugged her. "Call me anything. Just call me."

Miranda and Erin looked at each other and groaned.

THE MORNING OF THE WEDDING, Erin and Kelly were upstairs in Erin's room getting ready. They heard a commotion at the front door, exclamations from Gran, then seconds later Geena glided up the stairs in a Givenchy dress and a cloud of French perfume.

"Geena!" Erin threw her arms around her sister. She was as beautiful as ever, but Erin was alarmed to feel bones as fragile as a bird's beneath Geena's pale silk dress. "Why didn't you call? We thought you weren't coming."

"What! Miss your wedding? Never." Geena released one arm and beckoned Kelly. "Group hug."

Laughing and excited, the three of them embraced.

Kelly stepped back, saying to Geena, "You've lost a lot of weight."

"I know. Isn't it fantastic?" Geena's wide smile and full lips accentuated the hollowness of her cheeks, the glittering brightness of her deep blue eyes.

Kelly's eyebrows lifted, and Erin threw her a warning glance. *Don't get into this now.* Lips clamped, Kelly picked up Erin's veil and resumed a last-minute repair of the antique lace.

If Geena noticed their silent communication, she didn't show it. "Turn around," she ordered Erin.

A surfeit of happiness sent Erin spinning on the toes of her satin shoes. The long ivory dress molded her bodice and flared from her hips. Her mother's wedding dress that Gran had carefully preserved all these years.

"You look absolutely perfect," Geena declared. "Do you have something borrowed? Take my pearls," she said, unclasping them.

The long strand of rose-colored pearls added the perfect finishing touch. "I'm wearing Gran's veil, but these are gorgeous. Thanks, Geena."

"It's nothing." Geena threw herself onto the bed. "By the way, I'm sorry, sweetie, but I have to leave right after the reception. Julian is throwing a party at a resort in the Seychelle Islands, and I'm expected."

Julian Didier, the hottest new designer in Europe. Erin knew these social occasions were important to Geena's career, yet her dismayed glance met Geena's in the mirror. "I wish you were staying longer, but I guess it can't be helped."

From the window seat, Kelly sighed. "The new bride and the jetsetting supermodel. Then there's the small-town wife and mother."

"*And* hotshot real estate agent," Erin said.

"Come with me," Geena suggested to Kelly eagerly. "Julian won't mind, and I'd love it."

When Kelly shook her head, Erin asked, "Why not? You could use a break."

Kelly lowered the needle and veil to her lap. "I probably couldn't get a ticket this late."

"The flight's wide-open," Geena told her. "The airline agent said so when I booked my seat last week."

Kelly's eyes grew wistful. "The expense…"

"My treat. I insist." When Kelly still hesitated, Geena added, "You'd be gone less than a week."

"I always keep my passport up to date, just in case. Not that I've ever used it, but…" Kelly started to look hopeful, then slumped. "What would Max say?"

"Max is a darling!" Geena exclaimed. "He won't mind. Will he?"

Kelly turned to Erin, who could only shrug. Maybe Max would mind a little, but how could he begrudge his wife this opportunity? That was *her* opinion. Kelly knew her husband and the true extent of their problems, and she had to make up her own mind whether a week in the Seychelles was worth risking further trouble.

"There's only one way to find out." Kelly's chin rose as she made her decision. "I'll tell him I'm going."

NICK AND ERIN WERE MARRIED in the Lutheran church where Erin's parents had married and Erin and her sisters had been baptized. Kelly was matron of honor, Miranda was maid of honor and Steve stood as best man. Gran sat in the front row in her pink Chanel suit, a long-ago gift from Geena. Geena was beside her, clutching her camera and a wad of tissues. On the opposite side at the front sat Nick's family.

Townspeople filled the pews and stood three deep at the back of the church. Orange blossoms exuded heady perfume in vases on either side of the altar and in Erin's bouquet as she took her place beside Nick. After a simple ceremony the minister pronounced them man and wife.

Erin turned to Nick and lifted the filmy lace, suddenly breathless.

"At last," Nick murmured, turning to Erin as though he'd been waiting his whole life for the moment when she was his bride.

Afterward they walked down the block to the town hall for the reception to which everyone was invited. Nick carried Erik in his arms and the baby had Nick's little finger securely gripped in one small fist.

As they reached the hall, Nick turned to Steve. "I'm shutting off my pager tonight."

"Odds are you'll get interrupted, anyway," Steve said, with a knowing grin at the baby. "Don't worry, Tanya and I will hold down the fort."

Nick smiled at the fire department's newest paid recruit, a tall, strongly built redhead whose arm was linked with Steve's. "Just don't let the place burn down around you."

Tubby O'Conner and his five-piece band played a mixture of swing and rock, and guests danced and snacked from the buffet until late in the evening. As the reception wound to a close, Erin tugged Nick toward the exit. "I think it's time we left."

"Good idea." He nuzzled her neck until she shivered, then whispered in her ear, "The best is yet to come."

"Goodbye, darlings," Geena said, coming up to them as they lingered by the door. She hugged first Erin, then Nick. "Welcome to the family, Nick. I know you and Erin will be fantastic together."

"Thanks. Next time you come, stay longer."

"Will do." She planted a kiss on Erik's forehead. "Take care, little one. Wish I had a sweet baby like you." Then she turned to Miranda. "I'll send you something nice from Julian's summer collection."

Miranda attempted to remain cool, but this was too much. "Wow, thanks!"

When Erin started to unclasp Geena's pearls, Geena stopped her. "Keep them. They look better on you." She glanced around. "I'd better be off, too. Where's Kelly?"

"Coming. My suitcase is in the car."

Kelly glanced back at Max, balancing a sleepy little girl in each arm. His tense smile didn't reach his eyes, but he shrugged.

"Enjoy yourself, honey. If someone handed me a holiday on a plate, I'd take it."

"Thanks. Love you," she said, hugging him and the twins together. "I've said goodbye to Robyn and Beth."

"Wait," Erin cried as Geena and Kelly started to leave. "I have to throw my bouquet."

She turned her back and flung the spray of orange blossoms into the air.

Geena gave an astonished, full-throated laugh and held up the captured bouquet. "I'm going to be the next bride."

Erin and Nick said their own goodbyes and went back to the houseboat, leaving Miranda to settle in for the weekend at Ruth's house. A honeymoon would have to wait until Erik was old enough to be left. Which might be never, Erin thought, if Nick had his way.

Erik, tired from his big day, went to sleep while nursing, his eyes rolling back beneath his lids, a bead of milk sliding down his chin.

"Little glutton." Nick picked up his baby son from Erin's lap and carried him to the crib temporarily set up in Miranda's room.

He found Erin in his bedroom, working at the tiny satin buttons down the back of her wedding dress.

She glanced over her shoulder at him. "Help me?"

"I'd be only too happy to assist."

One by one the buttons came loose, revealing ivory skin and slender curves clothed in lacy undergarments. Nick grew hard and his fingers grew clumsy. He'd waited for this night willingly but impatiently. Now, finally, they were together and a minute's delay seemed an eternity.

Erin stepped out of her gown and Nick caught his breath at the sight of her long, shapely legs clad in gartered stockings and her slim ankles set off by ivory brocade high heels.

"Come here," he growled, and pulled her against him, taking pleasure in letting her feel how aroused he was.

She lifted her face to be kissed, and he captured her mouth in tender exploration. Free at last to touch, his hands moved over her breasts, the hollow of her lower back, sliding down the curve of her waist. Silk and lace and heated skin, she moved against him, pressing her hips to his. He heard moans, mingled sounds that came from both of them.

Breathless, a little dizzy, he eased back to catch his breath. Then frowned, puzzled, when he noticed two damp patches on his shirt.

Erin saw, too. She touched the wet circles of lace around her nipples and waited anxiously for Nick's response. Had he really changed, or would the sight of her milk put him off? Another man's baby had caused this.

His eyes darkened, and very deliberately he reached around and undid her bra. Erin held her breath as the fabric fell away, revealing full breasts and ripe erect nipples oozing milk. Nick slid a hand under one breast, cupping the curving weight. Slowly, he lowered his head and his mouth closed around her nipple.

Erin's eyes fell shut and her bones melted. She barely felt Nick pick her up and carry her to the bed. Then, with eager fingers she peeled back his shirt, hungry to see and touch. Heated skin, salty on her tongue. Hard muscles and curling chest hair. She felt the whisper of skin on skin and smiled into his eyes.

"Are you ready to make love?" he murmured, rising on one elbow to stroke a hand down her quivering body and slip beneath her satin panties.

Erin moaned softly. "I'll die if we don't."

He began to strip off his clothes. When he got down to his underwear, Erin started to smile. Sally Larkin was right and Tracy was wrong.

"What's so funny?" he said, lying beside her in black silk boxers.

"Nothing. Come on, take everything off."

Soon they were both naked, touching, kissing, leading each other to the edge of madness and desire.

"I don't want to hurt you," he breathed next to her ear.

"You won't." She cupped his face in her hands, watching his eyes darken with desire for her. Someday they would make another baby. But for now, they would make love. Pure, blissful love, blessed by God and the citizens of Hainesville.

Her eyes closed in ecstasy as he slid inside her.

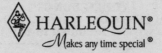